At one point, prophetically, Marie says, "Maybe salvation is like a fresh new supply of maxi-pads." Here is a mysticism my soul understands. Wondering what to get Joan of Arc for her birthday this year? This book. Also magic, the way it tracks us. And knows us before we know (see: tarot card XI, Justice). I would classify this book as red conjuration. Really, only this: I would like to convert to the Church of Marie, where the past, present, and future agree to disagree in the name of radiance. And too —these five words, the most extraordinary words I know, "For she began to write." *The Reconception of Marie* is a stunning book.

Selah Saterstrom, author of *Ideal Suggestions* and *Slab*

Teresa Carmody's *The Reconception of Marie* strikes a wondrous balance between comic absurdity and a tight grasp of the cost of rules, especially when rules are random and erratic. It's also a sly critique of the ancient human drive to turn the inscrutable into a force that can be known, controlled, and used against others. A beautiful, alive record of one mind coming into being, but not through any way you'd expect.

Paul Lisicky, author of *Later: My Life At The Edge Of The World*

THE RECONCEPTION OF MARIE

Teresa Carmody

SPUYTEN DUYVIL
NEW YORK CITY

This is a work of fiction. All the characters, organizations, and events portrayed in this novel either are products of the author's imagination or are used fictitiously.

ISBN 978-1-952419-22-5

Library of Congress Cataloging-in-Publication Data

Names: Carmody, Teresa, author.
Title: The reconception of Marie / Teresa Carmody.
Description: New York City : Spuyten Duyvil, [2020] |
Identifiers: LCCN 2020039080 | ISBN 9781952419225 (trade paperback)
Subjects: GSAFD: Bildungsromans. | LCGFT: Novels.
Classification: LCC PS3603.A7555 R43 2020 | DDC 813/.6--dc23
LC record available at https://lccn.loc.gov/2020039080

for my sister Karen

*For we wrestle not against flesh and blood but
against principalities, against powers...*
–Ephesians 6:12

*Grace fills empty spaces, but it can only enter
where there is a void to receive it, and it is grace
itself which makes this void.*
–Simone Weil

We prayed for angels to surround us in a hedge of protection but never imagined the angels to look like this: rainbow-striped wings in soft light. Gold, blue, red, and white. The wings are peacock-spotted, a dot on each feather. Eye-bright, globe-like. Fra Angelico painted this *Annunciation* in the North Corridor of the Convent of San Marco, Florence, sometime between the years of 1438 and 1450. We had never heard of Fra Angelico. We knew about Italy but didn't imagine it as a place we could visit, especially to look at a painting by some dead Catholic friar. We believed that art, like fancy schools and big cities, belonged to other people, not us. We prayed for angelic protection because that was in the Bible, Psalm 91. We knew the Bible. Or thought we did. It's our book, we said. We're US Americans, God's chosen ones.

1987, WESTERN MICHIGAN

A REAL CHRISTIAN

Today proves it: Jennifer Hartman and Angie have *definitely* lost their salvation. Real Christians don't act like them, which means they were born again for a grand total of two weeks and two days. Now it will be even worse for them because they know the truth and they've ignored it (2 Peter 2:21).

They were weird that night, too, not after they were saved but before. It started when Jennifer Hartman asked why my family isn't Catholic anymore, and Angie stopped laughing and looked at me as if she were super interested. I knew they'd been talking about me behind my back. That's why I invited them over but not Denise. Because, while Denise is my absolute best friend, I don't have to be with her every day for her to still like me. But if you're not with Jennifer Hartman and Angie every day, they will turn against you, and they're always making fun of Denise. Jennifer Hartman especially loves to gossip—she's the biggest backstabber I know. When she dislikes someone, she'll let herself hate them. Last year, she wouldn't say one word to Beth McNorton's face, not a single yes or no. She wouldn't even look at Beth—she hated her that much. Angie thought this made Jennifer cool, but Angie is stupid that way—Jennifer Hartman sows discord, and Angie dumbly reaps it.

Jennifer Hartman's family wasn't Catholic when they came to Sacred Heart. She didn't make her first communion with the rest of us, and she never talks about God or answers questions in Religion class. So when she asked why we quit going to Catholic church, I knew it was a set-up.

"Are you serious?" I said.

She nodded.

I prayed silently (the Lord is my strength and my shield, Psalm 28:7), and then I told her. I mean, I really told them. I said my mom quit going to Catholic church when she became born again, and while you may not know this about me, I'm born again, too. Now that Dad is born again, we all go to Mom's church, even Dad. Because there is more to God than what they teach at Sacred Heart. Do you know God gives us the whole story of history like one gigantic painting? If you look, you can see yourself in it and it within you. Our story begins with Adam and Eve and their fall and the promise of Jesus as the one true Messiah. He definitely lived, died, and rose again, and he *will* return someday, probably in the next thirteen years since that's the year 2000. When Jesus returns, the whole world, including made-up places like Michigan, will be destroyed, and God will win.

If you read the actual Bible, it doesn't say anything about Catholic priests or popes, and it especially doesn't include the saints. Saints are like pets Satan gives to Catholics to distract them from the real God. Saints even seem harmless, like kittens, puppies, or bunnies. Did you know that rabbits bite? And kittens turn into cats that scratch. The Bible says we should pray to God and God alone; therefore, when you pray to a saint, it's like talking to God's dog while ignoring the master. According to the Bible, no one will enter the Kingdom of God unless he is *born again*. And while Father Berne says there are different kinds of sins—mortal and venial, and venial aren't as bad—the Bible says *all* sins are mortal sins. Because the wages of sin is death, and death comes to everyone. I talked for an unusually long time, and Jennifer Hartman and Angie listened like they'd never heard the Bible before. I told them this was the most important news they'll ever hear; it is the truth of salvation, the reason they exist. Now that they know the truth, it will affect them forever. I stopped after the word "forever."

They were very quiet.

Maybe this was the first time they realized they are going to die.

We were sitting close together, cross-legged on the floor. Jennifer Hartman was drawing lines in the carpet with her index fingers, her hair covering the sides of her face. Nobody spoke. Then Jennifer looked up and asked, "Am I going to hell?"

For a moment, I didn't want to tell her the terrible news. It's a horrible feeling to realize your whole life has been a lie. I had to speak the truth. I said—and it's true that whatever you put in your heart, your mouth will speaketh (Matthew 12:34)—I said, "John 3:3: 'Verily, verily, I say unto thee, except a man be born again, he cannot enter the Kingdom of God.'"

Jenny looked down. "Does that mean I'm going to hell?"

Did she not understand English? Those words are perfectly clear. The air became so still, I could hear myself breathing. I nodded, but Jenny didn't see. She was looking at the carpet. She had drawn a crisscross pattern inside a box, like a checkers board, but the lines were diagonal, not up and down, a bunch of x's instead of a cross. I felt bad. I don't want the hell punishment for anyone. Maybe I am mad at Jennifer Hartman—maybe she's a conceited, stuck-up jerk who wants to be the center of everything, but I can't wish hell on anyone. I swallowed. It hurt. I spoke slowly. "That's what it says in the Bible."

She looked straight at me. Normally Jennifer Hartman doesn't make very good eye contact even though she has the prettiest hazel eyes. I thought she might say anything, rebuke me, cast me aside and call me names, but I didn't expect to hear what she said: "I want to be born again."

"Really?" I asked. My heart started buzzing, burning inside my chest, as Angie, who had been sitting so still, jerked her head up and leaned forward.

She wiggled her fingers and said, "Me, too."

I couldn't believe it! Although I know all things are possible in Christ, I never imagined Jennifer Hartman and Angie as Christians. I thought I would always be the only born-again in my class—it's what makes me different. And people love to hate Christians because that's what the world wants them to do, and most people can't bear to face the truth because the truth will set you free, and most people don't want to be free. But God is bigger than any lock and key; He can open the tightest heart. We don't even know how big God is. That's why it's stupid when Catholics paint pictures of Him, even if they're painting Jesus Christ. God-Jesus is too great for us to imagine, so any image we make creates an idol instead, a small earthly version of something we *can't* understand. When God says He's awesome, he doesn't mean "cool" but rather fearsome and wonderous. Sublime. Pastor Marks warns that most children construct an image of God based on their parents. That's why parents need to be born again and follow God's rules for parenting, such as spanking. That's biblical.

So is children obeying their parents, husbands loving their wives, and wives submitting to their husbands. I didn't tell Jennifer Hartman and Angie about that; we can pray for their parents later. Instead, I told them God makes it easy for us to know Him. They could become born again right then—it's that simple. Angie started doing spirit-fingers dance motions, rocking her shoulders back and forth, while Jennifer Hartman sighed and smiled. They're used to Catholicism, where every sacrament takes months of preparation and only a priest can make it official. I said there aren't priests in the New Testament, not among believers, anyway. With Jesus, everyone is equal!

We were still sitting in a circle. I said let's move closer and hold hands. I have, by the way, the largest hands in my class, bigger even than Pat Harrington's, and my feet have been size 9 since fifth grade. I hope I'm like Pickles in *The Fire Cat*, whose big paws helped him do big things, but there's also Cinderella's ugly stepsisters with their destined too-big feet. I told the girls to bow their heads and close their eyes. "Dear Jesus," I said, pausing to make sure their eyes were still shut. "Dear Jesus," I said again, "thank you for being here with us...." I continued to pray, working my way through the Sinner's Prayer, which we said together, sentence by sentence. They repeated after me.

When we finished, my heart was bursting with love for them, as their eyes sparkled, so beautiful and light. It's the lightness that comes when you've truly confessed and you know, beyond a shadow of the smallest doubt, you've been forgiven and blessed. Set free, you've let your sins go. I told them there are so many cool things about the Christian life, especially the music. Did they know about the Christian rock band Petra? Of course they didn't, so I found Michelle's tape and played "Thankful Heart." *I have a thankful heart, which you have given me.* Angie loved it so much, she memorized the words from inside the case as we kept rewinding and singing along, five or six times. Then we listened to Twila Paris, "The Warrior Is a Child." *I drop my sword and cry for just a while. Cause deep inside this armor, the warrior is a child.* I played that song only once, but I played it. It's the song that makes me cry the hardest.

Later, I told them about Pastor Jaime, our Youth Pastor who's so cool—that's another thing I like about our church. Pastor Marks is for everyone, but Pastor Jaime works only with teens, and it's the teens who will lead the spiritual battle to reclaim this nation because we're special—we still know right from wrong. Then Jenny found some cherry Lifesavers in her bag and kept offering them to everyone, including herself, saying, "Would you like a Lifesaver?" "Oh, no, thank you. I'm already saved!" We were being absolutely dorky, but nobody cared because that's how it is when you've led someone to Christ. You've shared your insides, your hopes and beliefs. You've admitted together that you're sinful, worthless human beings, that you're wrong and, by being wrong, can be put right. No one is cooler than anyone else, and there aren't cliques or popular girls because now we're all in the same club, the born-again club—we've let Christ come inside us and wash our sins away!

And while God does love all people equally, when He looks at a Christian, He sees Christ's eternal light inside them, which is, let's face it, special. Christ's spot is small at first, deep in the gut, and every time you do or think something sinful, Jesus shrieks in actual pain. In some Christians, He becomes so pinhead small, He pops and disappears. That's when they've lost their salvation—there's no seed left to grow. But if you read your Bible and pray every day, if you keep repenting your sins and living in His strength, not yours, you will mature in Christ, and He will grow larger and larger inside you as you become more and more Christlike. Eventually, His light will spread into your arms and legs, your fingers and toes. He will rule every part of you as you become a giant, glowing advertisement for Christ, fully occupied.

Unfortunately, Jennifer Hartman and Angie have gone the way of the lessening light. In fact, they're back to their old ways, even worse. They've even started reading *Teen Magazine*—and right in front of me, too.

But it wasn't always like this, especially the week right after the sleepover. Jennifer Hartman and I were always together; she wanted to know my opinion about everything. She told me her dad said being born again is baloney and asked what should we do. We decided to pray for him, that he would become born again. I reminded Jennifer of how light and clean and free she felt right after she was saved. She nodded, then started laughing because—she didn't want to say it, but she finally did—she said I sounded like a maxi-pad commercial—light and clean and free. "With wings!" I cried, and we laughed until Jenny snorted, which made us laugh even more.

Then I said, "No, it's more like laundry detergent. Because Jesus makes the dirt disappear, which is the opposite of maxi-pads. They get dirty when you use them."

Jenny shuddered and waved her hands in front of her face. "I don't want to see it," she said. "That's so gross!" But she's the one who brought up maxi-pads. When I think about it, maybe she's right. Maybe salvation is like a fresh new supply of maxi-pads. Because pads don't clean regular dirtiness. They catch blood and specifically the blood caused by original sin, as you're cleansed from the inside, which is much harder than washing your outsides or cleaning up your act. Plus, before you have your period, you can't *feel* the blood inside you. It's just there, building up, like in that movie Nurse Pam showed just the girls during her school visit. She said if the blood doesn't feed a fertilized egg, it becomes toxic inside you. You would probably die if you didn't get your period!

That's how sin works, too. We get so used to our sins, they become habits—it feels like we're not doing anything wrong, or that we could do anything different.

But once your period starts, you see the evidence on the pad and definitely know that the blood of sin was inside you. Which is both the same and the opposite of being washed in the Blood of the Lamb. You don't see Christ's cleansing blood, but after confessing your sins, you can feel the difference, the way your deepest self has been purified. Also, when you first start menstruating, you might not know that's what it is, just like some people think they're going to heaven when in truth they are bound for hell. I honestly didn't know I was getting my period the first time. There was brown in my underwear. Nobody said the blood might be brown. I thought there was something wrong with me, like I was losing control. It appeared three days in a row—this stain in my underwear. After the second time, I was so freaked out, because I couldn't feel anything happening. How could I not know I had to go number two? Or feel it happening? On day three, I began wearing a maxi-pad, which I thought was super smart—repurposing a pad for another leakage.

But I forgot to throw one away, so it was still in my underwear when Michelle opened our bedroom hamper that night and screamed so loud I thought of big hairy spiders, because we get those in our room.

"Mom," she yelled as she ran into the hallway. "You've got to talk to her."

Michelle says I left that pad there on purpose. She says no one can be that dumb. Sometimes I really ~~hate~~ dislike Michelle.

Jennifer Hartman and I talked about maxi-pads on Thursday, and we were still friends on Friday. But on Monday she didn't wait for me at morning recess, and Angie didn't look at me when I walked by her desk. I hadn't talked to either of them all weekend, even though I had called Jenny once and left a message. She never called me back. At lunch, I went to their table like normal. Angie scooted to make room; they were talking about some movie they had seen that weekend. Mom never lets me go to the movies, so if they had invited me, Mom would have said no. They kept talking only to each other, and I ate my sandwich (PB & J) in silence. That's how it was before they were saved; that's how they were on Wednesday.

But today during recess, they were huddled near the back doors of the school (it's cold outside), and I tried to join them. Jennifer Hartman said they were talking about boys. If I wanted to stand there, I needed to pick a boy in our class to like. There was no way I would do that. Because although Derek Cunningham is obviously the cutest, he's also the meanest and most competitive and clearly doesn't like me. So I said, "Cereal?" which is what Denise and I say instead of "serious." They did not smile.

Jennifer Hartman repeated, "Pick one if you want to stay." Her voice was low and steady.

"You really won't let me stand here?" They didn't answer. I forced a laugh. "It won't cost you anything," I said, "it's a free country." They didn't smile.

"You can," Angie said, "if you pick a boy."

I've known those guys since kindergarten, and I don't like any of them, not like that.

Angie rolled her eyes, and Jenny said, "Nice try."

I said it's true, and Angie squinted.

"That's not what we think."

Angie obviously likes Derek Cunningham, but he will never like her, not in a million years. Not with that pink fat face and straight orange hair.

"OK," said Jenny. "If you *won't* pick, then you have to leave."

I couldn't believe they were being so stupid. There are only five boys in our class. None of them are cute or smart, and I've known them forever. Why would I suddenly pick one to like, and why is liking a boy so important?

Jenny and Angie glanced at each other. They nodded and turned around in sync, like a practiced dance move. They actually turned their backs on me.

14

I stared at their long hair and winter hats. Jenny's is light pink with a white ball on top. Angie's legs are starting to curve out at her knees because of her fat; she was wearing the same biscuit-tan coat from last year. They stood still as statues. I could see puffs of white breath rising behind their stupid heads. There was nothing to do. So I left.

Do they even remember being saved? After they were born again, I felt God pressing on my heart, saying I needed to help them. They don't know other Real Christians, so who would be their model or spiritual guide? But, to be honest, I didn't want to. I didn't want to worry about whether Jennifer Hartman is reading stupid *Teen Magazine* or if Angie is listening to Michael Jackson or Poison. If you're the leader, you have to be better, purer, than everyone else because you're the example. People will call you bossy even though you're not.

I'm only the leader because I know what everyone is supposed to do.

We asked to be protected from the spirits of illness, of fear and poverty. These were not figures of speech but real demons who existed within a dimension we sensed but usually could not see. Humans were simply the newest cosmic creatures, whereas angels and demons—like the spirit of prophecy, the spirit of death—had been and would forever be.

When she was thirteen, she asked God to please reveal the truth of St. Thérèse's miracles. Did roses honestly rain from the sky as the saint's supernatural signature, as a way for the supplicant to know, with certainty, that Thérèse, and not some other saint, had interceded on her behalf?

Yes, there were questions, things that didn't add up. But we didn't get hung up on such details. The divine wouldn't be a mystery if God gave us all the answers, and faith exceeds rational thought. That's why it's faith: belief without any basis but itself.

That night she dreamed of an infant whose face turned into a blood-red rose. It was a sight as disturbing as any genuine paradox. Roses, she was learning, symbolized passion and purity, fertility and virginity, life and death. Transmutation. In the dream, she stared into the baby rose face as a center hole formed within its swirling petals. A nothing she fell into as she woke to another gray spring day.

In Fra Angelico's painting, Mary is marked with a light that moves from beneath her pelvis up through the crown of her haloed head. She holds her hands across her stomach as Gabriel, hands likewise crossed, speaks the word of God, which fills her womb with life. In Catholic school, we prayed the Hail Mary, repeating the angel's words. *Hail Mary, full of grace, the Lord is with thee. Blessed art thou among women, and blessed is the fruit of your womb, Jesus.*

At Children's Church, they taught her to put on a spiritual suit of armor. Everyone has one, they said, by which they meant Real Christians. Their instructions followed Paul's language in Ephesians. Gird your loins first, they said, and she wondered what other words they allowed when speaking of those more secret parts. Years later, she had a roommate who called flowers "plant genitals," which was, she noted, biologically accurate. There was also "the flower in your panties"—a euphemism her friend's mother used for menstruation. Yet spiritually girding her loins was different from wearing menstrual protection (or "equipment"—her sister's word for pads and tampons, even if she was talking only to girls).

Blessed art, full of grace—Mary's dress matches the light taupe color of the wall behind her. A cloak drapes her shoulders, covering her back and lap from the middle of her thighs down. She sits in a loge, or outside veranda. To her right, a doorless passageway leads to an inner chamber, where the light brown of its furthest wall nearly matches the color of her cloak's interior fabric. The cloak's exterior fabric is blue, her color, and the garment folds across Mary's lap in seeming alignment with the chamber's back wall. The painting's combination of color and line creates an optical effect, so Mary's body blends into the sand-colored building even as the architecture merges into her. She becomes a foregrounded figure and part of the background, which is not unlike her role in the story of Jesus's birth. She's a principal actor and the stage, as her body literally and metaphorically creates the context (time and place) for a child divine.

She was the only eighth-grade girl not to participate in the May Crowning Ceremony. It was on a Wednesday, and she wore her school uniform as she sat in the second pew next to Sister Mary Francis while the other girls, solemnly and slowly, dressed in white, proceeded up the center aisle and to the left, where they placed a crown of red roses and baby's breath on Mary's head. Or, rather, on her statue, which was, her mother said, an obvious display of idolatry. She didn't consider her classmates to be idolaters, at least not more than most people, who seemed to worship money and fame (thus the dogged pursuit of these became easily justified). She doubted her classmates cared about Mary or wondered how it felt to receive such startling information as, "You, dear child, are the mother of God."

We didn't use the word Protestant. Instead, we said "Christian," and there were two kinds of people: Real Christians and Non-Christians. Real Christians were born again; spirit-filled; faith-healing; talking, wanting, praising God with every breath. Real Christians lived like the Apostles in the Book of Acts—always preaching and converting others because that's what love looked like. A Catholic may be a Real Christian but probably isn't. Catholics called their priest "father," while Real Christians answered only to God, the Real Father who puts other fathers in charge.

We prayed for salvation because the world was ending, with a clear finish that God had ordained in linear time. This was spiritual warfare, and the fighting was growing increasingly fierce as the nation lost its Christian values: young people rebelling and fornicating, mothers neglecting their families, fathers ceding authority. It would only get worse, they said, before the apocalyptic dawn.

DRAWING LINES

When Sister Mary Francis said we had to diagram ten sentences a day for the next four weeks, I looked at Denise and rolled my eyes. We knew those sentences were coming. Michelle used to moan about them every day when she was in eighth grade. They're like eating canned spinach, she said, and Sister Mary Francis wants them perfect, with ruler-straight lines.

Canned spinach is disgusting. On the back of my ruler I've written M.C.L.N.Y.B.W.L.S.S., which is a code Pat Harrington keeps trying to break but never will because he's, honestly, not very bright. And my code is supposed to be more *intriguing* than breakable. Don't tell Michelle, but I've discovered that I like drawing lines with my ruler and splitting sentences apart. I like how each word has a place; that adjectives hang from nouns; that prepositional phrases create cul-de-sacs; how the line between a verb and a predicate noun is slanted, not straight, because people aren't consistent.

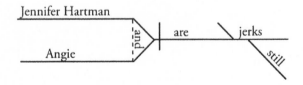

Which may *seem* consistent because of the word "still," but they weren't acting jerky two weeks ago when I thought we were friends. Maybe they think "friend" is merely a slot you slide a name into—all you need is a proper (and popular) noun.

Today they were passing notes about me. I know because every time they wrote or read a new one, they looked at me and laughed.

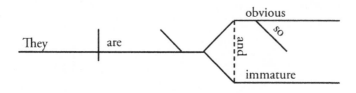

Unoriginal, too, since they were acting like Nellie Oleson from *Little House on the Prairie*, which is one of the two television shows Mom lets us watch. Nellie Oleson is mean, spoiled, and prissy. Even Michelle says she'd rather diagram sentences than be a Nellie Oleson.

Jennifer Hartman has new duck boots, navy and tan. Her feet are too small for her body. I kept looking at Angie's arm instead of her face. She wears short sleeves even in the winter because her extra weight keeps her pink fat warm. Before winter break, Jennifer Hartman said Angie looks like a pig in a blanket in her dog-biscuit-colored winter coat, and Angie told me that Jennifer Hartman had lice last summer but doesn't want anyone to know.

I've decided duck boots are ugly. I've always known that Angie can't keep a secret. Duck boots may be popular with high school preppies, like Michelle says, but everyone thinks pigs in a blanket are gross. Plus, there are at least two kinds of time: popular time and eternal. Angie and Jennifer Hartman want to suck me into popular time because that's where they're important, at least in their small minds. But everyone matters in eternal time. In eternal time, we are all already living. When I closed my eyes and opened my Bible and pointed, God gave me this sentence as proof:

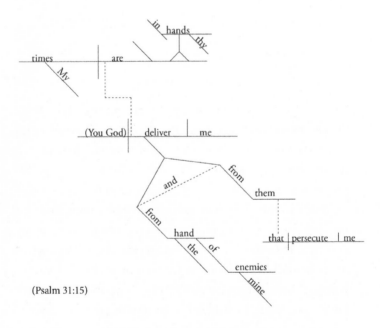

(Psalm 31:15)

WHAT GOD WANTS

1. **P**ut Him first. Love Him more than anything or any person. Remember: Nothing is good without Him, and, without Him, I am a full-of-sin nothing and my life is meaningless.

2.   Stay pure by saving sex for marriage. No compromises! Our bodies are gifts from Him, and once you lose your virginity, it's gone forever. Premarital sex automatically dooms your marriage because your husband will always know you didn't love him enough to save your most precious parts for him.

3.   Pray every day. How can I have a relationship with God if I don't talk with Him? This is also true for my future marriage. I promise to tell my husband what I'm thinking even if my words don't matter or won't change a thing. I bet the longer Dad is saved, the more he will listen.

4.   Don't complain! It's easier for people to hear you when you speak in a sweet voice. Maybe Mom can't learn this, but I can.

5.   Read at least three chapters of the Bible every day. How will I know what He thinks if I don't read every one of His precious words? Also, ask Mom for one of those read-the-Bible-in-a-year Bibles, and, if they're too expensive, I promise to buy one with birthday money, which is only five months away. I need to memorize as many verses as possible. So when they take all the Bibles away, like Pastor Marks says they will, eventually, I will always have His word—carved in my mind and heart.

6. Read one chapter of Proverbs every day, starting today with Proverbs 13 since today is January 13. There are thirty-one chapters of Proverbs, just like there are thirty-one days in most months. I agree with Pastor Marks—that's too strange to be a coincidence! See how He is always there, even in the details.

7. Never drink, smoke, or do drugs, as they leave permanent scars on your soul while opening doors for demons to enter your life. That's not the only way demons can attach themselves to you, but it's very common. I hate the taste of beer, but I've heard that Angie is looking forward to high school parties so she can drink and meet boys. She doesn't want to be a virgin when she graduates from high school. Can you believe that? Maybe she is already demon-oppressed.

8. Quit talking about people behind their backs. This is my #1 weakness and biggest character flaw. If I can stop, Jennifer Hartman and Angie won't accuse me of being two-faced, which I am—but only to them. From now on, when I am tempted to talk about Jennifer Hartman or Angie, I'll pray instead.

9. Be the best friend I can. Always be there for my friends, and always remember their birthdays even if they forget mine. Yesterday was Aunt Susan's birthday, but Mom forgot to call her, just like she forgot Michelle's birthday last year. That's what Michelle says, anyway. I seem to remember German chocolate cake.

10. Speaking of Michelle, I promise not to harbor a heart of bitterness or unforgiveness. I will immediately forgive anyone who hurts me because forgiveness is an act, not a feeling. If I speak forgiveness, the forgiving feel-

ing will come. I don't want to be like Michelle, who never forgives or forgets. And I promise to tell the truth, the whole truth, and nothing but the truth, so help me, God. After all, your life is a kind of testifying, so don't live a lie!

The truth was she wanted someone's attention, and in eighth grade, she was constantly seeking eye contact with any halfway attractive boy her same age. The boys gave her feelings she couldn't explain, and their comments, looks, and possible phone calls preoccupied her, filled her head with thoughts she could escape into, relief from her siblings, her friends. She worried about being somehow wrong, unavoidably ugly—would she ever have a boyfriend? Even as she knew that life was bigger than who you coupled with, if you coupled at all. She wonders, now, what created this worry. Probably some mixture of hormones and loneliness in a culture that primarily values females as virgins, mothers, or wives—that is, for their relationships to men.

Fra Angelico's Mary is the same size as Gabriel, and both figures are proportionally large in comparison to the veranda where she sits and he bows—so large, in fact, they would definitely have to duck in order to pass through the doorway behind them, if they fit at all. They seem to be around the same age—seventeen or eighteen, nineteen at most. Their faces are lineless; their cheeks, rosy. If we step back and consider their greater narrative context, we realize that neither figure is the age s/he appears in the fresco. As an immortal being, Gabriel's existence can't be captured in human years, so his representation, which is also rather feminine, can't be taken literally. According to Jewish custom of the time, Mary was likely betrothed to Joseph around the age of twelve, with their marriage planned for approximately a year later. In *The Golden Legend*, Jacobus de Varagine writes that the Holy Conception occurred when Mary was fourteen, though other sources say she was between the ages of twelve and fourteen. What we can say, with a certain amount of confidence, is that Mary became pregnant when she was the same age as a US American eighth or ninth-grade girl.

We sat through math and English, religion and history, longing and waiting for the bell to ring so real life could resume. On the schoolyard and in each other's gazes, we were what mattered. Our bodies were changing, our brains weren't fully developed, but on the schoolyard and over the telephone, we certainly knew what was really going on.

A Certain Truth

The whole truth starts with Jennifer Hartman—for as long as I can remember, she's been trying to be the leader instead of me. Look, I don't want to be bossy, but I hate it when a group sits around waiting for someone to tell them what to do. Especially when I already have an idea. It's not my fault that Sister Mary Francis puts me in charge when she goes to the office, like she did today. Maybe she knows I'm especially mature and won't mess up her desk, which is where I sit when she's gone. It had been less than ten minutes, and everyone was behaving until Pat Harrington coughed twice and called me a "goody-goody." Two of the boys laughed just as Sister opened the door, so she caught them herself. She asked me who started it, and I said Pat Harrington, as that's factually what happened. But I suspect he was inspired by Jennifer Hartman, who, right before this, walked up and around the room to sharpen her pencil, passing Pat's desk even though it's shorter for her to walk toward the back of the room. Pat has a crush on her, so I think she told him to say that; she probably passed him a note but then let him get in trouble all by himself. Because Jennifer Hartman is like that. She'll let anyone take the blame for her.

Here is my question: Are my problems with Jennifer Hartman just my opinion, or is there something *objectively* wrong with her? I would ask Mom, but she'll tell me self-pity is a sin. I'm not having a pity party about Jennifer Hartman (fact: it hurts when people misperceive you). I don't want to do the same thing to Jennifer Hartman (do unto others, Luke 6:31), so I'm going to write a true portrait, instead: everything good, bad, and in-between. Regardless of my personal opinion.

About Jennifer Hartman

Jennifer Hartman has long, curly brown hair, and some people think she's the cutest girl in our class. I think Denise is cuter, but nobody *sees* her cuteness because they think she's weird and they don't know about her hidden dimple. Jennifer Hartman's dimples are obvious every time she smiles and tilts her head to the side, like she's such an adorable puppy. Her eyes are hazel with flecks of gold, she never gets pimples, and some say she magically makes her freckles cute. Her nose is flat and small, and her nostrils are tiny and hard to see, which means she probably doesn't pick her nose. She parts her hair down the middle and feathers her bangs, using just the right amount of hairspray so her hair never looks hard or shiny but always stays lightly feathered, even during gym. She says her sister, Tammy, showed her how. All her jeans are either Guess or Jordache, and her watch is a real Swatch—not a fake, like mine. Jennifer Hartman believes that brand names matter, which is annoying and dumb because brand names mean more only if you believe they do. They say nothing about a person's insides. Only superficial people mistake the surface for all that's real.

We call Jennifer Hartman, Jennifer Hartman, because there used to be two Jennys in our class, Jennifer Hartman and Jenny Bryant, and even though Jenny Bryant left and went to public school, Jennifer Hartman stayed Jennifer Hartman. Sometimes I call her Jenny Heart-mean. When I told Denise that, she said, "But what does her heart mean?" That's what I love about Denise! She knows how to make everything even *more*. But Jennifer Hartman honestly believes she's better than Denise, just because Denise would rather laugh than be cool. Jennifer Hartman has a smashed-in Pekingese dog face. I've thought that since the first time we met.

She lives on Silver Lake. At her birthday party last year, we could see the water from her bedroom windows. She has her own room even though she's not an only child. Her sister, Tammy, is in my brother Mike's class, and Josh is in the sixth grade. Her bedroom is fully color coordinated. There are painted gold handles on her dresser to match her bed frame, and her blue and lavender gingham bedspread matches her curtains. She's been at our school since second grade, but last year was the first time I'd been to her house. I hope she's not having a skating slumber party this year since I haven't been invited. Last year, I used my own money to buy brand new ice skates from Meijer for $12.99 plus tax, and Jennifer Hartman's parents let her rent two movies—*Back to the Future* and *Children of the Corn*. Her family has cable and a VCR player, so Jennifer Hartman had already seen both movies at least once, maybe more. Everyone wanted to watch *Children of the Corn* starting at midnight, but I knew I wouldn't watch it no matter what, so I went into the kitchen and found Jenny's mom drinking white wine from a giant glass.

Her dad wasn't home yet, but her mom told me he was on his way and how, in high school, she and her best friend, Janet, used to plan their future wedding dresses and houses. "It was such a dream," her mom said. Later, when Jenny's dad still didn't come home, she said I could sleep in Jenny's room instead. She made Jenny stop watching the movie and help me. Jenny said don't worry, she won't let anyone play tricks on me. The most attractive thing about Jennifer Hartman is how she leans in and almost whispers. I always want to hear what she says.

Before going to sleep, I hid my bra beneath the mattress. Maybe that's why they put Denise's in the freezer instead. Everyone else slept in the living room, and now they're afraid of cornfields, which is sad because there are cornfields all around us, including one right behind the school. Satan used that movie to plant a seed of fear in their hearts. Jennifer Hartman likes to say, "Malachai's coming," in a creepy singsong voice that freaks Angie out and makes her laugh. Sometimes I think Angie *likes* to be afraid.

But you know what's scarier than horror movies? Real live demons. And those movies literally open a spiritual door for demons to enter your life.

The worst thing about Jennifer Hartman is how she talks about people behind their backs. If you join in, she'll use that against you. She was the first person to notice Nikki Boyle's strange smell, and once she said it, I could smell it, too, like old potato salad with too much pickle relish. Angie laughed when I told her about Scent la Boyle, then turned around and told Nikki that I gave her smell a name—even though Jennifer Hartman said it first. That was in fourth grade. I already felt bad because I was already ignoring Nikki. I didn't want to be her friend. Honestly, Scent la Boyle wasn't nearly as bad as the old pee smell inside her house, and I didn't tell anyone about that. I thought Jennifer Hartman should know that Angie told Nikki about Scent la Boyle, but Jennifer claimed she's never smelled anything sour about Nikki (liar!) and I should know better than to tell Angie anything because Angie can't keep her mouth shut—everyone knows that.

Another time, Jennifer Hartman said Angie's mom called her mom for advice on helping Angie lose weight because, the summer before sixth grade, Jenny and her mom went on a diet together, and each lost ten or fifteen pounds. Now Angie is the chubby one, and Jennifer Hartman's mom thinks Angie's mom likes having a chubby daughter because it makes her feel better about herself. Also, Jennifer Hartman said my mom needs to "lighten up." I asked why she cares about my mom. She said she doesn't. It's just something she heard her mom say. I don't care what her mom thinks. I didn't tell her about Mom getting rid of our TV. Maybe my mom gets overwhelmed and protective, but at least she doesn't talk bad about other moms, especially to her daughter.

Obviously, Jennifer Hartman is just like her mom. This happens.

Jennifer Hartman even tried to talk bad about Denise. She said since I'm Denise's best friend, did I know why Denise is so weird. But I don't think Denise is weird, not in a bad way. That's what I told her, and she twisted my words. She said, "Oh, so you *do* think she's weird." But I meant it in a good way, like how I'm weird, too, and how the exceptional is always misunderstood by the ordinary.

Jennifer Hartman wouldn't admit there are different kinds of weirdness. She looked at me as if I was stupid and said, "Don't worry. I won't tell." I started getting mad because the same word can mean two different things, like how "killer" can be both murderer and awesome. Jennifer Hartman just smiled smugly and tilted her formerly fat head, nodding as if I was a four-year-old telling her that my real mom is a movie star or something. I had to tell Denise what happened. I swore I wasn't talking bad about her. I told her I do think she's weird—but in the best way, like I am.

I didn't want Jennifer Hartman to tell her first.

Not Gossip

God gave me an insight! That even though I wrote both good *and* bad things about Jennifer Hartman, I am, in effect, still talking about her behind her back, which is wrong and exactly what I promised *not* to do. But God didn't stop there. He also showed me that it's okay to share my thoughts and feelings; my problem isn't that I wrote about Jennifer Hartman but that she's the only person I've written about. Motivation matters. If I truly want to understand my friends and how I feel, I should write about other people, too. Especially my actual friends, like Denise, who I was with all weekend. But first, let me tell you

About Angie Warbler

Angie Warbler is overweight. That's the #1 thing about her, but none of the girls will say so to her face. It's the boys who call her Bird Dog or Big Bird because her last name is Warbler, a kind of common brown bird. Angie used to be skinny and nervous. In first grade we called her Baby Bird because she shook and her skin was so light you could see blue veins in her neck. Something happened in fourth or fifth grade. She gained weight, and then more weight, burying the real Angie beneath a protective shell of flesh. I can still see the Baby Bird beneath her fake weight, but if something doesn't change soon, the fake weight will become permanent. Angie will become a fat person. She must face this problem within the next two years, or it will be too late.

Wow! I don't even know where that knowledge came from, but as I was writing about Angie, her situation became clear. I may have just prophesied so that my words are already true.

Angie has pale, straight hair she calls strawberry blonde. Her hair is red, not blonde, the exact same color as iron streaks in the bathtub or sink. I hate the smell of iron water. Angie's skin is very pink; her eyelids, almost red; and she wears robin-egg-blue eye shadow on top of her eyelids. She doesn't know anything about blending eye shadow. Once in seventh grade, she charged at Jennifer Hartman and bit her. It was the weirdest thing. We were walking back in after recess, Jennifer Hartman was with Beth McNorton, and Angie was ten feet behind them, alone. Denise and I were behind Angie.

That's how we saw her suddenly rush at Jennifer Hartman, grab her right arm in both of her hands, and bite hard on the back part, just below her shoulder. Jennifer Hartman shouted and pulled away. "Freak!" she yelled at Angie, who was blinking at Jennifer Hartman as if she didn't know her. Jennifer Hartman must have seen that look, too, because she pulled away and started walking like nothing had happened, her left hand covering the bite mark like it was something we shouldn't see. We didn't speak about it, either, but that's when the boys started calling Angie, Bird Dog. Angie lies. She says her mom will buy her anything, but her clothes are generic. Jennifer Hartman is the only girl in our class with Guess jeans. Angie wears the same headband every day; it's thin, plastic, and rainbowed.

Angie gets mad if we don't do what Angie wants, such as sitting at the blue cafeteria table every day just because it's blue. It's also near the trash cans, so the area kind of smells. Jennifer Hartman used to tease Angie about wanting to sit there, but now Jennifer acts as if that's the most special spot for her and her best friend, Angie. One time, Angie told me that if she had a sister, she would never share a room because there wouldn't be space enough for her collections. This was purposefully directed at me because, no matter what we're collecting—stickers, Smurfs, Strawberry Shortcake dolls—I always have less. But if Angie had an older sister, she would die from being turned into a nothing because I guarantee that Angie's sister would be the boss of them. Angie lives in a long, skinny mobile home that's set on a cement foundation. There are only two bedrooms. and you can hear everything through the walls, including farts and sneezes. Angie won't let you touch anything in her room, including her Cabbage Patch Kids. As if I care about dolls anymore. But those are so expensive, and Angie has five or six or seven, at least. I have zero. I think they're ugly. The last time I went to Angie's house was in sixth grade, on Columbus Day, because school was closed. Her dad said don't touch the stereo. Angie waited for him to leave, then said let's dance in the living room. I didn't want to, but she said don't worry—she knows what he means and does it all the time. We played Chubby Checker and danced the twist, which was actually fun until her dad got home and caught us. He locked us in her bedroom for the rest of the day. We played about ten thousand rounds of M.A.S.H., and our future husbands and houses and numbers of children kept changing, I really had to pee, but he wouldn't let us out.

Finally, Angie's mom came home about five. At first, she was mad at Angie, but then Angie's dad said Angie is just like her mother: a spoiled, fat "b-word." They started yelling and slamming doors, and Angie's mom said her dad should go off and kill himself. There was a loud thump, and Angie's mom cried, "Bastard!" Then it was quiet. Jennifer Hartman says Angie doesn't know her real dad, but Angie calls her dad "Dad," so maybe he is. In the room, Angie started laughing and making jokes that weren't very funny. We heard her dad roar away in his truck, and her mom went outside to smoke. We could smell the cigarette on the other side of the window. When she was done, her mom unlocked the door and drove me home. We stopped for doughnuts on the way, and Angie's mom said we could pick anything we wanted. I got a giant sugar-glazed doughnut with raspberry jam in the middle. The jam was sticky, and if you squeezed the doughnut, red squirted out the other side. They were so good, I remember. Angie and I got the exact same thing.

About Denise Cotter

Denise didn't go to our school until third grade. That's when Angie began talking about some weirdo in her reading group, and she pointed at Denise during recess. That same afternoon, I saw Denise on my bus. She had chocolate brown hair and was wearing blue barrettes with ribbons. I began watching her. She always sat alone or with Lisa Flannigan, who was in second grade and has gone to Sacred Heart since kindergarten. I know now that Denise's mom is cousins with Lisa's mom, so they know each other from family reunions. But Lisa is petite with long curly hair, and she has the best sticker collection, while Denise has a gap between her two front teeth and no stickers, and none of the third-grade girls liked her. Plus, Angie reported that Denise said the most bizarro things during reading group, like how plants will talk to you if you listen and how every animal likes a vote and veto when receiving a name. Denise wore one black shoe-lace and one white on a pair of dirty green tennis shoes. Her socks didn't always match, and they still don't. It's one of her things.

One day, I asked her to sit with me on the bus. I hadn't planned it, but when the bus pulled up to Denise's stop, I saw her outside, smiling. She wore her hair in a side pony-tail, my favorite. How come I didn't like her? I didn't know her. And I was tired of Angie, who always has to get her way. I sat up tall so Denise would see me, and when she reached me, I scooted over and patted the seat. "Wanna sit here?" I asked. She looked suspicious, but I patted the seat again and said, "Sit here." She glanced around, then sat.

And she was so nice! In our first conversation, she looked out the window and asked, "What do you see?"

I thought maybe it was a trick question because it was only the regular country: cows and grass, barns and trees.

"I don't know," I said. "What do you see?"

She looked and squinted, paused, and said, "I see brown shaped like cows and green shaped like leaves." Well, I wasn't expecting that! Looking out the window, the cows became more brown than cow, and there were so many shades of green.

Denise *is* weird. She knows how to make everything

strange even if nothing has changed. It's her gift. Besides, normal is boring, and at least she knows she's weird. She pretends to be a Russian spy who's lost her brain and is on a mission to find it. She uses a spying voice and writes notes in secret code but can't tell anyone—including herself—what the note says because she lost her brain and can no longer decipher. Sometimes she'll use the Russian spy voice for so long I can't find Denise inside. She plays body-dead for too long. too.

Denise is more developed than I am, and she wears braces. She has a dimple on her right cheek, and her fingers taper like Meijer's fancy candles. Her nails are always clean, and she understands about makeup and the seasons. Her mom sells Amway, so they have Artistry makeup, the best makeup ever. Artistry says every person is a season—just match nature's colors to your hair, skin, and eyes, and you'll know who you are. Wearing makeup is an art. Denise is a Winter, and I'm a Fall. She should wear black, red, and navy clothes, and her best eye shadows are brown, gold, peach, or purple. I should wear brown and orange clothing and various shades of brown shadow. Denise lives on a lake, and we go paddle-boating whenever we can. She has one younger brother and two half brothers from her dad's first marriage. I've gone to her oldest brother's house in Grand Rapids. He's tall and slouchy, and is her favorite even though he barely talks.

Denise loves MTV, and, lucky for her, there's cable on her side of the street. Her current favorite band is ZZ Top. I've seen their videos, including the one where they appear and disappear like ghosts (note: all ghosts are actually demons), and I have to say their beards are very disgusting. They are clearly trying to hide something while wanting a lot of attention for their way-too-long beards. In their video, they show up out of nowhere to supposedly help various pushovers unhappy with life. It starts with a girl who works at a shoe shop. ZZ Top gives her a key, and she's magically transformed into someone hot and horny (a gross but accurate word). In the next verse, there's a boy who's bored working at a country gas station until ZZ Top pulls up in a cool yellow roadster and gives him the key. He quits his job and goes to the city, where he meets the shoe-shop girl, and they go dancing like they're so free.

Do people actually believe that rock and roll will make them rich and sexy? Sometimes demons are so obvious.

Not that I think Denise agrees with ZZ Top's demonic message. She doesn't care about money or popularity, and she never talks about or even looks at guys. She is such a good artist. She draws half-animals, like the hippopotasnake, a hippo in the front with a snake's behind. Or the rabbit-lion, with rabbit ears and a lion's body and roar. Her drawings look like they could come alive at any moment. She makes the best adventure stories, too. Sometimes we'll go back and forth, creating a story about the world beneath the lake. There's a pink bear there, Bearly, who turns into a pink carp. That's how he travels from the door of his bottom-of-the-lake-bear-world to the top of the water, where he peeks out and sees us in this world. In Denise's picture of this moment, Bearly has a fish bottom and a bear top.

Sometimes Denise doesn't come back from the stories, as if she truly believes that Bearly exists. Even when I say, "Denise, earth to Denise," she'll just look at me with almost pity.

"Bearly loves you," she'll say. "He wants to help you, too." That's the only time she bugs me. I could almost say scares.

And that's her weirdness Jennifer Hartman and Angie talk about. Denise can go somewhere not here, and when that happens, I don't know where she is or who else is there. It's a feeling, but I can sort of see it—like the first time she took me to Mr. Henry's, or that time I came over and she'd hung sheets over her bedroom windows although she has very nice curtains. She'd closed the curtains and put the sheets over them. With duct tape. She duct-taped the sheets to the wall, all the way around—she wouldn't say why. The sheets puffed out and looked like great pillows with grey duct-tape borders. She laughed and said Bearly can't protect her. He's gone to the Grand Canyon, and she doesn't know when he'll return.

Denise thinks she's stupid because she can't do math and gets mostly B's and C's on her report card. I get mad sometimes when she calls herself dumb.

Note: It's good to have imagination if you can also be serious.

I love Denise's house. I was accidently-on-purpose there all weekend, and had to borrow her blue plaid skirt this morning since Denise's mom says jeans are allowed only at Saturday evening Mass. I haven't been to a Sunday Mass at Sacred Heart in forever—not since Dad became born again. Jennifer Hartman was there, and guess what? We three sat together in a side pew, with me in the middle. Jennifer Hartman kept offering us orange Tic Tacs, and we all went up for communion anyway because Tic

Tacs don't count as food. We passed notes about it. It's so stupid how Jennifer Hartman acts one way when Angie's there and a different way when she's alone. Hello? Who's the real Jennifer Hartman? Meanwhile, Denise doesn't know about any of this because she refuses to talk about people behind their backs—if I start in on someone, she'll change the subject. She gets this dazed look, too. Like she's gone to the place I wish she'd avoid. Denise always shares. She says she has to. If someone says, "That looks good," she'll give them half her Zinger or one of her crème-filled cookies. My mom won't buy sugary food, especially for lunches, so Denise usually brings an extra for me. She says her mom never notices anything, especially not that.

We stopped at Mr. Henry's house yesterday, but, luckily, he wasn't home. He's as old as her dad and lives alone on another part of the lake. Denise says he gets lonely, but I feel weird there, even though he buys fudge-striped shortbread cookies and milk just for us. Or for Denise and her brother, Ricky. He's also friends with Denise's dad. In the summer, he likes to stop by with a six-pack of Pabst Blue Ribbon, and they smoke brown-paper cigarettes and talk about boats and baseball. Mr. Henry is bald, his eyes are bright blue, and he's always grinning. His voice is quiet, so you have to stand close if you want to hear his words. He isn't very tall, but he has a big nose and very large hands. Mr. Henry has a go-cart, and last summer he let us drive it. That was pretty fun, and he didn't make Denise promise a specific time for her next visit, probably because he got distracted talking with her dad instead. Denise says Mr. Henry is sad because he doesn't have a wife or kids. That's what he told her. That's why he likes it when Denise and Ricky stop by to play checkers, or he'll take them swimming on his pontoon boat. Denise says she likes being Mr. Henry's friend and doesn't want him to feel bad. That's another reason I love Denise—she's the most considerate person I know!

We learned about cause and effect, and it sounded so simple. When it rains, the ground becomes wet. She sneezed, so her mother said gesundheit. Coughing can be suggestive; therefore, if someone coughs during Mass, the cough will catch and ripple around the room. Go ahead: try it. Cause and effect, our teacher explained, could be found within a sentence's syntax and structure. This is what we learned to look for: "so," "therefore," "when," "then," "since," "because."

She reasoned that if she confessed truly, the desire would disappear, quickly or eventually, according to her level of obedience and the mystery of God's unfolding plan. Because she should desire God and God alone, so all other feelings—arousal, anger, envy, yearning—were to be mastered, turned over to Him. "Humans can rationalize anything," said one Pastor. "Never trust your own mind." "It's better to be either hot or cold for Christ," preached another. "Because in Revelations, God says He will spit the lukewarm from His mouth." "I don't want to be, I don't want to be a casual Christian," sang the Christian rock duo DeGarmo and Key. "I don't want to live, I don't want to live a lukewarm life." Therefore, when people asked what she wanted to do or be, she often froze, panicked, and lashed out. What's wrong with me, she wondered through the dull fog inside her head.

After girding our loins, we were told to put on our breastplate of righteousness as the second piece of our spiritual suit of armor. This frontispiece would protect our hearts from deception and the enemy's lies; the enemy was, we learned, anyone who disagreed with our world-view. Like most parents and teachers, ours wanted us to believe what they believed—that's what they took to be true, and they wanted us to live in truth. Or that's what they understood as safety, and they wanted us to be safe. They wanted us to value what they valued, as that's what they understood as meaningful or good, and they wanted us to reflect their meaning and/or goodness back to them. For some parents, these beliefs and values were a source of solace and hope, hard-won through tears, loss, and prayer. Other parents inhabited their beliefs and values like a house they'd been comfortably born into, a structure they did not want to leave.

GOD'S VOICE

Guess who Michelle saw at the Stop-n-Go tonight—
Tammy Hartman and her mom. Tammy was wearing so much makeup, Michelle almost didn't recognize her. Or Mrs. Hartman, in her dress pants and high-heeled boots, her hair curled and perfectly sprayed. They were on their way to the mall in Grand Rapids—who goes to the mall on Wednesday night? And in high heels? Michelle thinks that whole family only cares about looks. It's true. That's why Jennifer Hartman wears brand names and never wants to sweat. But brands don't mean much if you can't be real. This explains why Jennifer Hartman can use words as if they have only one meaning and why she switches best friends every week or two. If you're superficial, you judge the surface. But God loves everyone, no matter what you wear or how much money you have—God judges you for your insides only. Pastor Marks says modest dress reflects a modest heart, and God made us modest first. I feel sorry for Jennifer Hartman because she will probably live her whole life trying to look a certain way in order to be loved, never realizing that God already loves her, sinner that she is.

It's hard to feel God's love when you're afraid to be yourself.

I wonder why Jennifer wasn't going to mall.

That's another reason I love our church: People wear ordinary jeans, and no one cares because it's most important to bring an open heart. At Sacred Heart or Assembly of God or Calvary, we always had to dress up because that's what's expected. The worst was First Pentecostal. There, all the moms and girls wear dresses and skirts, no pants, and they keep their long hair in buns or braids and aren't allowed to wear makeup or jewelry. The Pentecostals think that's the only way to be a holy female because one verse in Timothy says women shouldn't have fancy hair or expensive clothes. So Christians can be superficial, too. Because Mom's hair is short, and she'll wear pants to church if she's cold, and I definitely curl and spray my hair, but that doesn't mean we don't love Christ. In fact, I just realized how perfect it was that God called me to be full-body baptized at First Pentecostal. He could have chosen Branches or Calvary, but He called me there, at the church where we looked different. Maybe He was using me to make a larger point.

I was nine years old, and it had been raining for days. Outside, everything was mud, and our basement had already flooded once from water seeping in beneath the door since Dad still hadn't fixed the seal—though, by that point, Mom had been telling him to fix it for months. Mom said she was going to church anyway, and if it flooded while she was gone, he would just have to take care of it. She was ironing her ivory-colored blouse as she spoke, and I'd been bored all day, so I asked to go along. Mom likes it when I go to church with her. She was meeting her friend Julie Johnson for a Sunday evening service at First Pentecostal. Sometimes they show movies there, like the one about how Satan uses rock and roll and backwards masking to capture the youth. Bands like Slayer and Black Sabbath put subliminal, praise-Satan messages in their music, which allows demons to enter teens' lives. Obviously, I'm using "lives" to match the plural "teens," not because I believe in multiple lives or reincarnation— that's another demonic lie spread by "sweet-sounding" bands, like the Beatles.

You only have one chance to get right with God, one life that determines where you'll live for eternity. Also, you should know that, before Satan fell, he held the position of archangel of music in heaven, and his name was Lucifer, which means "light." Basically, Satan is a music specialist who can tempt people away from Christ's true light. He'll start playing his songs and all his beats, and, before you know it, you're dancing to Satan's rhythm, your body chained to his. It's really good to know this since you'll be judged even if you don't. That's why I like going to church with Mom, and, that night, I also wanted to wear my new white blouse and purple corduroy skirt with matching purple suspenders. Mom bought it at Meijer, and I'd never had a store-bought, coordinated outfit before. Purple, especially dark purple, is the best color ever. Wearing it made me feel good, which may sound superficial, but it's not.

Julie was waiting for us at First Pentecostal. She looks like Dolly Parton and wears her blonde hair in Dolly's same style, and even her you-know-whats are big. She is Mom's best born-again friend. She has five children and had one miscarriage, and, like Mom, she was praying for her husband to be born again. Her youngest daughter, Nancy, was the first of her kids to get saved, but I don't talk to Nancy much because she prefers Michelle, who is older than me so automatically cooler. I prefer it when Nancy isn't there because then Julie talks about her problems, and Nancy is one of her biggest. Last year, Julie caught her drinking beer, and Nancy is so sullen these days, Julie doesn't know what to do. Her words have little sighs in them—not sad sighs, like Mom's, but little breaths, like frightened hiccups. She otherwise has very clear pronunciation because she used to be a secretary in a law office before she met her husband, John. At church, Julie was wearing a white cotton dress with an eyelet pattern, and I'm pretty sure she was wearing eyeliner and lipstick because she sells Amway and her regular church is Resurrection Life, where the women love Artistry makeup and host an annual retreat. Julie looked beautiful and relaxed as she smiled right at me.

We found seats in a back pew. Everyone was singing. The songs are pretty good at First Pentecostal, but, overall, the Praise and Worship is better at Branches since we use drums and electric guitar. At First Pentecostal, it's just piano, and sometimes the pastor shakes a tambourine. He's tall with dark curly hair and bushy eyebrows. He likes to pace, shout, and stomp, and when he's preaching, his face turns bright red with righteous anger. He wants to save the world because people are dying and Satan is on the march. He sweats when he talks and sometimes spits.

That night the front of the church looked different. The wall behind the pulpit was slid open like a giant patio door, and there was a tall blue and white bathtub-style tank with steps on its side so a person could walk up and into the tub. After we sang, Pastor appeared alongside a woman with dark curly hair; they both wore long white robes. The woman was old but not old enough to be married. Maybe nineteen. She followed Pastor into the tank while two men wearing regular suits stood beside them, one on each side. Pastor prayed and dunked the woman to baptize her, and as she tipped backwards, the two men caught her and lifted her back up. She raised her hands in the air as she emerged and shouted several phrases in tongues as everyone clapped and the piano music started. Everyone was happy and shouting as we sang *It's joy unspeakable full of glory full of glory*. And Pastor slipped offstage through a side door. Oddly, I remember most of the songs we sang that night—and in what order. When the song ended, Pastor re-emerged, dry and dressed in a black suit and white button-down shirt, as if nothing had happened. The sliding walls behind him were closed, hiding the wet woman from view. Pastor said the Spirit of God was filling the church that night.

I knew he was right because Julie had gone into a prayer state. She was sitting with her eyes closed, rocking back and forth and quietly singing in tongues. Julie is sometimes like that for the whole service; she is especially touched by God and has the gift of prophecy. She can dream the future, like how she dreamt my dad would become born again long before Mom thought such a conversion was possible. In her dream, she said Dad was holding a Bible and walking outside to start the car, that we were leaving the house together, going to the same church. "I'm telling you," Julie said. "God has a plan." Mom and Julie were having this conversation at the kitchen table while I was in living room, listening and pretending to read. Six months later, Dad became born again. Isn't that crazy? So that night at First Pentecostal, neither Mom nor I were going to interrupt Julie. If she wanted to sit and quietly pray while Pastor was preaching, that was between her and God.

Pastor preached about the power of baptism in a way I hadn't heard. He said if you think you're saved but haven't been baptized, then prepare yourself for a big surprise because you won't make it to heaven. At first, I thought he was talking about being baptized in the Word, which is like being born again, but Pastor said no, some people think accepting Jesus into their heart is enough—that they're saved, done, and taken care of—and some churches even teach this lie, but the truth is that, if you haven't been baptized, your Christian journey hasn't begun! When Jesus started His ministry, what did He do? Get baptized in the river. Jesus called the disciples by baptizing each and every one of them. When the disciples began preaching after Jesus's death and resurrection, they baptized people and performed miracles in His name. Baptism is in the Bible! The Sinner's Prayer is not—that wasn't in the sermon but is good to remember.

Pastor said if you've haven't been baptized, you'll be banished, turned away.

My ears were burning, and my throat felt tight. I definitely want to go to heaven. Pastor started talking about the Trinity, how God is three-in-one and one-in-three, how you can't know the Holy Spirit unless you are baptized, how you won't know God unless you receive the Holy Spirit. The Bible says, "Except a man be born of water and of Spirit, he cannot enter the kingdom of God."

That's when I knew I had to be baptized. Because even if Pastor's teaching differed from what I'd heard at Branches, I didn't want even a sliver of a chance that I could go to hell. My chest felt heavy and full, like something familiar. God, I wanted to be baptized, but when I tried to talk, I couldn't move.

That's when Julie opened her eyes, turned to Mom, and said, "You have a child who wants to be baptized."

Isn't that amazing?!

I thought Mom would look right at me, but instead she said, "That's strange. Could it be Michelle?"

Julie shook her head like she didn't know.

I was standing right there. How could they not see me? Especially with the pounding so loud, I couldn't breathe. Or maybe I was holding my breath—because when I exhaled, I could move again. I tugged on Mom's ivory-colored sleeve.

"Mom," I whispered, "it's me."

She couldn't hear, but Julie looked, tilting her head like Dolly does while singing "Coat of Many Colors." I nodded, and she smiled. Her eyes were glazed from praise. Mom followed Julie's smile, scowling because that's always her first look.

"Marie?" she said. I nodded. She was worried, I think, that we were wrong.

But Julie had heard God's voice. There was no denying it. Julie said I had to tell Pastor. "Right now?" I asked, and Julie started turning me in his direction. My throat tightened again. I did not want to. "Maybe later," I said, but Julie insisted.

"God spoke," she said. I looked at Mom, who finally nodded.

I no longer believe that you must be baptized in order to go to heaven. That's what the Pentecostals think, but remember: they don't let girls cut their hair or wear makeup, either. And while it's a sin to be vain and conceited, wearing eye shadow doesn't mean you're either of those things, and not wearing eye shadow could also be vanity. Too, there are a lot of rules in the Bible that we don't follow because the times have changed. We eat of the cloven hoof, and people say oysters are delicious. God knows this. He makes oysters and "the times." It's more important to repent and turn your insides over to Christ. When you're truly pure, you'll want to mature in Christ, which means you'll want to be baptized. Like how I did when God called me. If I had listened to my scared feelings, I would have missed His call.

So as the congregation started singing *just a closer walk with Thee,* I slipped from the pew and walked up a side aisle, around to where Pastor was. I didn't go onto the altar but stood on the side, waiting for him to notice. I could feel everyone's eyes. When he finally noticed, he slowly walked over and leaned down. I asked him, "May I be baptized?"

He looked at me with hard, brown eyes behind rimless glasses. There was sweat on his forehead and grey curls in his black hair. "You want to be baptized?" he said. His teeth were big and square, and he smiled when I whispered yes. Then he motioned with his giant hands, and two larger men suddenly stood beside me. They took me, one by each arm, to the area behind the sliding wall. They told me to wait.

I did not have to tell Pastor about God's message to Julie. Maybe when he looked at me, he could hear God's call.

A few minutes passed. I was cold. My nose started to

run. I sniffed, and a lady appeared, her grey hair wrapped in a tight bun. She smiled with her mouth closed, touched my arm, and called me "dearie." She was wide, bearlike. Her voice was low. She gave me my own white robe and pointed at a door I hadn't seen. "Take everything off," she said.

Alone in the bathroom, I paused at my underwear. They would want us to wear underwear for something holy, right? The robe felt heavy and stable. Protective. Little weights were sewn into its bottom seam, and later I understood they helped the robe hang straight even while in the water. The bathroom floor was pale blue linoleum and very chilly on my bare feet as I folded my skirt, shirt, tights. Outside the bathroom, the bunned woman was waiting, rubbing her hands. She smiled in my direction while avoiding my eyes. She led me to the side of the tank, where Pastor motioned me forward. He told me to go in first, that he would enter behind. He whispered instructions: He would pray, then dunk me. Just relax, he said. Follow his lead. It's weird when Pastor whispers directly to you, how you become more of a body than part of the flock. Pastor kept preaching. He said God is doing great things—another soul has come forward, another terrible sinner.

Someone said, "Praise Jesus." I knew my mom was out there. Everyone was looking. I did not want to look back.

Pastor said, "Thank you, Jesus, and I baptize you…" and as he spoke, he pushed down on my forehead while his other arm held the small of my back. I couldn't help it. I grabbed my nose and pinched it closed to hold my breath. Relax, I heard his voice say inside me.

When I came up, people were singing. I lifted my hands

and whispered, "Thank you. Jesus." I wanted something more, but that's all I had.

Mom was quiet on the way home. I could feel my underwear, wrapped in seven layers of paper towels and stuffed in my coat pocket. The rain was heavy. It was difficult to see. I rubbed my hands against my tights. I didn't tell Mom about the underwear. She hadn't smiled when I returned to the pew. Maybe she was suspicious, even angry. Did I love Jesus? Or was I trying to avoid hell? Maybe I stole Michelle's prophecy, like Jacob did to Esau. Maybe Julie's message wasn't for me. Why didn't I speak in tongues? I didn't know that, in order to speak in tongues, God needs you to move your own mouth. But as we neared the Icy-Cream in Comstock Park, Mom slowed the car. "Well," she said, "Let's see if it's open." And like that, everything was light. We always beg Mom to stop there, and she always says no; it's wasteful to buy individual cones when you can buy a gallon for less. Then we were inside Icy-Cream, and she said I could get whatever I wanted. It took me forever to decide on a double-dip waffle cone with black cherry and bubble gum because both flavors were different shades of pink. "Are you sure?" said Mom. They looked so pretty together. And Dad loves cherry things.

I licked the ice cream and knew I'd made a mistake. The bubble gum was too sweet; the Chiclets impossible to chew; the cherry tasted like rotting maraschinos on ice. Mom turned the car heat on high. I see now that I had acted superficial, like Jennifer Hartman, by picking ice cream flavors based on looks. Because being pretty doesn't mean you're good. I don't want to be like Jennifer

Hartman, my heart filled with daggers. I chose the ice cream, so I had to eat the whole thing. Otherwise Mom might never stop again. Not for me or for anyone. I ate every bit of that waffle cone, each sour cherry and every piece of Chiclet gum. They were tiny, hard, unchewable. But once I swallowed one, the rest knew how to follow.

Every priest and pastor, every Vacation Bible School teacher and youth group facilitator, the church camp counselors and radio commentators, the televangelists and visiting missionaries—they said that, with baptism, you receive new life. With salvation, your old self passes away. The old self, they assumed, was a dirty, unwanted thing. A source of pain only. They didn't speak of the grief or mourning that's part of the loss and letting go necessary for rebirth to occur. A transition sometimes chosen but often not. The inevitable change of shifting situations and bodies, of adversity or growth. Puberty, graduation, illness, a new job, a failed marriage. And then, of course, there is death itself. The religious teachers spoke of death—but only literally of the one death, the final one. Never death as a necessity for renewal, death as a passageway toward life. The religious teachers wanted a world clearly ordered. To children and adults, they preached a simple Bible, with one true story to tell.

STORYTELLING

In the beginning, after God created the world, He looked at the stars sparkling in the heavens and the starfish sprinkled in the seas. He saw red canyons and green mountains, tall needled trees. There were short brown bushes and tiny black fleas, crab apples, tangerines and elephants' knees. Yes, God looked out and saw all of these, and He smiled and sighed because He was pleased. But something was missing, one most important thing—for God's new world needed a king!

Well, not a king exactly, but it rhymed, and I couldn't resist. By the way, rhymes are a mnemonic device used in poetry to help you remember the words and know what sound to expect, even if you don't understand the poem. Mrs. Kirkwood taught us that last year. Nowadays, not all poems rhyme because they're written about today's world, which is filled with wars, nuclear bombs, and social upheavals—things that aren't very rhyme-ie. No one knows what's happening anymore, and they shouldn't know what to expect in a poem, either. Maybe God didn't expect to be lonely in His new world, so He made Adam to keep Him company. Or maybe God made the world so He'd have an excuse to make Adam—in His image, with an eternal soul and a pleasant face. Of course, He's God, so He always knew that Adam would sin. But God let Adam name the other animals anyway, and they lined up, one or two of each kind, and walked, crawled, flew, or swam before Adam, who spoke their first name. We don't know what those names sounded like because

Adam didn't speak English (was English even invented?) but some other language, even earlier than ancient Greek or Hebrew. I bet his poems rhymed, too.

After Adam finished naming the animals, he sighed so loudly that God asked him what was wrong. Adam said the animals were cute and everything, but none of them were his type, like him, if you know what I mean, and when God went home to heaven every evening, He left Adam alone.

"No one understands me," said Adam. "And when no one understands you, it's almost as if you don't exist." Then Adam began to almost-cry ("almost" because Eden was still paradise, so no tears allowed). Adam said, "When You leave tonight, I'll be so lonely!"

God understood. So that night, when Adam fell asleep, He snuck back in, took one of Adam's ribs, and made Eve. Note: In Genesis 1, Adam and Eve are made at the same exact time. But in Genesis 2, the story is repeated, with Adam made before Eve and the whole rib part, too. I asked Pastor Jaime about this—I mean, how can the Bible, which is the Word of God and Absolute Truth of the Universe of All Time, have two different versions of the same story? He warned me against getting caught in details. God included both stories because they're both equally true. In both, he explained, the word "man" comes first. Pastor Jaime says God used one of Adam's ribs because ribs are on the sides of our bodies, and men and women should stand together, side by side. Ribs are also located under the arms, so God used one of Adam's ribs to show that men are supposed to protect women, physically and spiritually, by putting their arms around them. That's why men are the head of the household, and women, the helpmates. Or sidekicks. Eventually, I want a husband who is strong in God and will take care of everything, but I don't want to stay home, canning vegetables and nursing babies. I'd rather be doing something—like building schools in Swaziland or leading a women's prayer retreat. Also, I want to marry someone cool, like Pastor Jaime, though he's too tall and big for me. He played football in high school and looks like a bison. I like bison, but I don't want to marry one. I would rather touch a deer.

But here is another contradiction. In Genesis 1, God made the trees and other animals before man, and in Genesis 2, He made the trees and shrubs afterwards. And while this may seem like a little detail to Pastor Jaime, changing the setting changes the whole story. That's also from last year's English class.

The point of my story is that God doesn't want to be alone. He made Adam and Eve so He'd have someone to hang out with, even though He knew they would betray Him. Everyone messes up. Like tonight. Mom made mashed potatoes, and I was taking big bites because I love mashed potatoes. And then my body couldn't help it. I have a cold. I coughed. Potatoes went everywhere, which was so gross, little spots of mushy white on everyone's plates. Mikey and Michelle freaked out, jumping up from the table like frightened cats. They said I'm the most disgusting person alive, and Michelle yelled at Mom, saying, "Why do you let her do that?" "You were eating like a pig," she said to me, and Mikey accused me of slurping.

I was sniffing because my nose is stuffy. Not slurping. But I hate how gross I am. Mom and I got up to switch everyone's plates, but Michelle and Mikey said they were done. It was already gross to be sitting there because Dad came in late from the barn and Mom wouldn't warm the food. He said he had to finish that job if we want to pay bills, but Mom thinks he'd get more done if people didn't just stop by. They always bring beer, too. I don't know whose truck that was. I saw it leave, and Dad came in a while later. What if there is something seriously wrong with me? I know you're supposed to cover your mouth when you cough. Michelle says most people live their whole lives without coughing mashed potatoes onto other people's plates. That would never happen to Michelle, it's true.

We make mistakes. It's part of our condition. And no matter what you do, you'll sin again, perhaps more. After dinner, Dad went back to the barn, and Mom went to bed with a headache. God, meanwhile, knew He didn't want to create Adam and Eve to be robot zombies, automatically programmed to love Him. He didn't want them to be users, either, loving Him just because He gave them the fowl of the sky and the fish of the sea. No, God wanted Adam and Eve to love Him for who He was and is—His true self. That's why He gave them freedom to make their own decisions. He said, "I made this Garden for you. Stay as long as you like, and eat whatever you want. Eat from all of the trees and all of the bushes, but I have one rule: Do not eat from this one tree in the center of the garden. If you eat from this one tree," God said, "you will surely die."

At first, Adam and Eve were so pure, they followed His one rule because they didn't want to hurt Him. They had so many trees to choose from that they didn't need to eat from that one forbidden tree. Death didn't exist in Eden, which, when I think about it, means that Adam and Eve didn't *know* what "to die" meant. Everything in Eden was beautiful and good. All the animals were kind and trustworthy—there weren't predators, and even future carnivores didn't eat meat. So when Satan showed up, disguised as a snake (and remember: back then snakes had legs), Adam and Eve didn't realize they shouldn't trust him. How could they? They were being tested.

In a sermon, Pastor Marks said that Adam and Eve should have suspected two things: 1) The snake was speaking their language, even though none of the other animals could talk, and 2) The snake contradicted God, which was the biggest sign that something was wrong. They listened to Satan and let in a seed of doubt. They began to question. Does God really love us? Why doesn't He give us all the fruit? What is He hiding, and does God mean what He says? The only way to test the truth of God's word was to break God's rule and see what happened. Thus, they ate: first Eve, then Adam. Pastor Marks says women are more insecure, which is why Satan spoke to Eve first, and Adam went along because man's main weakness is woman. The Bible says they ate the fruit and "saw it was good." "Good"—maybe to taste. It probably was delicious.

This is why you should listen only to Christian music and take advice only from other Christians. If you're faced with a temptation, like singing along to Huey Lewis and the News on the school bus—which Denise and I did today because David brought his boom box—and while you're singing, you feel pangs of wrongness eased by a small whining voice saying, "Oh, it's just some song—it's not like you're the one who's playing it on your boom box. You don't even have a boom box"—STOP! Think about whose voice that might be. Satan or any of the other fallen angels (now demons and evil spirits) can whisper bad ideas directly into your head. Of course, it probably won't be Satan himself because, as ruler of this fallen world, he's busy commanding a whole demonic army and is more preoccupied with things like abortion doctors and homosexuals.

But like they say in *Pigs in the Parlor*, Mom's book about demonic war strategies, if you have a thought like "Everyone thinks I'm gross, weird, or uptight," or "I need to touch myself in order to fall asleep," a demon is in the room with you, speaking into your mind. (Question: Can demons use your sister to put thoughts in your head?) To cast those demons out, say, "You are a liar, demon. I reject those thoughts about myself." Then cover your mind with the blood of Jesus, bind the thoughts, and command the demon to leave. If you don't do this, you are essentially allowing the demon into your life, and the longer it talks to you, the more you will believe it. The more it will control your mind, even as you will be the person punished for believing the demon's lies. Demons are already banished from heaven. They're trying to get everyone else banished, too.

I quit singing on the bus today. Denise noticed and quit singing too. She told David to wear his headphones because we didn't want to hear his song. She asked what was wrong, but I didn't answer. After a while, I asked her if she ever thinks about hell. "I don't think much about anything," she laughed. I didn't want her to go into her Russian spy voice, so I looked away instead of laughing with her. After a minute, she said, "Maybe hell is on earth."

I don't know what she means, but she's wrong. "Denise," I said, "hell is real. Just imagine if you were the wick of a birthday candle and the flame never went out."

She shrugged and laughed again. "You could wish not to go there!"

When I didn't respond, she said, "They say war is hell."

But maybe there are wars you have to fight, like defeating Hitler and freeing the Jews.

Demons will always use some nugget of truth to hook you—like how, in Eden, Satan didn't tell a 100% lie. Adam and Eve did become more like God: Their eyes opened, and they became aware of evil and good. They knew they were naked, and when God came that evening for their nightly walk, they felt ashamed and scared. They hid from God. Adam and Eve's sin was "original," the first sin and the reason humans are hungry, arrogant, selfish, and conceited.

God can't stand sin. Sin to God is the noontime sun to an albino baby or a bee sting to Lisa Flannigan. She used to go our school, and she was so allergic, she had to carry a needle and medicine so that if she got stung, she could give herself a special shot. Otherwise, she would quit breathing and immediately die. That's like sin to God. It's suffocating, searing. If you're thinking, "Well, He's God. Why doesn't He make Himself *not* allergic to sin," let me tell you that God can't do that, because even though He technically can, if He did, He wouldn't be God anymore. It's self-regarding, and God can't be God unless He has something, like sin, to rule over. It's also not His fault that Adam and Eve sinned, causing the rest of us to become so beast-like and dirty that God can't stand the sight or smell of us. God still loves us—no one loves you more than God does—He just can't be around sin, and we chose sin over Him. From the oldest, most wonderful gingerbread grandma to the youngest, sweetest most milky baby—we are all sinners, doomed to hell.

But there's one exception. Aborted babies automatically go to heaven because those babies were never born, so they don't have original sin. By the way, just because something is legal doesn't make it right. Abortion is always wrong, and it wouldn't be fair to punish an unborn baby for a mother's sin. Though that sometimes happens in the Bible, where the consequences of sin are passed down, yea, even to the third and fourth generations (Numbers 14:18). But the Bible is talking about living people, not dead babies. Also, laws matter because they shape our morals and daily lives. For example, ever since "no-fault" divorce became legal, only one marriage out of every two lasts. Not that I think divorce should be illegal. People should not have to stay married if they don't want to, and, also, not everyone believes divorce is morally wrong. But if you're a Christian, you probably should think so. Divorce is different from abortion because abortion is murder, and that's breaking one of the more serious Ten Commandments. (Is disobeying your mom the same as murder? Is remarrying after divorce adultery?) On the radio they said more babies have been killed in this country from abortion than the total number of Jews lost during the Holocaust. Note: I'm pretty sure Jewish Holocaust victims are also in heaven. God has a different arrangement with the Jews. And it wouldn't be fair to go from a concentration camp to actual hell. In fact, one of the main reasons Christ died on the cross was so Gentiles can become God's chosen people, too. If we so choose.

It would seem that babies who die as miscarriages also go to heaven, but I wonder about babies who die during childbirth. And what about babies who die days, or even hours, after they are born? Catholics hurry and baptize newborns, to wash away original sin so the baby will definitely go to heaven. If a baby dies before she's baptized, the Catholics say she's in Purgatory. But guess what— Purgatory does not exist. That's a place Catholics made up—it's not in the Bible. So what else about their faith is false? I bet the prince demon of the Catholic church started that lie, and now millions of Catholics believe they can make it to heaven by doing good works and through the prayers of others. In *Pigs in the Parlor*, they say that Satan, or one of his managers, assigns a specific demon to every church for the sole reason of messing that church up. It's scary, but you can bind the demon and purify your church. You have to get the whole congregation to do it. There's power in groups.

When I think about it, maybe all babies go to heaven. Somebody can't be saved until they are old enough to reject Christ, and babies and toddlers can't make that choice, so it's not fair to make them burn forever. Even though I've known some really mean toddlers. On the other hand, everyone has original sin, so maybe babies do have to burn. It's the same thing with people who are mentally slow or not fully developed—unless, of course, that person did something really bad. Like my dad's cousin's son. He kept bringing his thing out and playing with it, especially when there were girls in the room. Mom wouldn't let Michelle and me be near him. Eventually, they sent him to a special home with guards, which my dad's cousin did not want to do. The State of Michigan said it was either that or prison, then sent her a bill. God doesn't want to be separated from us, either, so when He kicked Adam and Eve out of the garden, He told them He'd give them Jesus to pay the price of their sin.

Wait—is God more like the State of Michigan or like my dad's cousin? And what about Jesus, as He is the person paying the bill, literally with His life?

Sometimes, rather than trying to figure out God's logic and all His rules, I just praise Him with songs and cheers, which is what He really wants—for us to worship Him, to call Him amazing and terrific, a tremendous, perfect God. Here's something I made up at Vacation Bible School (VBS) one year. Break into two groups. and the first side shouts, "Who's the God with all the might?"

Side 2 answers, "That's right, He's Jesus Christ!"

Side 1: "Who's the Lord who shines so bright?"

Side 2: "Outta sight, my Jesus Christ!"

"He'll make everything all right?"

"Get tight with Jesus Christ!"

At the nondenominational Protestant church, we didn't talk much about Mary. Her obedience, we learned, was her most important quality, as was Joseph's, who stayed beside her even as she carried another's child. God spoke to them, our pastor said, and they listened, thus fulfilling their divine roles. Obedience, he explained, along with repentance and forgiveness, is always a choice. The more you love your Father, the more you'll want to obey.

At the Convent of San Marco, Fra Angelico placed his *Annunciation* at the top of a stairway, yet, depending on the day and size of the crowd, it's one of the more difficult frescos to see. The stairway is wide, carpeted in red. At the top, thick double doors open from the landing, and the viewer, the seeker, passing through these doors, ascends toward the painting. In the Gospel of John, Jesus says, "I am the door; by me, if anyone shall enter, he shall be saved." Here, all are welcome to walk through the Christ portal and meet the divine. Yet in the Gospel of Luke, Jesus warns of the door's inevitable closure: "You will stand outside knocking and pleading, 'Sir, open the door for us.' But He will answer, 'I don't know you or where you come from.'" Here, she worried about possible estrangement. How far could she wander into the forestlike world of secular thinking? For, increasingly, she couldn't stomach their particular Jesus, but she was scared, so scared, to lose sight of their door.

In college, a friend accused her of proselytizing. "You don't know what that word means," her friend observed, and she admitted, with a flush of shame, that no, she did not. Her ignorance made the friend laugh harder. "It means you like to convert people," the friend proclaimed. Which was confusing as she hadn't spoken to the friend about anything Christian and wasn't certain she still believed in their God herself. Or, more precisely, she had given up so many of the so-called Christian rules, for following them felt like stuffing herself into an unnaturally small, one-size-fits-all box.

"I'm suffocating," she said to herself. "I don't want to wear a pink hair bow," she said to her mother. She liked going to concerts, smoking some weed, not shaving her armpits or legs. Yet if the spiritual realm remained all around us (she felt it, yes), then who's to say that their God and His awful teachings didn't exist? She tried not to think about it. She didn't say this to the woman who had been her friend—because after talking about proselytizing, the two women only saw each other at parties, where they smiled tensely and said hello.

Mary and Gabriel peer, mouths closed, into each other's eyes. Insight: a radical realignment in perception. Time collapses, as what has been and will be comes into presence. Into this moment. The here and now. A viewer can step back and survey this scene from a distance. Or she can fall into the gap between the painting's two figures, unfixed as she looks from one pair of eyes to the other, a penetration sensed yet unseen. For how do you visually represent that which occurs within the vast internal cosmos?

Learning the word "zealous" also felt significant. "You are," observed an early roommate, "rather zealous about your friends." She hadn't realized how much she'd been talking about the small group she'd left behind, a mix of high school and community college students she knew mostly from the twenty-four-hour diner. Because that's where they'd go to drink coffee, do homework, smoke cigarettes, and talk politics and art. Like her, they listened to punk and alternative music, and like her, they mostly came from fundamentalist Christian or deeply religious families. They were all experimenting with new rules to live by: eating vegan or vegetarian, refusing makeup or conventional ideas of beauty, resisting capitalism and environmental calamity by shopping for secondhand clothes.

There is a Corinthian column between the angel and Mary, and, according to Georges Didi-Huberman, this object signifies "the uncrossable distance" between sacred and ordinary time, as well as "the mysterious journey through which the Incarnation has crossed every conceivable threshold." If experience exists within the intersection of time and space, then perhaps the Annunciation, this moment announcing the divine within, occurs as space from one dimensional realm intersects with time from another. A moment in which both an insurmountable barrier and the crossing of this barrier become true, possible but not inevitable, apprehended but not fixed. Surrounding Mary and Gabriel, four additional columns link via a series of arches, which are, in turn, connected by a thick black line. On the online site *Art and the Bible*, someone writes, "The purpose of the black line between the arcs of the loggia is unclear. They do show that Angelico had good control of linear perspective."

She likes to imagine the black line as a sacred geometric hologram made visible.

She learned the word "theodicy" while driving home from a tutoring job at a community college. She was listening to an audio course entitled "Philosophy and Religion in the West." "Theodicy," the professor explained, was coined by the German mathematician and philosopher Gottfried Leibniz to describe the logical problem of how a good God, all-knowing and all-beneficent, can allow for suffering and evil in the world. If God is love, how can there be hell? If God created each of us, how can He say, "I do not know you."

One time she asked her devoutly Catholic grandmother (the one she could ask because this grandmother had found deep acceptance) why, if God knows all things, including the future, did he create Adam and Eve if He knew they would sin, fall, and bring us all down? Her grandmother said she didn't know. That she'd never thought about it like that.

From her spiritual suit of armor, she learned that "to shod" one's feet meant putting on footwear, in this case "with the preparation of the Gospel of Peace." This implied walking shoes and readiness, she supposed, to go out and tell others about Christ. Of course, this was not a word for everyday conversation, for most would find her deeply strange if she said something like "Let me shod my feet before we go."

In a college seminar, she learned Freud's concept of repetition compulsion: that a person unconsciously repeats a behavior or situation, including trauma, out of "the desire to return to an earlier state of things." She wasn't 100% sure of Freud's meaning, but she began noticing patterns within her life. Her intimate female friendships, for example, often ran too hot to not turn cold. At parties or other social events, she somehow always disclosed her restrictive, religious childhood, even as she tried to focus the conversation mostly on others. Yes, some part of her was still at Children's Church, Bible camp, or Sunday service, forever putting on her armor of God.

CHECKLIST

"Friends," by Michael W. Smith, came on the radio while I was drying dishes, and I wondered if it's even possible to be forever friends with someone if you're not both born again. Otherwise, how can you be honest? Like last year—we got in so much trouble for the slam book. Jennifer Hartman and I had the idea from *Facts of Life* (of course it was Blair's book), and our first question was, "Do you want to do a slam book?" Everyone wrote yes, because the first rule is you can't look in the book unless you write in it, too. We asked the same questions about everyone. What are the best and worst things about her? The prettiest and the ugliest? What is something she should change? That's how I know they think I'm bossy and that people actually like Jennifer Hartman's tiny smudge nose.

We wrote in the slam book for three days before Beth McNorton told her mom, although she swears she was only asking for help and didn't realize her mom would tell the whole school. I thought maybe if Angie saw how everyone thinks she's spoiled and babyish, she would start acting more mature, and if Jennifer Hartman knew that people felt bad when she whispered to another friend right in front of them, she would stop because who wants to intentionally hurt someone? That's honestly why I wanted to do the book—so that everyone could improve. I definitely want to get braces because more than one person wrote that my teeth are ugly. The slam book was final proof of something you already suspected.

Still, Mrs. Kirkwood made us write a secret letter that only she would read, describing how it felt to read what others wrote about us and how that influenced our own writing. Afterward, she said that everyone's feelings were hurt and that some people began writing mean and untrue things because they wanted revenge. Mrs. Kirkwood asked who started the book, and I wanted to confess—with Jennifer Hartman—but she said if I told, she would hate me forever. But I couldn't stand not telling the truth, even if Mrs. Kirkwood probably knew that only one or two girls in the class are charismatic enough to start a slam book.

She took away recess until someone came forward, saying she'd keep us inside for the rest of the year if necessary. She didn't look like she was bluffing. So I confessed. I said it was all my idea. I never told on Jennifer Hartman, I swear. Mrs. Kirkwood was disappointed. She expected more, especially from me. Then Mom grounded me for two weeks, and for the first week, Mrs. Kirkwood made me clean the classroom every day during recess. Now Jennifer makes it sound like it was only my idea and that I pressured everyone to participate. Mom knows that's not true. She said you can tell a lot about a person by how they accept responsibility for their actions. It's hard to be a ringleader. It's even harder to know who you can trust.

How to Tell Your True Friends

1. Do you feel bad after talking with your friend? The first step in recognizing a true friend is to know that some friends are false. True friends like you for who you

are; false friends want something else, like to feel popular at school or the answers for their math homework. If a friend is always asking for favors and comes to your house to hang out but never invites you over, pay attention! She is probably a user.

2.   Does your friend spread rumors or make fun of you behind your back? Does she laugh when others tease you or roll her eyes when you complain? If so, she's not a true friend. Because true friends will tell you about your annoying habits—and to your face, too. I told Denise to quit calling herself stupid, and she said I can act like I'm better than everyone else. I'm happy Denise told me because I honestly don't believe that. But maybe it's confusing when I'm the person always put in charge.

3.   Is your friend happy for you if you win a prize? I have had this problem a lot because I happen to win a lot of prizes. Just last year, I won the Catholic Diocese poster contest, the Sacred Heart holiday poem prize, and the Project Business community essay contest. After the Project Business award ceremony, Derek Cunningham said I'm the only person dorky enough to write an extra essay, and if he had entered the contest, he would have won. (Guess what, Derek. I get better grades than you, too.) Meanwhile, Denise said, "Congratulations," and we went to Meijer, where I spent the $50.00 of prize money on stickers and new sticker books for both of us. Photo albums with protective sheets work best.

4.   Does your friend act one way when she's alone with you and another when she's with her other friends? Will she sometimes ignore you or pretend she's too busy to say hello? True friends never ignore each other, and true

friends don't keep their other friends selfishly to themselves. Angie always talks about her cousin, Cheryl, who supposedly is the coolest person ever. But she won't let Cheryl meet us, even when we ask. I suspect she doesn't want Cheryl to see how we think Angie is annoying. I'm sure Cheryl finds her annoying, too.

5.   Does your friend invite you to her house? Does she ever call, just to talk? These are signs that someone likes you. If you're the only person making invitations and telephoning, then it's a one-sided friendship and maybe not a friendship at all. On the other hand, does your friend invite you somewhere—Saturday afternoon all-skate, for example—and tell you while you're lacing your skates that she was going to invite someone else but really wanted to be the cutest girl at the rink, so she invited you instead? Jennifer Hartman did that last year; she said she was going to invite Stephanie Conroy but changed her mind at the last minute. She used her whisper voice when she told me and didn't wait for my response. Can someone become so ugly on the inside that they're outsides turn ugly, too?

6.   A true friend truly wants what's best for you. That's why true friends share Jesus Christ with each other. If you know your friend is going to hell, you need to help her. That's why I led Jennifer Hartman and Angie to Christ—I want to be a true friend. I really do.

Staying Gold

Michelle and I went to the library after school, and she showed me the best books—like *The Outsiders*. It's so good, I read the whole thing last night. Ponyboy almost turned into someone he's not because it hurt so much when Johnny died. Johnny was his best friend. A true friend. It wasn't fair because there were two gangs in their town—Greasers and Socs. The Socs had money to go to college and wear madras shirts. The Greasers had nowhere to go, no money, and were considered scum. If Johnny hadn't accidently killed that Soc, the Soc would have killed Ponyboy. I'm so glad Ponyboy found Johnny's message in the book and realized that, by giving up on everything, he was letting himself change, and Johnny would have hated that. Ponyboy had to stay gold, or Johnny would have died for nothing, for a Ponyboy who no longer existed. I'm glad I'm not a boy. Every boy has to fistfight at least once, or he'll be a pushover forever.

In a back aisle, I also found a bright green book called *Sons of Africa*, by Elmer Schmelzenbach, who used a simple prayer to change his life and the hearts of those around him. He was a missionary in Swaziland, just like the missionary who led me to Christ. I was in second grade, and we had been going to Awana at Grace Baptist for two months, which felt like forever because we always played dodgeball and the boys aimed the ball right for your head. I got hurt every week. But that night we had a special presentation, so Mr. Hoekstra, the director, said no sports—we were in for a treat. I hoped that meant cookies, but Mr. Hoekstra said, "Let's show Dr. Winkle what we've got." That was his cue for us to sing the only song we ever sang at Awana; we sang it every week, and every time we marched in place and pumped our arms as we sang.

Firmly Awana stands
Led by the Lord's commands
Approved Workmen Are Not Ashamed
Boys and girls for His service claim!
Hail, Awana, on the march for truth!

Note how I underlined the first letter of each word in the middle line: "Awana" is an acronym. That night, everyone sang as loud as possible. Except for Mikey and Michelle. They were there because the Awana van picked us up at the end of our driveway and Mom gave us no choice but to go to Awana every Monday night. Mikey and Michelle hated Awana; they called it stupid with a stupid name and a stupid song. Why do they say "workmen" when it's a club for children? They made fun of everyone's singing. They would have laughed at mine, too, even though Jesus wants us to sing. That's what Mr. Hoesktra said. He watched us, and he sang, too, pointing at anyone not singing loud enough, smiling and encouraging them to be louder. That night, some children were probably singing and marching on the outside while their insides wished to stay quiet. It's better if your insides and outsides always match.

We finished singing, and Mr. Hoekstra asked if anyone knew about Swaziland. Nobody answered; I'd never heard of such a word. Mr. Hoekstra asked if anyone wanted to guess where Swaziland is located, and someone shouted "California!"

Everyone laughed, but Mr. Hoekstra said, "Raise your hand." An older red-haired boy lifted his and suggested Africa. "That's right," said Mr. Hoekstra. And like other African countries, there are lions and tigers and elephants in Swaziland—and many people who have never heard the Good News of Jesus Christ. He paused. I pictured the skinny black boy, shirtless and ribs popping visible, that I'd seen on the cover of *National Geographic* and wondered if *National Geographic* just takes pictures and leaves. Denise said they do, but that seems too mean, especially since they are taking the boy's picture because he is starving. He should at least get a sandwich or something. "We have a guest today," said Mr. Hoekstra, "who has traveled all the way from Swaziland just to be with us tonight. Please welcome Dr. Bob Winkle!"

I'd never seen a real-life missionary. He was pale white and wore a dark brown suit with darker brown shoes and square toes. He had a long, skinny nose, not very much red hair, and was super tall. He called us boys and girls and said we could call him Doctor. He knew a thing or two about healing bodies, thanks be to God, but his main work in Swaziland was healing souls. He never imagined living in Swaziland. He said that, as a boy, he wanted to be a policeman or a baseball player. But at college he went to a Campus Crusade for Christ meeting, and that's where he found Jesus. He rejoiced when God knocked on his heart's door and whispered, "Seminary." But at Seminary, God knocked again, and this time Dr. Winkle heard "Missions."

Dr. Winkle said, "OK, God. If that's what you want. But please don't send me to Africa." He thought that Africa was filled with dangerous insects and deadly disease and that everyone there would hate him. But it's not the physical illness that makes Africa scary. It's the spiritual sickness, the witchcraft. Someone could put a spell on you, and there are spirits ruling that land that have been there for thousands of years. They are very well organized, with a stronghold over the people, which is why God is always sending missionaries to Africa. It's one of the most intense spiritual battlegrounds, but God loves Africans and wants them all for Himself. God knows what's best for those who follow Him. And when Dr. Winkle prayed about his first missions, he heard the dreaded word "Africa."

At first, Dr. Winkle was upset with God. He'd done everything God wanted and felt like Africa was punishment. Why did God want to punish him? "But," said Dr. Winkle with a smile, "God knows each one of us better than we know ourselves." Then he leaned toward us and gave a big exaggerated wink. He did this a few times that night. Because, I suppose, his name is Dr. Winkle.

Dr. Winkle had a question for us: "How many of you brush your teeth every night before bed?" Everyone raised their hand. He asked, "How many of you brush your teeth every morning before school?" Everyone raised their hand. "All right, kids," he said, "be honest—how many of you would skip brushing your teeth if your parents didn't make you brush them?" I didn't raise my hand. I always brush my teeth unless I forget. But so many kids raised their hands. They would admit that? Dr. Winkle walked toward a large poster board leaning face against the wall. He turned the poster board around and held it high: a picture of a giant-sized mouth with swollen red gums and dirty yellow teeth. The teeth had black spots on them. Some of them were sideways, some were chipped off, and almost all of them were brown at the top. I swear there was green fuzz. That giant mouth was the ugliest, grossest, biggest mouth anyone has ever seen.

"This," said Dr. Winkle, "this is what happens to your mouth if you don't obey your parents and brush your teeth twice a day, every day."

"And do you know what I've learned—that if you don't obey the Word of God every day throughout the day, your soul will rot just like your unbrushed teeth. Your insides will shrink and decay. You'll get black spots of nothingness, soul cavities and spirit puss. If you're a Christian who's not following God's exact plan for your life, you'll have so much pain, you might start wondering if Jesus truly exists. He does, but you've closed your eyes to Him, so it seems He's nowhere. Open your eyes and quit walking around like the blind! Accept His plan for your life— He made you—and just like your parents know what's best for your physical health, God knows what's best for your soul. Because God made you. When you accept God's plan for your life, boys and girls, you'll have more joy than you can imagine."

Dr. Winkle held up a second poster board that had been lying behind him. It was a beautiful smile, the teeth perfectly straight and white. The top lip looked like the tip of a heart, and the gums were so pleasantly pink that my belly hurt. "If you follow God's will for your life," said Dr.

Winkle, "your soul will be as pearly white as both these teeth and the gates you'll walk through on your way to heaven. In heaven, that's where you'll find your reward."

Dr. Winkle smiled. His teeth were perfect, complete with a gold cap!

Dr. Winkle followed God's plan, so his insides and outsides matched. He loved Christ, found the truth, and once he accepted God's will by moving to Swaziland, he "stayed gold," like Ponyboy. Wow! I'm really bringing it all together today. That's what Sister Mary Francis says we should do in our essays. Here's an optional essay question: Would you rather be a Soc or a Greaser? Why? Can a Greaser ever become a Soc? Do Socs secretly envy Greasers?

Fra Angelico painted three dots on each plank of the yard's wooden fence: one on the bottom, another in the middle, a third near the top. The fence creates a barrier between the courtyard and the lush growth of bushes and trees in the forest beyond. The wild outside. There, the sky isn't blue but yellow, green, and brown—the same earthy colors found below. Tips of leaves echo the light bathing Mary, so the yellow of her tunic and the yellow of the wall are also the yellow light of the trees. In the courtyard, small white flowers bleed red.

She learned her social class at college. Before that, she'd considered her family basically the same as those around her. They didn't live in a fancy neighborhood or have money for vacations, restaurants, or new clothes, but they always had food on the table, and, most significantly, they owned their own homes. At college, it became clear that class was about more than money. There was education, geography, culture. The unpaid internships you could or, in her case, could not take. The way you held your body, how you spoke, what you expected or imagined as a possible future. Her automatic habit of saving everything because she might need it later. She called it thriftiness, and it masked a fear of not enough.

DEAD ON ARRIVAL

I went for a walk after school, but instead of entering the slush and mud of the woods behind our house, I walked up the road toward Mr. Johnston's. I never go in that direction. Maybe the Spirit of God was leading me because, halfway up the hill—right beside those blackberry bushes Mikey and I hid behind that time we were berry-bombing passing cars until this mean lady stopped and chased us, calling us poor trash and saying we could have broken her windshield (with a berry? Really, lady?)—right there beside that bush, I heard a soft sound. I held still until I heard it again. The thicket was tangled, even without leaves, but I managed to push aside the thorny branches. There she was—a cold and hungry kitten. So skinny and sick, when I put her in my jacket, she shook, so scared. She moved her mouth but couldn't make a sound, not even a squeak. I made a box for her in the mudroom with a washcloth and blanket, and she's sleeping there now. I've been sitting next to her, reading my book by Elmer Schmelzenbach. Zionism, by the way, is the main religion in Swaziland, blending Christianity with native beliefs.

Isn't it amazing that I heard the kitty? God must have opened my ears because she's definitely lost her voice, even though I definitely heard her cry. Her fur is purple-grey, and thick yellow-white gunk keeps collecting in the corners of her blue eyes. I've cleaned them four times. She's lying on her side like a grease rag and can't lap milk or water. Mom gave me an eyedropper to feed her milk right into her mouth, though most of it seems to dribble down the other side of her face, which is wet. So wet.

Mom told me not to name her until we know whether or not she'll live, but she's alive now, and some people, like Mom's friend Julie Johnson, name their miscarriages. They say the soul is supposed to enter the fetus right from the start, kind of like how the sperm enters the egg. Except that simile doesn't seem right. It suggests that the sperm has the soul while the egg has the body, which makes men sound more important than women since boys have the eternal part and girls have the flesh, which dies. The truth is everyone has both, body and soul. Michelle took one look at my kitten and pronounced her nearly dead, and Mikey says you should only name cats after candy bars. But frankly, I'm tired of Mikey's names and of the cats always belonging to him. The rule is whoever finds the cat gets to name the cat, and that's who owns the cat (if Mom lets us keep the cat). But Mikey and I were together when we found Snickers, who I wanted to name Sophia because she was small and dainty, with long yellow and white fur. Mom agreed with my name, but Mikey called her Snickers and carried her around like a baby, cuddling her in the crook of his arm. He snuck her whole cans of tuna fish—Mom would have been so mad—and always changed her water. She loved him most, following him everywhere and even coming when he called her name.

Snickers was our best cat ever. She let anyone hold her, and she slept in the funniest positions, on her back with her legs spread wide. You know how cats run off to have their babies in secret hiding places? Our first cat, Butterfingers, had her babies in the storage-shed wall. We could hear them crying, and Mom said they'll die in there, so

Dad used a power saw to cut a hole in the wall and fish the babies out. We were afraid he would accidently slice the babies open, but instead he pulled out four kittens, safe and so cute. Though Mom made us give them away, all of them, even one to that stupid family who stopped because of the Free Kittens! sign at the end of our driveway. Before their car doors slammed, we could hear their mom scolding them to hurry and pick one out. She dropped her cigarette on the doormat in our garage, and the kids kept pushing each other. The tallest one had something wrong with his face, though Michelle said it was only a bruise. None of the kittens wanted to go with them, but Mom let them have one. She showed the biggest girl, who had white eyelashes, how to hold the kitten and told her that if she loves it gently, the kitten will love her back. The girl smiled at my mom while her mom said, "You *would* pick the runt." But my mom knows how to pet a cat.

Snickers had her babies in the living room wood box, and she let us watch. She was lying on her side, meowing long and low as ripples moved down her body like waves. If cats sweat, I swear she was sweating—everything was wet. Her fur was sticky behind her ears and on the sides of her nose. Finally, the first kitten came out. Did you know baby kittens live inside a clearish sack inside their mother? It's called a placenta, and it makes every newborn kitten look like a peeled grape with a kitten inside. The mother eats the placenta to free the baby. Well, that's what is supposed to happen. But Snickers ignored her first baby. Mikey was worried the baby couldn't breathe; he wanted to use a pencil to peel the placenta, but Mom said to leave Snickers alone. She needed to birth all the babies, or they might all die, even Snickers. It's better to lose one baby than all three; sometimes the oldest is the sacrifice.

Snickers had two more kittens after that. She licked the second baby right away, and she licked the third one, too. The cleaned kittens looked like wet, sticky rats with closed slits for eyes. They were ugly and cute. One was caramel with black stripes, and the youngest was orange and white, like Snickers. Then Snickers began sniffing the first kitten, and she began to lick its sack. Then she started eating the placenta, but she didn't stop there. She ate the baby. We wanted to make her stop, but Mom said don't mess with a new mother, so we watched her lick and gnaw until the baby was half gone. She ate its bottom half. Mikey was so mad—he said he could have saved the kitten. Michelle said the kitten was DOA, dead on arrival, which makes me think of original sin. Are we DOA, too? When Snickers stopped eating, she turned back to the living kittens, and they settled into her stomach, finding her nipples and beginning to nurse. Mom scooped up the dead half-kitten in newspaper, and we buried her in the backyard. A stone marks her spot. Mikey and I called her Baby Ruth.

I miss Snickers since she ran away. Mom should have let her stay in the mudroom like the winter before. It didn't smell that bad of cat. Because Snickers was special. Not an ordinary cat. Cats don't get lost: They leave. Mikey says Snickers froze to death, and Mom knew Snickers would leave but didn't care. Mom could have saved her. He's still mad—that's how much he loved Snickers. But I hope he learns to forgive because unforgiveness can eat your heart alive. Which makes me think of Snickers's dead kitten.

I'm so glad I found this kitty before she died, my little purple-grey. How amazing—that I saw her. Oh, I know! I'm going to name her Iris because her purple is like the flower, and an iris is also part of the eyeball. May baby Iris help me to more fully perceive.

GROW OR WITHER

I am not 100% sick, but I'm not lying, either. I have cramps, and if I think about headaches, I might get one of those, too. Nothing was due at school today, and there weren't any tests, so it doesn't matter if I miss. Every time I get up, I check on Iris. She needs me like no one else does. I reread most of *The Lion, the Witch, and the Wardrobe*, which is an allegory for the story of Christ, though it's difficult to concentrate when Mom's listening to the radio. She likes for us to overhear the preaching, as if we're not already saved; she says there's always more to confess. I don't know. Maybe I'm just not that busy. They're playing "Mirror," by Evie, right now, and earlier I heard Beverly LaHaye. Mom has a whole row of her books. Mrs. LaHaye makes everything sound easy, like God definitely has a Christian husband picked out just for you. Her voice is low, I noticed—low and smooth, like that apple tree in Denise's backyard where the bees built a hive. Filled with honey.

Beverly LaHaye is exactly the opposite of the women at First Pentecostal. She says women should make themselves pleasing to God and to their husbands. There isn't any reason a woman shouldn't groom, trim, and paint the marvelous body God gave her. To improve your marriage, put God first. With God as your roof, your marriage will be safe and dry, and happiness, your interior design. Beverly LaHaye says there are four main personality types. Once you know who you and your husband are, you can easily turn your personality-based weaknesses and strengths over to Him, and He'll make your marriage better. I can't remember all four types right now, but I guess I'll look them up later in Mom's copy of *The Spirit-Controlled Woman.*

I don't want to write about boys, and Christian boys are especially dorky. If a cute one ever does show up at church, he always likes one of the other girls. I can't blame him. Like Tina Kinney, with her pixie face, or Diane Scofield, who has the best hair, down to her waist, thick and golden blonde. If we were friends, I would ask if I could braid it. Pastor Marks says it's better not to date until you meet your future spouse—that one person God prepared especially for you, *created* as your perfect fit, like Eve for Adam. The worst is to be unequally yoked.

At youth group, Pastor Jaime showed us what happens when you date a nonbeliever. He made Trevor Christenson stand on a chair while Tina Kinney stood on the floor beside him. "This is a couple," said Pastor Jaime. Jeremy made fake love eyes toward Tina, and everyone laughed—especially Tina, who laughed out loud, a real laugh with teeth. Trevor is super tall, and Tina is barely five feet, so they look funny anyway, standing next to each other, but the chair made their differences even greater.

Pastor Jaime said to imagine that Trevor is a Christian, and Tina, his unsaved girlfriend. Trevor wishes Tina were saved because she is so cute and sweet. Trevor nodded and winked at Tina, which made everyone laugh again. Tina *is* cute—she's petite even if her mouth and nose are big, and her hair is bobbed and perfectly permed. She has a preppy style but in a good way, with lots of pink and mint green, though there is something horselike about her mouth. Tina rolled her eyes because Trevor is such a clown, but he's also kind of cute. Only kind of, like a vague cuteness. Pastor Jaime said that Trevor thinks if he brings Tina to church or youth group, she'll be saved and there won't be a problem. Trevor told Tina he's a Christian, and Tina told Trevor she wants more meaning in her life. "I made Trevor stand on the chair," Pastor Jaime continued, "because, as Christians, we're living on a higher, sanctified level, where we answer to God."

Pastor Jaime told Trevor to pull Tina onto the chair with him, which would "bring her up to your level." To do this, Trevor could pray for or with her. He could beg her to join him or just lean over and pick her up, as if she were a little girl. But Pastor Jaime told Tina that she had to resist Trevor because she likes it where she is and doesn't want to change. Not really. So Trevor did everything he could. He prayed and persuaded, pulled and tugged, but Tina didn't move. Then Pastor Jaime told Tina to bring Trevor down to her level. He said Trevor doesn't want to change, either, and he should try to stay on the chair, in the place of sanctification. But it only took one good tug for Tina to topple Trevor, and he fell fast and right on top of her, as she almost collapsed under the weight of him. It was so funny, and Tina made an umph sound, which made us laugh again. Pastor Jaime said an unbeliever will always bring you down. There is no such thing as standing still. You're either rising in Christ's estimation or falling in His eyes. Growing or withering. And until we get to heaven, there is no such thing as not changing. No one stays forever fixed.

One date with an unbeliever can push you further from God.

Wait! Iris just meowed! Her little voice is the cutest, squeakiest ever, and she will definitely be healed in the name of Christ. I'm sitting in the mudroom now, next to her box. And, yes, I definitely want to marry a Christian, so I should probably date only Christians. But if it's all right to talk to non-Christian boys in person, what about on the phone? (Not that I talk to any boy on the phone—because I'm definitely not the biggest flirt in our class, regardless of any stupid survey. I know Angie made the one from yesterday because it was her chicken-scrawl handwriting, and she passed it to everyone before tucking it into my folder while I was diagramming a sentence at the board. Question: Is Marie the biggest flirt in our class? 14 yes, 2 no. I don't even know what they're talking about, except that, yes, I will talk to the boys in our class because I've known them since kindergarten. But since the start of seventh grade, there's this weird unspoken rule that girls shouldn't draw attention to themselves while real boys make nasty comments about boobs, butts, or legs, which is just gross.)

Also, you might both be Christians when you begin dating, but then one person backslides, and then what? Or what if you're both Catholic, like Mom and Dad when they married, but then Mom became born again when I was just a baby? She hated it that Dad was still Catholic because he made us go to Mass, and Mom knew it was bad to pray to Mary and the saints. That's idolatry. Mom came to Mass for my first communion but didn't receive communion herself. She didn't want me to keep my rosary from Grandma C, either—she said it was my choice, but praying to Mary is a sin because you're elevating her to God's throne. You should pray to God and God alone. I gave my rosary to Mom, and she probably burned it. Along with all our owl decorations, including Michelle's owl clock. Its eyes moved back and forth at every tick tock. Michelle was pretty mad, but Mom said owls symbolize witches. We also had owl potholders and a ceramic figurine Mom got from Ginny and Vi. She used to bring me to Bible study at their house, but one day she said there was evil there. That's all she said. She wouldn't explain. She didn't call them witches but quit their Bible study and burned the owls on the same day.

I liked Ginny and Vi. Their eyes smiled consistently. They kept a goat and an herb garden and made real Christmas candy from scratch—potato candy covered in chocolate. You would never guess it was potatoes; the candy was soft and sweet on the inside with a mint taste, delicate. It was much better than store-bought ribbon candy, which looks pretty on the outside but tastes like only sugar. Ginny drove a truck, and she and Dad once discussed the best places to get gravel in the area. I heard Ginny and Vi were asked to leave their church.

I think it's weird for Dad to be the sudden spiritual head of the household just because he's finally born again. Mom has been studying the Bible for ten years longer. Of course, she doesn't say that to Dad's face, but she told Julie Johnson. They were sitting in the kitchen together, drinking coffee. When she noticed me, she added, "But the Bible says wives are to submit, and children, obey your parents." Why isn't there room to ask questions? Especially when there are other facts to consider. Like how I've been saved longer than Dad has, so it's annoying when he tells me something about the Bible as if I don't already know.

She began to understand the authority of claiming and naming time. The Catholics, her mom said, mapped so-called Christian holidays onto the earth-worshiping pagan calendar—because they wanted numbers, her mother grumbled, more than purity within the church. On the radio, preachers agreed that the Easter bunny, Christmas trees, and trick-or-treating were still-living branches of wicked, Satanic roots. Meanwhile, her mom's church began hosting a Hallelujah Party—dress as your favorite biblical character—instead of Halloween. This was considered different from the Catholic cover-up. We were reclaiming our lives for Christ.

Years later, at the Philadelphia Museum of Art, she remembered her dream of the baby rose face. She was looking at a triptych of the martyrdom of Saint Barbara. On the rightside, two ugly-faced jailers held the saint between them. The men looked stupid, with ruddy faces and large noses, like underclass laborers who do as they're told. The saint's bare breasts protruded from holes cut into her plain garment; her nipples had been sliced off, and blood dripped, like tears, onto her torso and thighs. Staring at the saint's mutilation, she felt a vulnerability in her own breasts as she instinctively pressed her forearms against them, reassuring her body as whole. The felt nausea, she realized, was an empathic sensation; when she relaxed, space opened, and she could lean in to better examine Saint Barbara's wounds. Instead of nipples, each breast became a bleeding red rose. Ah, she thought, so there are flowers here, as well.

INFLUENCE

I just heard Dr. Ralph Hayes on the radio. He says homosexuals are still on the rise, especially in New York and Dallas, where they want to make their own sin seem OK, even attractive, so they've developed a new rainbow curriculum that teaches children "it's OK to be gay"—they actually want kids to believe that! Why call it rainbow when it has nothing to do with Noah's Ark or pots of gold? Dr. Hayes says the battle is especially fraught in Texas because Texas has the biggest textbook companies, so if that state adopts the curriculum, then schools across the nation will begin teaching homosexuality, like a sick spirit blanketing the land. We must pay attention and fight back! We must call homosexuality what it is: sin. You can't be gay and be saved. Dr. Hayes is right about that. Only the Christian news will report this, but put the pieces together, and you'll see—we are living in End Times. It's going to get worse. Listening to Dr. Hayes, I felt almost frozen. It hurt to swallow. Because homosexuality is that scary and bad.

When I first heard Dr. Hayes, I didn't even know what a homosexual was. That was back in third or fourth grade, and his show was on the radio while Mom and I were driving home from the grocery store. When we pulled into the driveway, I finally asked Mom—What's a homosexual?—and she got that look on her face of pure sickness. If vomit had a look, it would be that. She turned off the car and paused for so long. When she spoke, her voice sounded funny.

"They are men who love other men," she said. She didn't wait for my next question. I felt confused, like I had asked something bad. I figured it had to be dirty love, like those magazines we found in the burn barrel by the barn. Those pictures had mostly naked girls with gigantic boobs and close-ups of guys putting their giant dongs into hairless down-theres. If homosexuals were men, I didn't have to worry about becoming one. That was the good news. Then everyone started calling homosexuals "gay." Dr. Hayes never uses that word. I looked it up in the dictionary (I once looked up "tits" and "humping," too, which was unsatisfying). It didn't say anything about homosexuals, only "happy, merry, lively mood," as in "now we don our gay apparel." Question: How does a word change its definition?

Last year, I heard Mom and Michelle talking about the girls on the high school softball team. Michelle won't go into the locker room if they are there. She says the school should do something; it's disgusting and wrong. They quit talking when I came into the kitchen, but I honestly didn't understand the problem until I heard about lesbians. Dr. Hayes says it's fashionable for men to dress like women (note: Boy George) and for women to dress like men (I think he's talking about that woman who sings "Sweet Dreams Are Made of This," but she wears makeup as well as suits). Dr. Hayes says Satan uses clothing to plant seeds in someone's life. It may be "cool" for a man to pierce his ear or wear makeup, but those things will open a door, allowing the spirit of homosexuality to walk right into your life. I understand what Dr. Hayes is saying, but I also think clothing is fashion, and fashion is an art. When

Michelle wears Grandpa's big mohair sweater, she looks fashionable, not gay, even though it's a man's sweater. Plus, it's maroon and grey and has amazing texture.

But I should remember that Satan always starts small. On *Talk Back with Bob Larson*, Bob Larson told a story about a boy who was trick-or-treating on Halloween when a group of people invited him to join their animal sacrifice. He thought it was a joke, or "trick," until they actually killed a small white rabbit, which freaked him out so hard he left. But not before he became demon-possessed! In fact, we know this story only because Bob Larson performed an exorcism, and he always makes the demons state their name and point of entry since he needs that information to cast them out. The demons don't want to tell, of course, but Bob Larson commands them to speak in the name of Jesus. Otherwise, Bob Larson might not close the right interior door.

You might think it's just trick-or-treating or wearing eyeliner, but Satan can use that moment—he really can. Everything you do, every word and action, has a price, and demons are passed down through your ancestors, as well. If your relative was a witch, you might have a spirit of witchcraft inside you. Or a spirit of thievery. Or drunkenness. After all, demons need to stay somewhere, and your family has already given them a home.

I haven't told anyone this, but Denise stole a candy bar from the Trading Post. It happened the last time I spent the night. We walked to the store on Saturday—it only takes seven minutes, and we were thirsty. We bought a two-liter of Mountain Dew because that's so obviously cheaper than individual bottles. Her mom gave us exact change. We were walking home when Denise asked if I wanted some Kit Kat. "Did you buy that?" I said. Because I hadn't seen it on the counter.

She looked at me strange, her head tilted. "Don't tell," she said. We were already across 14 Mile Road and around the curve, in that area that's all trees. Denise was half-smiling.

I said, "Don't tell what?" She didn't say. She looked at me sideways with extra meaning, but I still didn't understand. She held out the Kit Kat. "Wait, did you buy that at the store?"

"I got it there." She looked at me again and raised her eyebrows.

That's when I heard what she was saying. I stopped and stared at the back of her head because she was still walking. It took her a few steps to notice and turn around. "We have to take it back," I said. She looked as if she didn't understand, her eyes going cloudy like they do when she plays Russian spy. I said, "Denise, you know it's wrong."

She sucked in a deep breath, then sighed. She looked down. "But I already tore the wrapper," she said, right before she tore the wrapper. Which, to be honest, made me burst out in laughter. I couldn't help it! I knew it was wrong, but Denise is so dorky and literal, and suddenly I just wanted it to be okay between us. Denise never follows the rules; that's what I love about her. She opened the Mountain Dew, and pop fizzed all over, which made us laugh even harder.

"You have sticky fingers," I said, which was especially funny because Denise always spills on herself and her homework. It drives Sister Mary Francis mad.

We couldn't return the candy bar; it was covered with Mountain Dew. And we couldn't quit laughing. Oh, well, we said, and we ate it—it would be double-wrong to waste food. But later, while we were lying in bed, I told Denise I don't want her to go to jail. She doesn't know why she took it; she said it was her first time and promised not to shoplift again. I believe her. But I've noticed that, ever since that day, I've had thoughts of stealing. It's happened twice now, once inside Meijer and again at the Stop-n-Go. I'm looking around, like any normal shopper, when suddenly I think, "It would be so easy to steal." I've never had that thought before. Or I'll notice that I'm looking at the mirrors or cameras and wondering how they work, if I can trick them. It's almost as if these thoughts come from outside my head. Now I'm worried that moment with Denise opened a spiritual door to my life. We should've returned the candy bar. We should've gone back to the Trading Post, confessed what happened, and paid for the bar or worked it off. I don't want to be wrong. I feel cold.

Am I focusing too much on demons? Pastor Marks warns about their strategy of weaseling into the center of your conversations. Like how it's easier to complain about someone than to be grateful for everything you've already received. Can I cast my own demons out? God says we should pray in a private place, like a closet (Matthew 6:6), which means some secrets are desirable. I'm going to confess and bind the spirit of shoplifting. Also: God is so amazing. Look how He just used homosexuality to lead me back to Him.

Fra Angelico is not the only Dominican friar associated with the Convent of San Marco. In 1481, twenty-six years after Fra Angelico's death, Girolamo Savonarola arrived in Florence for his newly appointed role as lector, or teacher. Evidently, his early sermons landed flat, so he changed his preaching style, became more imaginative and imagistic, more focused on hell and doom. He was preaching in a world pulsing with change: new technologies (the printing press), an emerging social class (merchants), rediscovered forms of thinking and style (ancient Greek and Roman works brought by Byzantine scholar-refugees fleeing Constantinople). But what some experience as exciting possibility, others feel as anxiety: about loss, ruin, uncertainty. Savonarola spoke to this fear, preaching the end of the world and a need for purification. Modeling himself on Bernardino of Siena (1380-1444), he revived "Bonfires of the Vanities," whereby the devoutly religious gathered to burn objects thought to be sinful: mirrors; playing cards; cosmetics; musical instruments; works of astrology, divination and magic; and anything associated with Mardi Gras. They burned art of all varieties, including books by Dante, Boccaccio, and Ovid. Artists began offering their own works for the fires, as Savonarola's followers—known as the "weepers"—conducted pressure campaigns, effectively trolling influential people, insisting they be either for or against.

In a literature class, her professor described reading as a way to imagine yourself into the world of another. When you read, the professor said, put aside evaluative postures such as do I agree or disagree? Is this true or not? You can consider those questions later, when the book or story is done. Instead, let yourself wonder as you move through the text—about the experiences and perspectives you're encountering. Let the world you're meeting be true. How would your relationship to an oak tree differ, for example, if a spirit did actually live within the tree? The ancient Greeks named such spirits Dryads, or tree nymphs. What if the nymphs aren't metaphors for life but a form of life itself?

Or consider F. W. Murnau's adaptation of Goethe's *Faust*. In this film, Mephisto hides a golden chain in Gretchen's bureau drawer, where the object radiates an unseen influence, such that young Gretchen becomes susceptible to Faust's charms, falling in love with the alchemist who has already sold his soul to the Devil. Some deals are better left undone. What would it be like, her teacher asks, to live in a world where objects carry such weight?

In his sermon "The Art of Dying Well, Ruth and Micheas, Sermon XXVIII," Savonarola urges a consideration of one's own death as a means to bolster faith. Thinking about death, he argues, will lead to a consideration of afterdeath, and the possibility of hell, where you must stay "not a hundred years, nor a thousand, nor a hundred thousand, nor a hundred million, but forever and ever to infinity."

The unseen influences were all around us: at the movies, in the music, on television. And always: in the ads. So pick up your faith (i.e., your shield) as part of your spiritual armor. It will protect you from the enemy's lies. Because the enemy wants you to burn forever, just as fire naturally seeks more fuel. To effectively use your shield of faith, hold it between yourself and your attacker. Let your faith become a barrier purposefully erected. Let your faith separate good from bad.

With time, she wondered: What is the difference between protecting and obscuring one's heart?

Savonarola's sermons were like so many she had heard as a child, with the same logical fallacy, though it took years for her to understand that a consideration of death does not necessarily lead to questions about afterlife. In fact, the first time she truly faced death—that is, when her father died suddenly from a heart attack—she began asking what makes a life worth living. Before another year had passed, she left her on-again-off-again boyfriend of many years, the one who couldn't kiss her on the mouth or read her writing because he said he probably wouldn't like it. She left him, having already decided he would be the last man she would date—because during those off periods, she'd been more attracted to women. Yes, she'd had several affairs. Sexually, but also emotionally and spiritually. Two years after her father died, she was living with a woman and absolutely in love.

When she began teaching, she told her students that we read with our bodies. We observe behaviors and form hypotheses about the people around us, which subsequently influence our future observations and actions. Belief creates what we see. If we consider someone a good person, we tend to view their actions in a positive light. If someone fits into a category we consider more trustworthy—a pastor or parent, a lesbian or an artist—we are more likely to listen, more willing to hear.

In 1497, Pope Alexander VI excommunicated Savonarola, purportedly for refusing to join the Pope's Holy League against the French. As his long-envious rivals rose to power, Savonarola began to write, composing what some consider to be his spiritual masterpiece, *Triumph of the Cross*. In it, he claims that, while faith is a gift from God, he would prove his arguments with reason alone. "Such a mode of procedure," writes Savonarola (in a translation by the Very Rev. Father John Proctor), "must, surely, satisfy everyone who is not absolutely foolish." When another Franciscan friar challenged Savonarola's divine mission to trial by fire, all of Florence gathered to witness the spectacle. Who would be God's chosen favorite? Yet as the priests and other contestants weren't exactly excited about the prospect of walking through fire, they kept delaying the start of the trial. When a sudden downpour ruined the event before it could begin, the crowd became enraged, and blaming Savonarola, a mob descended onto the convent of San Marco.

The male religious leaders talked as if faith meant certainty. But faith, she came to realize, becomes more meaningful with doubt.

Under torture, Savonarola confessed to making up his prophetic visions and teachings. Later, he recanted his confession, only to reconfess, and on May 23, 1498, he was condemned as a heretic and sentenced to death. Savonarola hung that day in the town square, alongside Fra Silvestro Maruffi and Fra Domenico. To prevent their devotees from gathering relics, the friars' bodies were burned, their ashes spread in the Arno river.

ALAS, MY DAUGHTER

Mom got mad at us for being lazy slobs, so she opened the front door and threw out anything that wasn't properly put way: my hairbrush and books, Mikey's work boots and tons of dirty socks. Michelle freaked out because the wool sweater she bought last week was lying in the snow—she says Mom ruined it forever. Michelle got a job at Mrs. Field's Cookies in the mall, so she didn't have time to pick up anything but her own stuff. That's what she said, anyway, and she was griping, too, about having a dirty apron. She says if she gets in trouble at work for lack of cleanliness, it's Mom's fault. It's already dark, and Mikey is still at wrestling practice. I certainly wasn't going to leave everything in the wet snow. Like Michelle did. She could have picked up my library books, at least. They're drying now, but my English notes are totally ruined. I'll have to recopy everything. Michelle says I shouldn't leave homework lying around, but it's the same thing with her stupid sweater and work apron. Mom went to bed with a migraine. We have an English paper outline due on Monday, and Sister Mary Francis wants us to follow the guidelines perfectly, zero mistakes. I'm writing about religion in Africa or, more specifically, about Zionism in South African countries, including Swaziland.

Note: I don't want to be a complainer like Michelle.

I'm going to focus on the positive instead. Like Iris—she's still alive! She's eating regular kitten food, which I soak in mother's milk replacement. Even Michelle admits that Iris is a cat miracle. Because faith heals! Elmer

Schmelzenbach knew that, as did the Reverend J. A. Dowie. He's the man who started Zionism and—real fact—it began in the United States. (I learned this from my new library book, *Zulu Zion and Some Swazi Zionists*.) The Rev. J. A. Dowie lived in Illinois, where he founded Zion City in 1901 and began calling himself John Alexander, First Apostle. One of his early converts was a Dutch Reformed minister, the Rev. P. L. LeRoux, who began preaching faith healing to his own congregation. Until the Dutch Reformed officials found out and kicked him out of the church. Because they did not want to admit that faith healing is as real today as it was during biblical times. When God closes one door, He another opens. The Rev. P. L. LeRoux became a full-time Zionist preacher, traveling to Swaziland, where he converted Swazis as God healed them of their sicknesses and sins. The Rev. P. L. LeRoux wouldn't allow ordinary doctors into his house, and once his daughter was so sick she almost died. But God worked a last-minute miracle. God likes to work last-minute healings.

The Rev. P. L. LeRoux describes this incident as just like when Abraham almost sacrificed Isaac, though the Rev didn't tie his daughter to an altar after she gathered wood for the offering. God just let her get sick. God wanted to test the Rev's faith, like He did Abraham's. But what if his daughter had died? Because it could have been like Jephthah, who asked God to help him win a battle, promising to sacrifice the first creature who met him on his return home as a show of gratitude and faith. That's where the story turns, because of course he won—he had God's help—but it was his daughter, his only child, who ran out to greet him since Daddy was finally home. When Jephthah saw her, he shouted, "Alas, my daughter! You have brought me very low!" And then he killed her as the sacrifice he promised.

God let her die. I don't know why. Maybe some tests are too hard, and girls are more naturally sacrificial.

Because I have noticed it is mostly boys in the Bible. I don't think God loves them more, but they are male, like God, so it's probably easier for Him to imagine them in leadership positions. Also, I think the Rev. P. L. Le Roux was wrong not to ask for a doctor. As Pastor Marks says, "God made doctors and medicine, too," so going to the doctor doesn't mean you lack faith. A sound body is a sound house for the Lord.

Like a clean house holds sound minds. I read that in one of Mom's how-to-keep-your-house-clean books. Here's a simple tip: Close your cupboards and drawers, and your kitchen will instantly look neater. Mom is still sleeping. Because if she's not mad about being messy, she's depressed.

Repeat after Me

There are many ways to witness to a Zionist, but here are the two steps you should always take. One: learn about their leader. Two: speak truth to their lie.

Zionist Leader: Johanna Nxumalo was the first Swazi who converted to Zionism. She had prophetic dreams and used cards and crosses to heal the sick. She could, as if by magic, sniff out troublemakers and demons, including witches and wizards, so it was always spiritual warfare at her church because demons tried to trick the new Christians into believing they smelt evil, too. Then the real demon-sniffers, the ones blessed by God with this gift, would resmell everyone as they separated the real psychic smellers from the fakes.

Truth to the lie, or what to say while witnessing to a Johanna Nxumalo follower: I'm sorry to break the news, but it sounds like Johanna Nxumalo mixed witchcraft with biblical teachings. All you need is the name of Jesus to cast a demon out. Using cards and crosses may be idolatry because you're putting your faith in those tools instead of God, plain and pure. Also, what would evil smell like? Sulfur? Porta-potties? Or something more tempting, like chocolate cake?

Zionist Leader: Khambule wanted to be Moses and was able to deceive people because they hadn't read the Bible, so they didn't know Khambule was plagiarizing Moses's life. God gave Moses the Ten Commandments on stone tablets, so Khambule said he could see messages in stone, too. It started when he found twelve stones, each with a letter on it, one for each of Christ's disciplines. Then Khambule built an arc of the covenant (just like Moses) and put the stones in the holy of holies (again like Moses). He made up strict rules about polluting the body, so everyone at Khambule's church didn't drink beer or eat meat because even chicken wings have blood in them. His followers weren't allowed to touch corpses, so they couldn't kill animals or bury their dead. True fact: Khambule also wrote in a diary!

Truth to the lie, or what to say while witnessing to a Khambule follower: Obviously, Khambule was a plagiarist; just show his congregation the Bible, and they will know the truth. Maybe Khambule found messages written on stones, or maybe his neighbor wrote on the stones to trick Khambule for a good laugh, like when Michelle and Mikey spray-painted rocks and told me they found gold in the sand pit next to our house. I didn't believe them until I saw the stones myself, which were big and sparkly. Michelle still calls me gullible, but I was only four years old. I hate it when people misrepresent. I wonder if Khambule's arc of the covenant was plated in gold like the one in the Bible. I'd like to tell his followers they can eat meat if they want to, including bacon, since the God of the New Testament wants us to be free. Then I'd show them Acts 10 and Peter's vision (while in a trance!) of the sheet filled with animals. God says, "I made everything—call none of it common or unclean."

Zionist Leader: <u>Timothy Cekwane</u> (Church of the Light, South Africa): Mr. Cekwane always loved God, and when he saw Haley's Comet, he believed it was the spirit of God moving like a mighty wind. He immediately threw off his amulets and began speaking in tongues. Blood trickled from his unwounded palms in the same spot where nails pierced Christ's hands as he hung on the cross. Mr. Cekwane made his congregation wear red robes every day, all day, even though most Zionists wore white robes and only while attending church. Mr. Cekwane's church lasted a long time—maybe it still exists. When Mr. Cekwane died, the deacon whose hands bled like Mr. Cekwane's became the new pastor because that was God's obvious sign.

Truth to the lie, or what to say while witnessing to a Timothy Cekwane follower: Please be careful. You may truly love God, even as you've been taught a bunch of lies. I think that's what happened to Mr. Cekwane and why he wore amulets when he was younger. It's good that he listened to God and threw the amulets away, and, while I've never personally heard of someone bleeding from their palms, it definitely sounds like a miracle. Maybe there's nothing wrong with Mr. Cekwane's church. Except that God doesn't care about our clothing, with one exception: don't dress like a slut. Skimpy clothes invite a spirit of lust into the room. At Branches, we wear jeans. Including designer, if you're lucky.

Zionist Leader: <u>Ma Mbele</u> was a prophetess who could read people like a book. If someone came into church carrying hidden native medicines, Ma Mbele would jump up and say, "There's *umuthi* in the house!" She prayed and healed many sick people, especially hysterics. Sometimes she made animal sacrifices, and when her husband traveled, she always knew if he met a lady friend. She could see him even when he wasn't physically present.

Truth to the lie, or what to say while witnessing to a Ma Mbele follower: I hate to tell you this, but Ma Mbele's powers probably came from Satan, not God, who doesn't require sacrifices of flesh, and that's just weird about Ma Mbele's husband. It sounds like divination, even if Ma Mbele doesn't mention a crystal ball or bowl. Her husband probably wasn't Christian, or she wouldn't have to worry that he'd be unfaithful. On the other hand, at Branches of the Vine we prophesy like Ma Mbele and cast out evil spirits all the time. Question: Are evil spirits the same as *umuthi*?

Zionist Leader: <u>Paulo Nzuza</u> (another spirit church): The Holy Ghost descended on Paulo Nzuza on the ninth day of May, 1917, and the Lord said, "Paulo Nzuza, you are part of the holy family of Jehovah." So Paulo Nzuza prayed and studied scripture, and on June 17 of that same year, the Lord said, "Go preach the Good News."

Paulo Nzuza received direct messages from God, including the one-true-meaning of 1 Corinthians 14:27. If someone speaks in tongues at Paulo Nzuza's church, a second person interprets the message while a third writes it in the church's special book of prophecies.

The truth to the lie, or what to say while witnessing to a Paulo Nzuza follower: While it sounds like Paulo Nzuza was truly anointed by God, it makes me nervous when anyone claims God's one true meaning of the Bible. Even if I agree with his interpretation, God always has more than one meaning, and no one human can know everything about God. We're too full of sin, and God's too full of glory. Usually, people who say they have the "one true way" are cult leaders. I wonder what Paulo Nzuza's special book of prophecies looked like. I imagine it was green leather and covered with crosses, one big one in the middle and four smaller ones in the corners. But, unlike Ma Mbele, who literally saw things that weren't there, I know my picture isn't real. This is the clear difference between imagination and conjuring.

Zionist Leader: <u>Isaiah Shembe</u> (South Africa, Zulu): Isaiah Shembe was in a cave when God called him to leave his sexual sins and start a church on the mountaintop. Shembe's church believed his conception was holy because his mother didn't have or want a boyfriend, and one day she ate a flower in the forest, and the Holy Spirit filled her womb. Later, she married Shembe's father, and the Holy Spirit left her body to make room for the baby. Sadly, that baby died. As did the next one and the one after. She had so many miscarriages, she probably quit naming them, and she definitely thought God had abandoned her. Until she conceived Shembe, even though she was technically too old to have children, just like Elizabeth bearing John the Baptist. Or Sarah with Isaac. This is how Isaiah Shembe came to be the youngest and the eldest, and why he also received the blessings of both.

Shembe drove out demons, and his church followed many Old Testament rules. They didn't wear shoes inside or eat communion bread made with salt. If a woman was menstruating, she wasn't allowed to eat with the group or shake hands with men. After a man slept with his wife, he had to bathe in the river three times, at morning, noon, and night.

When Shembe died, his son, who was also named Shembe, took over the church. While doing research for *Zulu Zionists and Some Swazi Zionists,* the Rev. J. A. Dowie met this younger Shembe at a special service for barren women (Shembe and the Rev. J. A. Dowie were the only two men there). Younger Shembe moved up and down the aisles while women prayed in tongues and touched him. Some women were immediately slain in the spirit while others began to scream until Shembe cast demons from their wombs in the name of Jesus.

Truth to the lie, or what to say while witnessing to an Isaiah Shembe follower: If Shembe was special from the start, why did he fall into sexual sin? If Shembe's mother was so pure, why did Shembe struggle with a spirit of lust? How did she know the Holy Spirit was in her womb? It's not like Mary and the angel Gabriel, who spoke to Mary as God's messenger. Why do so many of the Zionists follow so many rules? God definitely doesn't want menstruating females to be put in time out, or how would anything get done? It's embarrassing enough to have your period, and if you get angry and happen to have your period, people say they don't have to listen because you're on the rag. Even if you have very real and worthy complaints. If God wanted everyone to know about your period, He would have made it happen somewhere more publicly noticeable, like the palms of your hands. He would not have given someone the idea for tampons, menstrual pads, or white pants.

I don't want people to know my private life with my husband! Why do men have to bathe but not the wives? Guys want girls to kiss on them because guys are always horny—they can't help it—but if a girl talks to a boy, they call her a flirt or even a slut. If a man from Shembe's church bathed three times in one day, it could only mean one thing; if a man is doing it a lot with his wife, do the other men get jealous? Does the wife look weird? Is the cleanest man also the dirtiest?

From cultural anthropology, she learned about animism—the idea that places, objects, and creatures carry a spiritual essence—and she began to see an inexact-yet-still-there parallelism between animistic beliefs in other cultures and the focus on demons in her own. In Northern Thailand, for example, families kept spirit houses—small replicas of their actual homes—as shelter for their deceased ancestors, who continued to watch over them and their abode. This relationship with spirits was more intimate and personal than her mother's belief, adopted from various Christian broadcasts and books by writers such as Frank Peretti, that certain spirits—i.e., demons—ruled certain locations. So every church, abortion clinic, university, and nation-state had a legion of demonic rulers, which US Christians, surrounded by angels and wearing their suits of armor, were fighting in that spiritual warfare more real than our visible lives.

Her mother, like the US Christians she listened to, would probably call Thai ancestor spirits "demons in disguise." Her mother's belief pained her for the way it valued white Western spiritual narratives over other cultural ways of knowing and seeing. Who was she to say that someone's ancestors didn't stay to help or watch over their descendants, protecting, keeping them in line. She refused to dismiss these Thai beliefs as primitive or false. Just as she wouldn't call her mother ignorant or delusional. Such a judgment limited the conversation to *who is right* and *who is wrong*, rather than trying to understand another's perspective, how their various threads of beliefs wove into the larger meaning-making tapestry of their life.

She saw parallels between a nation always at war (officially and/or covertly) and the emphasis in that nation's white Evangelical Christian culture on constant spiritual warfare. She wondered about the militarism found in many praise-and-worship songs (she knew the lyrics were biblical, but there were other verses—more about love, less about battles—they could have sung). At least her spiritual suit of armor was imagined rather than an actual six-piece plastic play set, as now sold by one of the larger Christian publishers. Modeled on the armor worn by medieval knights, the play set includes a helmet (of salvation) and a sword (of the spirit), and is, as the package says, a way to "share your faith and beliefs with your children." (The pictured children are white, and red is "for boys," purple, "for girls.") We wrestle not with flesh and blood, they quoted, but with principalities, with powers. Against spiritual wickedness in high places.

She could see such wrestling within her mother, who radiated the kind of deep-seated shame that thrives in households marked with violence and other abuse. Her mother says she's forgiven those who hurt her—that's the end of the conversation. Her mother may have forgiven them, she thinks, but has she forgiven herself? Like how a child often believes her father's explosive anger is actually, somehow, her fault. Or that her mother's shame is somehow, actually, her fault. Such beliefs are irrational and powerful. An attempt to gain control over the uncontrollable and scary. If it's your fault, there must be something you can do.

From anthropology, she learned *taking seriously* as a methodological approach to difference. Instead of translating another's beliefs or worldview into one's own, thereby grounding your beliefs as more foundational or "true," *taking* another's beliefs *seriously* presupposes their beliefs to be true and tries to understand them—in and on their own terms and within their context, knowing that some part can't be carried over. Like how every language has untranslatable words and idioms. Because the conceptual equivalent simply doesn't exist in another tongue. She learned this from studying Thai.

Yet she also felt her mother's faith as a phenomenon exceeding her mother's childhood trauma. Her mother experienced the supernatural: prophetic dreams and visions, intuitive insights, sudden healings, a return to her own beating heart. She sensed a deep knowing within her mother and wished they could talk about their lives as they are, rather than as something good or bad, black or white, *of God* or *of the devil*. She wished there were space for various intensities of luminescence, for civil twilight, the astronomical dawn.

HORROR VS TERROR

I didn't know about Teen Right to Life until I was at their conference today, and while I know abortion is wrong, I didn't know that abortionists and feminists have a plan to keep it in place. It's like they want to see babies die. I wrote letters to my senator and congressman, telling them to make abortion illegal now. They had paper and pens (black or blue) right there at a table so that you could easily write your note and address the envelope. I didn't know what to say, so they said to copy their sample letter. I asked the girl if that was plagiarizing; she laughed and said no. "Abortion is worse," said a boy, who was addressing his fifth envelope. He kept counting them aloud so that everyone would know. The truth is most people don't understand that abortion = murder. You are killing a life. They showed a movie of an actual abortion, called *The Silent Scream*. That baby fetus was only twelve weeks old, and he knew he was in danger; they showed us the ultrasound image on a TV. The doctor and nurses used metal instruments that looked like tongs and pliers to pry the woman open and get inside her. I wonder if the woman having the abortion has seen the movie.

The man showed us the baby's arms, mouth, and nose, he pointed with a pencil because they were kind of hard to see. "The baby was calm in his sanctuary," said the narrator. There are a lot of similarities between a sanctuary and a womb. When they put the suction tip inside the woman, the baby became more violent. He kicked and tried to get away. That's what the man said, who wore glasses and a suit. He said the baby's heart beat faster because this child was threatened with extinction. They were going to suck his body apart, piece by piece—because that's how they do it: legs first, then stomach and shoulders, then arms, and, because the head might be too big, they use tongs to squish it until it breaks or bursts, like a balloon or pimple. But before that happened, the man paused the picture on the monitor. He said the baby's mouth is wide open. "Look," he said, "at that silent scream." I wish he would have pointed straight at it because it was also a little hard to see. Which was probably just me not looking at the right area. They made abortion legal before we had the technology to watch exactly what happens, but now that we know, we must make it stop. Even the doctor and nurses in the movie watched the ultrasound. After, the man said, they were so upset, they quit performing abortions. Women can become sterile or castrated from the operation. The clinic doesn't tell you that, but it's true. Everyone at the conference got a postcard of a baby in a womb. They gave us the real facts: some girls use abortion as birth control, and some girls have more than one abortion. This is another reason to save sex for marriage. If I lost my virginity as a teenager, how many more guys would I sleep with before I found the one?

I'm so glad Mom signed me up for that conference. I didn't know where we were going until I was already inside. Other than the girl at the letter table, I didn't talk to anyone. I would have brought Denise; she would have liked it. They had blueberry minimuffins, but I didn't eat one. I didn't drink the orange juice, either, which had pulp. I didn't know where to stand or sit, and we had to move around, depending on who spoke in what order. First there was breakfast and some people talking, then a big talk and the movie while we sat in rows of metal folding chairs. I didn't stay for the afternoon session because Mom registered me for the morning only. That was okay. I was ready to go. Not because I don't care about abortion— it's clearly the most important issue of our time! But it's weird to be somewhere all alone, especially when everyone else is with their friends. I was wearing Michelle's hand-me-down jeans and one of Dad's white t-shirts with my new pastel-colored flower jacket. I used babysitting money and bought it at the mall, not Meijer, but I still didn't fit in. I didn't stick out, either. It wasn't like church, where we hope everyone will become born again.

I didn't know what to do at the conference. I wrote my letters early, during breakfast, because I was standing near the letter-writing table and the girl smiled and said her name was Ellen. She had the best dark brown curly hair. And a button-down shirt. If I had written my letters later, I would have told the politicians about the baby's silent scream or the womb as a sanctuary. After the movie, they said we need to organize protests and speak for the babies since they can't speak for themselves. I got a precious feet pin, and Mom loved it so much I gave it to her. It shows the actual size and shape of a baby's feet at ten weeks in the womb. The feet are so tiny and cute—you can see all ten toes, perfectly formed. But without toenails because the pin shows bottoms only. I used to suck my toes when I was happy and clap my feet when I ate squash mixed with carrots. Michelle says of course I would like such disgusting things.

Mom wants to move Iris's box outside, but I talked her into indoors for one more week. Iris is too skinny, and it's too cold; I don't want her to run away, looking for somewhere warmer. If it were up to me, she would always live inside, and I would always know where she was and never worry about losing her. That's probably how Mom feels about me. Just think—if God loves a stray kitten enough to save her small life, how much more does He love an unborn baby? The #1 solution for stopping abortion is to pray for 1) deceived women and 2) the strength to stay pure.

SEEING PATTERNS

Today at lunch, Jennifer Hartman and Angie waved me to their table. I thought maybe they wanted to be friends again, and, honestly, I was willing to give them another try. Instead, they told me their new rule: they've banned themselves from sitting with me. "We thought you should know," said Jennifer Hartman, her face turning red with laughter, "so you can help us follow our rule."

That's when Angie burst out laughing. "You keep the best rules," she said, though laughing so hard she could barely speak.

I asked if they were serious. They were looking at each other and laughing so hard, they shook. I felt so stupid. "This is stupid," I said. I turned and walked out of the cafeteria as if it didn't matter. But feeling hot and weird, like I'd been slapped for no reason.

I should have said "stupid and immature." I locked myself in a bathroom stall and stood on the toilet seat so no one would see me. I did not cry.

Because I've noticed how the girls in my class always need someone to hate. In second and third grade, no one liked Alice Schrauben because she was spoiled and there was something seriously wrong with her skin. Her hands and arms were covered in giant flakes, and her face was objectively ugly, wide with eyes so tiny, they sunk into her head like some kind of baby pig. I felt sorry for her, so one time I actually sat with her for lunch, but she complained that the smell of my peanut butter sandwich made her sick. She couldn't believe I had carrot sticks and an apple because her mother gave her a different Little Debbie snack cake every day. Her mom also cut the crusts from her sandwiches even though crusts are the most nutritious part. She said I should throw a temper tantrum and break things so my mom would give me better lunches. But we don't buy chips or store-bought cookies—that junk isn't good for you—and if I acted like a brat, my mom would rightfully spank me. I left Alice Schrauben to her bratty fatty lunches.

Though I did go to her birthday party later that year, and I remember everything in her house was white, all the furniture and even the carpet, so I guess her father doesn't track in grease and dirt all the time. Alice's party was like something from the Brady Bunch, with a lacey white tablecloth and pink plastic plates with matching teacups and silver-colored plastic forks and knives. There was Hawaiian Punch and bakery white cake with three tubs of ice cream—chocolate, strawberry, and pistachio. ("Isn't that unique?" That's what Mom said when I told her, which meant something else.) Next to each plate was a tiny pink bag with a drawstring top. Jennifer Hartman's mom called them party favors, which I've only seen in books. I opened mine right away—candy corn and jelly beans. They tasted okay but slightly stale. I'd already eaten mine when Jennifer's mom said they were probably holiday leftovers. "It's good to be thrifty," I said, and she looked at me with crooked eyes.

I didn't talk to Alice at her party. Everyone was dressed in jeans, but Alice wore a fancy pink dress with a silver ribbon that tied in a bow on her back. Her mom wouldn't let her open presents while we were there, even though

Alice begged. Her mom said, "Don't be tacky." Alice said she wanted us to leave, and her mom told her to be quiet. Because first we had to eat cake, and, before cake, there was pin-the-tail-on-the-donkey, which I thought was a bit babyish, especially because Alice's mom grabbed your hand if you got anywhere close to the edge of the paper, which made everyone jump, hard. She didn't want her walls marked up with little dots. I pinned my tail on the donkey's forehead, and when I took off my blindfold, Alice's mom said, "That's the worst one yet!" No one talked to Alice on Monday.

To compare: I went to Nikki Boyle's house in fourth grade. Michelle said, "Seriously? The Boil?" Nikki flunked first and fourth grade, so, by that point, she already wore a bra. Her house was obviously poor and country; everything sagged, nothing matched, and it smelled of cigarettes, boiled ham, and old toilets. Her mom sat in the living room, drinking from a big plastic 7-11 cup and watching *The People's Court*. But the Boyles had three horses—Scotch, Alphonso, and Bucket—so we were outside all day anyway. Nikki knows everything about horses, and the more we were around the animals, the more normal she seemed. Scotch and Alphonso were brown, and Bucket was black mixed with grey. We brushed and fed them hay, and gave them carrots from our hands. Nikki competes in horse shows. She knows how to jump and canter. She said someday I could ride one, too. I liked being with Nikki and the horses and didn't mind the manure and flies, but I realized when I got home that I couldn't actually be friends with her, or everyone would hate me. On Monday, I pretended she wasn't calling my name. By

Wednesday, I thought of her only when I saw her, which didn't feel very nice. So, luckily, that Friday Denise and I became ketchup-sauce sisters on the bus. Then Denise and I were always together, and I barely noticed Nikki, even when she quit coming to school. At least I was her almost-friend, if only for a weekend—that was more than anyone else in my class had done.

Alice Schrauben doesn't go to our school anymore, either. And except for Angie being overweight, there isn't an obvious girl to hate. It's always the gross girls who are left out first because their grossness might rub off on you. I'm not saying this is right, but that's how people think. In sixth grade, no one liked Becky Parker because she was unusually short and bossy. She had to be right about the stupidest things, like Zingers being better than Twinkies because she liked Zingers more. Last year, everyone but me and Denise hated Beth McNorton, even though she was an eighth grader, because she was a big flirt who stuck her boobs out when she walked. "For my posture," she said, which was only partially true. Beth started taking dance lessons when she was only four years old. She's an only child. She offered to teach me two routines. Last year, we were practicing the jazz one when Jennifer Hartman and Stephanie Conroy walked by and started laughing.

"Don't look at them," Beth warned. "They're just trying to feel better about themselves." Girls can be stupid and jealous, she said. She also told me that I'm a natural dancer, with a dancer's body, especially my thighs. I think Beth was right about more things than I realized. Because even though I am not obviously cute, I'm not ugly, either, and I consistently receive the best grades in the class, which probably makes some people feel bad. They may call me bossy or stuck-up, but I know I'm not better than anyone else because everyone matters equally, and I'll definitely let another lead as long as they actually do it. I always pay attention to others' feelings, which isn't true of Angie. She won't share and will actually gloat if she has something she thinks you might want. In fact, if you want to know who is really stuck-up and selfish, here's how you can tell,

1. To begin, you must understand that being stuck-up and selfish are similar but not the same. A selfish person may not be stuck-up, but a stuck-up is always selfish. Stuck-ups honestly believe they are more important than other people and automatically deserve better and more, which makes them selfish. They prioritize status over people. You can easily tell if someone is selfish if she won't share or if she compares amounts too closely. Stuck-ups are afraid of not being good enough; selfish people, of not getting enough.

2. Stuck-ups divide the world into "betters" and "lessers"; a stuck-up wants the "betters" to like her but only to confirm her popularity. This is why Beth McNorton wasn't stuck-up: she smiled at everyone and didn't care about being popular. But Jennifer Hartman fake-smiles, especially at Denise. She moves her mouth, but her eyes stay as flat as a cup of pop that sat on the counter all night. Contrarily, Jennifer Hartman gave real smiles to Stephanie Conroy because Stephanie was clearly the cutest girl in last year's eighth-grade class. She also had money. Mom says Grandma C fake-smiles at her and thinks Dad mar-

ried down because Mom was country and poor. Grandma C is a bit of a snob, which is the adult version of stuck-up, with a different set of manners.

3.   Selfish people call others selfish. If you give a selfish person a pair of fuzzy blue slippers for her birthday, she will complain that you regifted them from Aunt Susan and call you selfish, even though the slippers were brand new, still in their package, and she wears them almost every day. Also, if you lend your red marker to a selfish person, and the marker runs dry while she's using it, she will get mad at you instead of apologizing, like she should, for using up your red marker coloring in the Red Sea, which isn't actually red. Angie seriously did get mad at me in fifth grade and wanted me to ask Mrs. Correll if I could borrow her red marker. She called me stuck-up for being teacher's pet, but stuck-up would be if I bragged about it. It's not my fault if teachers happen to like me.

4.   Stuck-up people often have more money and wear designer jeans and brand names. It's hard to be successfully stuck-up if you're poor. On the other hand, a selfish person may be rich or poor. Or, to put it another way, stuck-ups are usually stuck-up because they have something more to begin with, while selfish people are selfish because they want more than others, which goes back to their fears. (Note: What are you afraid of?)

5.   Some stuck-ups literally stick their noses in the air, especially if they're conceited, which means they not only believe they're attractive but that physical looks are more important than character. Jennifer Hartman walks like that. Not me. So when we came in from lunch today and Angie said, "I'm Marie," in her stupid high-pitched

fake voice, then stuck her nose in the air as if that's how I walk, she's being delusional. Obviously, I'm going to act as if I don't see them. They've banned themselves from sitting with me! Which leads me to my final point, that

6.   Selfish people and stuck-ups cannot imagine what it's like to be someone else, especially someone they consider lower or less than. Once I told Jennifer Hartman to put herself in Nikki Boyle's shoes, but all Jennifer Hartman said was, "Her shoes are ugly." Jennifer Hartman was especially mean to Nikki Boyle, which is probably another reason Nikki left our school in the middle of fourth grade. I felt sorry for Nikki Boyle, but that's not a good reason to be someone's friend.

∷

Her mother liked to visit other churches, was curious that way, which is how they ended up attending a week-long evening series on the End Times at a local Seventh-day Adventist church. The preacher mapped various scriptures from Revelations and Daniel onto historical events and locations. This nation-state is depicted by the lion; that one, by the eagle's wings; here are the ten horns and the seven seals. The preacher called the Pope the anti-Christ and said anyone who worshiped on Sundays, as opposed to Saturdays, was outside of scripture and going to hell. She knew her mother didn't agree with this teaching but couldn't ask why the sermons, in their totality, were still theologically okay. When she was older, she noticed how her mother found a familial comfort in shaming messages of fear; even later, she found similar messages of doom and exceptionalism in early US American sermons, including Puritan typology, which also mapped the Old Testament onto the New Testament, onto this particular national ideology, this new world land.

A girl at church saw demons dancing in the hallway; the next morning, her parents found pornographic magazines under her brother's mattress, the source of demonic entry. A teenager saw a demon running up the stairs; he prayed for protection and felt the demon leave. The source was left unexplained. Another time, this same teen saw an angel's left arm, hovering there in the stillness. God revealed only part of the angel, he explained at church, because his personal faith wasn't strong enough to stomach an angel's full awesomeness. A father woke one night to demons taunting him—calling him a pig, a slob, a brute of a man. He cast them out in the name of Jesus, and they had to submit to the name of Christ and leave. That same night, the mother, asleep on the couch, dreamt of their two daughters mocking the father—calling him a pig, a slob, a brute of a man. She confronted the girls, who promised to speak of the father with only kindness and respect.

They taught her to put on a spiritual suit of armor because they wanted her to live free of spiritual attacks and oppression. "They" meaning her parents, her mom and dad. Who knew about the women and men in high places—the politicians, radio preachers, and best-selling Christian authors, the people who founded biblical institutes and ministries that mimicked corporations, small empires whose ideological influence was felt across the land. Like sex, fear sells. Like shame, fear becomes more powerful when we are unable or unwilling to see and name fear as part of the human experience, a psychic energy each of us must face.

Mapping Time

Creation, or What God Made Each Day	TIME	Books of the Bible	What Happened
Day #1: God separates light from darkness.	6000-1395 B.C. *These numbers are from an Appendix in Mom's Bible.*	Genesis – Deuteronomy In *The Way* (the Bible they gave us at VBS), it says the first five books are called the "Pentateuch."	God made the world and chose the Jewish people. He gave them light and left the rest of us in utter darkness. This was the beginning of our known world but not the beginning of God, which means God existed in a preworld where lightness mixed with dark. Which means there wasn't "light" and "dark." Does this mean that Light = Dark?
Day #2: God separates water from air, makes some water "above" and some "below."	1395-1095 B.C. *Day 1 = 4605 years, but Day 2 = 299 years. I guess God can make time*	Joshua – Esther *The Way* calls these the "history books."	These books are about the beginning of Israel and God's call to Abraham to be "best," not "average," like how God separated "water above" from "water below." In these books, the Israelites get their first king, even though God wanted them to live kingless. Mom said it's my decision whether or not to be confirmed, but if God didn't want to appoint a king, he wouldn't want me to pledge allegiance to the Catholic church. Note: God will give you a leader if you demand one, and most people want to be led.
Day #3: God separates water from dry land; green plants appear.	1095-975 B.C. *Someone are busy or having fun. but fly by fast when you you are bored or unhappy how days are longer when stretch or pass quickly, like*	Job – Song of Solomon *The Way* calls these "poetry" (I call them my favorites). Maybe there's a	These books express timeless human emotion. When you are sad, it feels like happiness doesn't exist anywhere. When you are in the middle of the ocean, you can't see the land. David wrote the Psalms, Solomon wrote the Proverbs, and when The Byrds sing "Turn! Turn! Turn!" they are quoting from Ecclesiastes.

		connection between what God created on Day #3 and how poetry is usually about nature—i.e., plants!	
Day #4: God creates the sun, moon, and stars.	975 B.C. – 0 *invented the number 0. Does that mean the idea of 0 did not always exist?*	Isaiah – Malachi (the prophets)	God created everything in the sky while giving us these books of prophecy. Question: Does astrology exist because demons twisted God's plan for prophesy into the zodiac? Well, I think it's okay to read your horoscope sometimes in *Teen Magazine* or the newspaper. I'm a Virgo.
Day #5: God creates birds and fish.	0 – 33 A.D. Life of Christ, birth to death. *Does time move faster as you grow older? Being thirteen feels like forever. Someone also invented clocks, which correspond to the rotation*	Matthew, Mark, Luke, John. (The Gospels tell the same story from four different perspectives)	The fish is a symbol for Jesus, and when Christ was baptized, the Holy Spirit descended on him like a dove. In other words, birds and fish are made just as Christ arrives.
Day #6: God creates animals and humans.		Acts – Revelation (Most of these are letters!)	These books describe the building and teaching of the Christian church, or people, while also prophesying the end of time. Now, consider what animals and humans do best. Answer: They make things and tear them down. So God matches Day 6 to these books of the Bible, right before the end of time.

Day #7: GOD RESTS.	2000 (or so)	This is where the Bible ends and the Book of Life begins. Though what exactly is the Book of Life? (*Find out.*)	During this period, there will be 1000 years of peace on earth. Then Christ will return (again), and Satan will be free to reign for a short period of time. There will be major fighting. God will send fire from heaven and destroy sin, sinners, and Satan. When the fire goes out, God will create a new heaven and a new earth. And the whole story may repeat, especially because the final battle ends in fire, which is the ultimate mix of light and darkness: fire brings warmth and life, alongside destruction and death. What if the world and God are caught in a loop of endless creation and destruction? What if God, who calls himself Word, keeps repeating, like a cassette tape of songs played on auto reverse. If God is the song, who is singing? If God is Word, who hears the song?

of the earth. Looking at my chart, I feel like the Bible and history are more complicated than I am writing. Because, while I can see how some things match, it also feels like I am the one drawing lines, making stuff up. Matches that are sensible and not. Maybe non-sense is the mystery of Christ.

She learned other systems for tracking time. Thailand followed the Buddhist calendar, which meant they were 543 years ahead of the United States. The millennium, she realized, had already happened in Thailand, and no apocalypse—what a relief! The United States followed the Gregorian calendar, named for Pope Gregory XIII, who introduced his calendar in October 1582 as a corrective to the Julian calendar's eleven-minute miscalculation of the solar year. The error was slowly misaligning natural phenomena and named Christian holidays, so that Easter, for example, was moving away from the vernal equinox. If Christ's resurrection is about light piercing the darkness, then church leaders wanted this holy celebration to align with the sun's crossing of the celestial equator and the felt experience of days growing longer and nights, shorter—at least in the northern hemisphere, which is where the Pope lived. Several Protestant countries protested the Gregorian calendar, refusing until the 1700s to adopt it, as they feared it was part of a larger Catholic plot. England and its American colonies held out until 1752, when they skipped eleven days in September, so that Wednesday, September 2, was followed by Thursday, September 14. Business can become usual when you're keeping time together, and most of Western Europe had already adopted Gregorian tracking. The Calendar (New Style) Act in the British Parliament also officially designated January 1 as the start of the legal year, as opposed to March 25, Lady Day, or the Annunciation, which had been the British new year since 1155.

It's easy to forget about other ways of being in time. To fall into what seems a natural rhythm of dreading Mondays and expecting something good to happen on Fridays.

Pierre Bourdieu says the cultural becomes natural "by negating itself as such," so that what is actually learned, or "artificially acquired," becomes "second nature, a habitus." In other words, we don't think of it as *culture* as much as how things are done. This includes how we order our days, tell our stories, greet and judge each other. Habitus: how we physically embody the "norms, values, and behaviors of a particular social group."

On the night of her millennium, she had to go to church. It was the only way to soothe her nervous system after hearing so many sermons, for so many years, about the year 2000 as the time of Christ's Second Coming and Final Judgment—it will be scarier than the movies and will happen in the blink of an eye. Everyone else seemed worried about Y2K and the computers. Or they wanted to dance because they loved Prince (or the artist formally known as), and it was 1999. She told her friends she was staying home because they would laugh at her, she knew, for "being religious." She told herself that she existed within just one of the world's thirty-eight different time zones, so midnight came every hour, somewhere, and each midnight was true. She found a Unitarian Church with a candlelight service, and, wearing a dress that once belonged to her Aunt Susan, she went alone. There she sang with the Unitarians, an elderly group that her mother would surely scorn as spineless liberals. She pushed this thought from her head and relaxed into their acoustic guitar music, the prayers for world peace, the dark wood pews and bland walls. At the stroke of midnight, the stars still shone, and, outside the tall plain glass window, evergreens waved in the winter breeze.

A DECISION

It was a (repeat) awful day. Denise wasn't at school, and the seventh-graders were playing a new game and didn't have a role for me. I'm trying not to notice. And now we have to do a book report on a saint. Sister Mary Francis assigned it this morning and strongly suggested writing about the saint you're choosing for your confirmation name since they will be your patron protector and guide for life. I'm not getting confirmed. I'm not going to tell Mom about this assignment because she'll get upset, and I don't want to have another problem with Sister Mary Francis. After all, she let me sit in the classroom during recess so I could read. That's when she asked about my confirmation papers (again).

My face went hot, and my mouth hurt. I'm not going to be confirmed, I said, but I must have whispered because Sister told me to speak up. I said it again, a little louder, and she looked me in the eye for so long I could hear my own breathing and the sound of kids screaming outside. She blinked twice and said, "Is that your decision?"

I nodded, I think. She asked again, and I said, "Yes."

"Yes, what?"

"Yes, Sister." I really have to do a good job on this report. Because I do make my own decisions, even if I'm not picking a confirmation saint. Reading someone's book is not the same as praying to them. I picked St. Teresa of Avila, who is the patron saint of Spain, plus headaches, bodily ills and sickness, opposition to Church authorities, loss of parents, lacemakers, people in need of grace, people in religious orders, and people ridiculed for their piety. I got this list from Sister Mary Francis's chart entitled "Patron Saints and Their Meanings." I get headaches, and I want grace, which is something like mercy. Right?

St. Teresa had fainting fits, and although her family told her she was physically too weak to live in a convent, she ran away and secretly joined a nunnery. Her dad was really mad about her leaving until he realized she was following God's will, not his, so he gave permission for her to stay. Note: If St. Teresa had always obeyed her father, she never would have become a saint. This makes the question of wanting something difficult.

Yet St. Teresa describes her family as "naturally good." She had two sisters, nine brothers, her dad, and a mom who died when Teresa was only twelve years old—that's practically my age. She writes that she alone was prone to wickedness. She loved to read her mother's chivalric romances, but, unlike her mom, St. Teresa couldn't control her reading. She says the books made her vain because suddenly she cared about hair and fashion, which are passing things of this world, instead of God and goodness. Her second weakness was her bad cousin, who was easily bored and loved to gossip. After St. Teresa's mother died, her cousin visited all the time, and the servants goaded the two girls into talking about their vanities and others' affairs. Teresa's father and older sister did not like this cousin but couldn't tell her to go home because she was family, even though (according to St. Teresa) this cousin was leading her astray.

St. Teresa is basically describing peer pressure, which isn't as bad as St. Teresa makes it sound. She wrote this book as an adult, and let's be honest: Grown-ups love to warn children about choosing their friends carefully, even though most adults don't really know how to have friendships. If you're truly friends with someone, you stick with them regardless of their faults or difficulties. You want to hear their problems and help them. Because you know who they really are.

Truthfully, St. Teresa is kind of boring. She worries too much about whether or not people like her, though, according to her, they usually do. One interesting fact: In St. Teresa's time, priests had affairs. Her confessor was having an affair with a woman when he began falling in love with St. Teresa. (Everyone liked Teresa!) The affair-woman gave the priest a small copper figure, making him promise to wear it as a demonstration of his love. And because the affair-woman had cast a spell on the figure, no one could make the priest throw it away. But after Teresa learned about the copper enchantment, she was able to convince the priest to hand it over as proof of his friendship (remember: he had a crush). And while she says she doesn't believe in enchantments, she threw the figurine into the river. As it disappeared, the priest suddenly changed; it was as if, according to Teresa, he had awakened from a deep slumber, only to realize he actually hated the other woman. (Teresa is always right, according to Teresa.)

SKATE PARTY

I thought Angie was bad, but her cousin, Cheryl, is worse. She's a ninth grader at Cedar Springs, and she came to Angie's birthday skate party today, which wasn't a private party with the whole rink to ourselves but a reserved table during open-skate Saturday, from 1-4 p.m. I'm glad. Because this stupid school isn't the whole world, and other do people exist. Angie invited everyone, even the seventh-graders she doesn't like. Probably for more presents. Cheryl doesn't look anything like Angie. She has ash-blonde hair and is really developed, if you know what I mean. She shows them off, too, by standing super straight and pushing her shoulders back. She and Angie wore matching Pepsi t-shirts, and Jennifer Hartman dressed in the same shades of candy red and baby blue. Clearly preplanned. All three wore blue eye shadow, and Jennifer Hartman and Cheryl crimped their hair, which honestly looked kind of cool. Angie tried to wear hers in a banana barrette, but it's not really long enough, so it looked more like a messy nest, which is kind of mean but true.

But the stupidest thing happened in the bathroom. I came out of a stall, and Cheryl was putting on lip gloss, looking at herself in the mirror. I didn't know she was Cheryl because I had just gotten there. It was only 1:05 p.m. So when she asked if I went to Sacred Heart, I thought she was some random girl. I said yes, and she said, "Are you here for Angie's party?" She glanced at me when she spoke. I said yes, and she began washing her hands. She glanced at me again. "Were you invited?" she asked. Her lips were pressed together in a creepy smile, and her eyes were blank green slits.

"Of course," I said, but my face had gone hot and crawling.

Cheryl wiped her hands, throwing the crumpled towel at the trash can. She missed but didn't pick it up. "You really are clueless," she said. She opened the door, then looked at me again. "Just because you're invited," she said, "doesn't mean anyone wants you here."

How can Cheryl hate me when we've never met?

I went straight to the rink, which was particularly crowded. There were metallic red hearts hanging from the ceiling and red and pink streamers on the walls. The fact is I can skate. Unlike Jennifer Hartman, who was going slowly around the edge, acting dramatic and scared about falling, just to make up for her lack of grace. I can turn corners by crossing one foot over the other (winged shoes). Not even Angie can do that—or her dumb cousin. I decided to ignore Angie at her own party. Denise had finally arrived, so that's who I danced with for the hokey-pokey, and they played "Pour Some Sugar on Me" and "Another One Bites the Dust." Denise and I sang while we skated. We shook our hips and shimmied our shoulders. I wanted the other girls to see. There were more couples' skate songs than normal (Valentines), and Pat Harrington and Jennifer Hartman skated two or three of them together, but they looked ridiculous. Pat puffed his chest out like a rooster, winking at the other boys while Jennifer wobbled and held his hand. It was so embarrassing. Pat Harrington is so gross.

Later, I saw the two of them coming out of the hall-way by the restrooms. There's a weird little dark arcade room there, but I doubt they were playing Ms. Pacman. I talked to Denise and David Robles only. Though I did say "please" and "thank you" to Angie's mom when she gave me a piece of cake. It was store-bought and heart-shaped, chocolate with white frosting and pink flowers. It said "Happy Birthday" and "Angie 14!" in red. I had an edge piece. Angie's mom wouldn't let her have seconds, but all the boys did. Denise did, too.

There weren't any cute boys at the rink today, and maybe God sent Cheryl to show me what happens when you believe other people's words more than your own experience. That's how people become prejudiced, too. Because Cheryl is obviously judging me based on Jennifer Hartman and Angie's lies, rather than anything I did or said directly to her. It was a bad day, but it could have been worse. I could have quit skating. Sometimes you see a person's true colors right away. It saves time.

She returns to the Convent of San Marco and Fra Angelico's painting on the stairwell and its title, which isn't unique to this particular work. *The Annunciation*. An announcement or declaration given by Gabriel, God's messenger, to Mary, God's mother and mother of us all. The annunciation calls to mind Hermes, messenger of the Greek gods. Hermes for hermeneutics, the energetics of interpretation, the god of transitions and boundaries, one who can move between worlds. Patron of thieves, graves, and heralds, of herdsmen, roads, and travelers. (Years later, at her mom's new church, she heard a whole sermon that located all of Greek mythology within the textual gap between Genesis 1:1 and Genesis 1:2. The preacher kept calling his sermon conjecture, admitting it wasn't biblically sound. Yet he preached it anyway, as a possibility of what might have happened, what could have been.)

Standing in the stairwell, she notices how the outer layer of Mary's cloak matches the blue seen through the inner chamber's window. This same blue is shadowed in the garden grass and outside the fence, in the wilderness beyond. In this way, Mary's garment brings the materiality of the world—fiber, tissue, water—into this sacred moment when Mary's body—bone, breath, blood—becomes infused with the Word divine. The annunciation: the speech act by which Christ comes to live among us—i.e., the moment when divinity, already present, is revealed and thus perceived. In language. As word: matter and spirit, sound and breath, scripted and willed.

Just as emotional or sexual abuse requires emotional or sexual healing, spiritual abuse necessitates spiritual healing. She came to this understanding slowly, painfully. Through language. For she began to write.

In a Dream

It was so vivid, I woke and wrote it. This is what I did.

1. Gather the materials, including two bread bags (no holes), two white candles with holders, a Bible, your diary, a favorite pen.

2. Open your diary and look through everything you've written. These words came from inside you, including all the words other people said. In this way, your diary makes your interior exterior. In my dream, I heard this sentence: Your diary is a version/vision of you.

3. Go into the bathroom and lock the door. Begin filling the tub. Place the two candles on the floor, one on either side, so you can kneel between them. Light them as you speak Psalm 23 aloud. The Lord is my shepherd; I shall not want.... Thou annointest my head with oil; my cup runneth over....

4. Place your diary inside one bread bag. Tie it shut. Place that bag inside the other. Tie it shut. Say another prayer, thanking God for His blessings. Speak your prayer aloud as you submerge your diary under water, saying, "I baptize you in the name of the Father, the Son, and the Holy Spirit, Amen."

5. Dry the bags, then untie them, one after the other, and take your diary out. It is time for a new name. Hold your Bible and close your eyes. Slowly turn the Bible around in your hands, asking God to guide you. Stop, and let your fingers feel for the page they want. The passage you point to will include your diary's new name.

6. John 20:18 says Mary Magdalene came and told the disciples that she had seen the Lord and that he had spoken these things unto her.

7. May she be known as Mary M.

I wrote down my dream this morning, and today at school, Denise told me about Meribear, who is half Mary and half bear. She's Bearly's cousin and can protect me the same way Bearly does Denise. Then Denise gave me this:

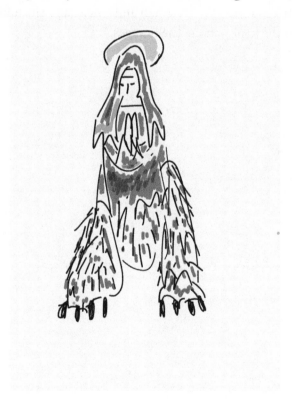

Denise swears she made up Meribear last night by drawing her. She likes to start with a blank mind, and when she looked at the completed picture, she realized Meribear was for me. Isn't God amazing? Are psychic connections real? I told Denise how I'm ignoring the rumors, and she said, "What rumors?" Which made me laugh. If I don't react to Angie and Jennifer Hartman, their words lose power. Yesterday I discovered a secret spot for reading during recess (by the side door near the kindergarten class). That's where I go when Denise is absent, which happens a lot lately. She says it's cramps. I finally told Mom about Jennifer Hartman and Angie, and she told me to be the apple among the oranges.

Compare and Contrast

I got Sister Mary Francis's permission to switch saints for my book report. I couldn't stand St. Teresa's whining! The worst is when she advises parents to marry their teen girls off to boys who are of "lower degree," rather than having them live in convents with nuns who don't worry about every single rule. Liberty means having the freedom to choose, and when you choose to forgive or pray or sing with joy, it means more because you chose it. Now I'm reading about St. Rosa of Lima, Peru, the first American saint and patron of needleworkers, florists, gardeners, embroiderers, and people ridiculed for their piety. She also helps anyone struggling with vanity (i.e., being conceited) because her own face changed so many times. Her book was written by Sister Mary Alphonsus, so it never sounds like St. Rosa is bragging. Maybe it's easier to look better (or worse) through the eyes of another.

St. Rosa

Rosa's birth name was Isabel, and her mother
was Marie. She became Rosa while still an infant
because one morning her face mysteriously
changed into the shape of a rose. Her mother
saw it! Thus, Isabel became Rosa by divine
intervention.

Rosa was tormented by her mother, who was,
in fact, very bitter. She mocked Rosa, accusing
her of spending too much time in prayer,
and pressured her to marry. Her mom valued
religion more than true faith. Rosa wanted to
join a convent, but the Virgin Mary wouldn't
let her. Rosa was praying in the church when
Mary appeared and told Rosa to follow God by
suffering at home with her mother.

Rosa built a cell in her family's garden, where
she went to fast and pray. "Cell" is her word, not
mine.

Me

My middle name is Rose, but no one calls me that. My name means both "of the sea" and "bitter." Mom named me for her mother and likes to warn me against growing into its meaning. I've experienced divine intervention, most recently in the miraculous healing of Iris.

Michelle torments me with her criticism. She says I put on a "goody act" just to get what I want. But Mom is more likely to say yes if you help her clean the house before you ask. Note: We know the Virgin Mary can't actually speak to you, so whose voice talked to Rosa?

I don't have my own room or anything, so I hate being stuck at home. The bathroom door is the only one that locks. I'm probably going to start fasting.

St. Rosa

People were beginning to talk about St. Rosa—
but maybe in a positive way. They visited her
cell to ask for prayer or insight. Once, a local
nun began freaking out about the mosquitoes
in Rosa's garden, but St. Rosa told the Sister
she would be bitten only three times, one bite
for each day that Christ our Lord was dead. Of
course, that's exactly what happened—even the
mosquitoes obeyed (and loved) her.

St. Rosa had clear blue eyes.

She was born with the help of a midwife at her
mother's house in Lima, Peru.

Rosa became a nun, married Christ, and wore
a gold wedding ring. I'm going to look at Sister
Mary Francis's hand tomorrow to see if she wears
a wedding band. God made Rosa live at home,
suffering with her mother.

Me

I don't mind mosquitoes, but I hate spiders.
Pastor Marks once told me I'm destined to do
great things for God. I shook his hand and said
thank you.

Michelle and I have the same color blue eyes, but
whenever we say so, no one believes us. Until
they check for themselves. How would we not
know the color of our own eyes?

I was born at a hospital in Grand Rapids,
Michigan, USA. Michelle brags about her lower
birth weight. I've nearly always been taller than
Michelle, too.

It's weird to marry Christ because marriage is for
Eros love, and Christ is Agape love. God doesn't
need you to suffer, but if you're a mom, he wants
you to stay home with your kids. I don't want to
be a housewife, so maybe I won't have children.

St. Rosa

St. Rosa tortured herself by sleeping on a bed of broken glass and eating her own bile. That's what's left after you've thrown up all your food. Her mother said that eating bile was stupid, but Rosa wouldn't listen. Did her suffering impress God?

St. Rosa wanted to be a (male) missionary but could only be a (female) nun. So she prayed that the (male) friars would do missionary work for her (female).

Nobody liked Rosa when she was alive. But as soon as she died, everyone began calling her a saint. They rushed to see her body, and someone stole her pinkie finger for healing luck. The priests had to lock her body in a special vault, or she would have been divvied into pieces.

Me

We don't need to eat bile; we are bile.

I thought about being a missionary, but girls are usually missionaries' wives, and missionary men are so dorky and definitely not cute. This is why they travel to find wives.

Except for Denise, no one likes me. Mom says self-pity is a sin. Is it easier to like someone when she's dead?

St. Rosa

St. Rosa really loved Jesus but not because she wanted special attention or power. That's how she's different from St. Teresa, who really wanted to become a saint. St. Rosa was physically beautiful, so she used pepper spray and lye to permanently destroy her face. She knew young men looked at her with lust in their eyes, so she permanently scarred herself to save the men from temptation. St. Rosa genuinely wanted to bring people to Jesus, even though it was Mary who spoke to her. Who told her to stay.

Rosa was afraid of the dark until she realized that her Divine Groom (Jesus) was always with her. She experienced many demonic attacks and had amazing visions, including a beautiful rainbow coming from the source of all goodness, which is God.

Me

Can you imagine washing your face with lye?!!
Michelle says I want to be the center of attention,
but I think Michelle does. I hate it when people
look at me because they always find something
wrong. Overall, I think my looks are more of a
minus than a plus.

I know Jesus lives inside me, but I'm still afraid
of the dark. I try to pray every night, and I'll sing
praise songs whenever I feel something in the
room. This happens a lot, especially if I'm alone.
I would say it's a ghost, but Pastor Marks says
ghosts are actually demons, trying to trick us into
believing our dead relatives are real.

Part of me wants to have visions like St. Rosa. But
I'm scared.

And the day came when the risk to remain tight in a bud was more painful than the risk it took to blossom.

–Anaïs Nin

1987, FROM MICHIGAN TO FLORIDA

She began by writing a zine about girlhood friendships. She called it a zine because she printed and stapled it herself, like what the Riot Grrls were doing, but while their zines looked punk and had DIY list instructions for making menstrual tea and homemade pads, her stories hung in seemingly more conventional paragraphs and read like something between fiction and non. Personal. Narrative. She wrote about Denise and Veronica. She was lonely, and writing was a way to reunite. To come to some understanding. She remembered Angie and Jennifer Hartman turning on her in the eighth grade and how later, at a special reunion Mass for graduating seniors, they still refused to speak to her. Cheryl was there, too, glaring as if there were more between them than one day at the skating rink. Stupid, she thought, and Jennifer Hartman and Angie continued to whisper. She began to write that story and recovered a memory of leading them to Christ. She began writing that story and uncovered the thing she couldn't look at. She began by writing about the girls in her class, and then she was writing the antiabortion rally she hadn't, until that moment, remembered attending. Eventually she found the Teen Life folder still saved at her mother's house. In one brochure she read, "Sleeping around cheapens sex—don't be afraid to say you're saving it for its real purpose."

She began as they drove to Florida, adding to the writing she had already begun. It was her first time traveling out of state. Her aunt had invited her to join their family vacation as the babysitter for her young cousins, ages three and five. A few months earlier, at Meijer, she had bought a pale blue journal with a duck-duck-goose pattern across its front. She wrote as they drove South; as her cousins napped; as she hid in the bathroom, hating her ever-complaining aunt.

She began with a list of memories and a desire to write: Her first communion, that second baptism, Father Berne's homily against Protestants, her mother's disdain for the Rosary because "praying to Mary is a sin." She began writing a memoir, but then her thirteen-year-old voice stepped in, which made her laugh and cringe in equal measure. A writing professor warned against keeping this adolescent point of view. "It's just so difficult," the professor explained. "Especially in nonfiction." But she didn't want to write like that professor, whose "no" became another obstacle to push against. She began again by deciding on fiction. She put away the manuscript and read for two years: novels, mostly, and books about language, the Bible as literature, mystic saints. She remembered some of these saints from before, when she was thirteen and had to read their lives in secret, away from her mother's prohibiting eye.

She began by recopying the Psalms, one per day for 150 days. She called it preparation for writing. She was building something that she didn't know how to make. She was learning her material along the way. Faced with uncertainty, she put her faith in neuroscience. Someone said the brain is plastic—if you practice anything for thirty minutes a day, you'll become an expert in ten years. So that's what she did. She began repeatedly, day after day, writing on notebook paper before moving to the computer. And though she was still writing the same book ten years later, she could see a difference in her sentences, in her relationship with language, in the sound of, and space around, the words.

Ohio

I am sitting in the very back seat of Aunt Susan's van. Big news: I'm going to Florida! Bigger news: Denise became born again!! I've been praying and packing since it happened, so this is my first chance to write. I decided to fast last Friday: nothing but milk and water from the time I woke until sundown. If St. Rosa can do it, so can I. (She also eats her own bile, but that's too much to prove.) Friday morning, I put on my armor first thing, and whenever I felt hungry or weak during the day, I prayed Elmer Schmelzenbach's prayer: "Lord, I leave this situation to you." Then I pictured Iris, who Mikey has promised to feed while I'm gone. Because before I found her, Iris hadn't eaten for several days. But God saved her and made her cuter. (Remember this.) Denise invited me over last-minute, and Sister Mary Francis let me use the phone in the office to call and ask my mom. She said yes. The fasting was working. On the bus, I told Denise about the fast, but she didn't care about eating because she's on a new diet that allows food only right before bedtime. It's difficult to sleep if you're hungry, and Denise suffers from insomnia. She says it's because she's a teenager, and that's why she keeps getting sick and missing school, too. It was so funny to confess our fasting diets, only to find out they were practically the same. Denise and I are electric and on the same wavelength, birds of a feather flocking together. Denise has already lost five pounds. Not that she was fat, but she does want her cheeks to be more defined, and I agree. To distract our heads from our stomachs, we power-walked almost to the opposite side of the lake, but, luckily, Denise suggested turning around before we saw Mr. Henry's house. I didn't want to see him, either. He always wants to feed us. Bologna sandwiches, hot dogs, mint chip ice cream, jelly doughnuts. He always has chocolate sauce, too.

Denise just got cable, so we watched *The Karate Kid*. Isn't Danny cute? I love the final scene, where he wins the championship by copying a crane. Because it's more than the gold medal or the glory of beating a rich jerk—Danny is facing and fighting his own demons. Which aren't actual demons (I don't think) but his beliefs about himself. Before bed, Denise and I ate one low-fat carrot muffin each, and I drank hot chocolate, which tasted so good. Denise made us split a gallon of water to flush our bodies while helping our skin and organs stay clean. We turned off the lights, and Denise asked if I ever get scared. I do. Especially in the basement or if I have to take the garbage out at night and I can feel something right beyond the edge of seeing. She asked what I'm most scared of. "Demons," I said, "though I know they can't actually hurt me because with God I have 100% protection." She said she didn't understand. I paused. Maybe I didn't understand, either. Because the fear feeling doesn't go away. Not right away and usually not until I change locations. I didn't tell her that. I said that putting on my spiritual suit of armor helps refocus my attention. "Also," I said, "you can pray a hedge of angelic protection around you." When angels are there, nothing can hurt you. If you sing or quote scripture—like "resist the devil and he will flee from you" (James 4:7)—

the demon has to leave. Automatically. He has no choice.

Denise said that's so cool and she wants a hedge of protection. I told her spiritual powers aren't nearly as important as accepting Christ into your life. When you're a Christian, spiritual gifts are side dishes to Jesus as the main course. You can't command demons unless Jesus lives inside you, and He doesn't live inside you unless you're born again.

Denise was quiet. "Sometimes," she said, "I think I'm really bad."

I thought about her stealing the candy bar from the Trading Post. "We all mess up," I said. She didn't answer.

"Denise," I said. I could hear her breathing. "I want to ask you something."

When she finally spoke, her voice was low but soft. "What?" she said.

I didn't want to upset her. "Tell me," she whispered. I could feel her wanting. I took a deep breath.

"It's just...." And now I was whispering, too. "Are you 100% certain that you're going to heaven?"

She didn't answer. I could hear air blowing from the vents and a car passing by, not on her street but further away. Then Denise began to cry. "It's okay," I said. "You can tell me anything."

"I want to,..." she whispered. Everything felt suspended. I could hear a whir in the air. "I want to...."

In the waiting, I began to pray that God would fill her with His light and peace, that she will know herself as a child of God because there is nothing she needs to do or say to earn His love, that she is loved already, that she is love. I paused before continuing with a few phrases in tongues. She didn't stop me. She was lying very still. When I paused again, she rolled over and whispered— her face so close to mine, I could feel her hot breath. She said, "Marie, listen." My face stretched toward hers like a flower toward the sun. "Marie," she said, "I want to be born again."

Isn't that amazing?

I gave her a big hug. Then we sat up, cross-legged and knee to knee, as I spoke a hedge of protection around us before leading her in the sinner's prayer. I could feel the calm, God's peace, enter the room. I promised to give her a Bible and help her look up Ephesians 6:10-15 so that she can take notes about her spiritual suit of armor. She was still kind of crying, but she also felt relieved. I could feel it. When we laid back down, she asked me to spoon her. I did. She smelled like lavender and night air. We were wearing dad-sized t-shirts and underwear but no shorts or pants. After a while, I could feel her sleeping. I really love Denise.

KENTUCKY

Last night we stayed at a Best Western just past Cincinnati, and now we're almost to Tennessee. Crossing state lines is so weird. The land looks the same on both sides, and you know there's a border only because there's a metal sign on the side of the road. The "Welcome to Kentucky" one calls this the bluegrass state. This was a slave state, since we're now officially in the South. When I think about it that way, a made-up border made such a big difference. Isn't that weird? And so sad. Uncle Steve is a dentist, and he and Aunt Susan have a TV in their van. Nicholas is watching *The Fox and the Hound* for the second time today. Aunt Susan and Uncle Steve are the richest people I know. Their house in Traverse City is practically brand-new, with a skylight in the kitchen and the parlor. No one uses the living room, and there is beige wall-to-wall carpeting throughout the whole house (except the kitchen, which is tile). They also have central air-conditioning and a redwood deck that wraps around two sides of the house. Aunt Susan is five months pregnant. Of Mom's sisters, she's the only one who is born again. She likes it when I babysit because I discipline the kids with scripture. She told Mom that, and Mom told me.

I've never stayed in a hotel before. Our room had two double beds covered with rose-colored bedspreads, plus a dresser, desk, and nightstand in matching dark wood. There was a free "Best Western" notebook and a green hardcover Bible in the nightstand drawer. When I told Aunt Susan somebody forgot their Bible, she said it's from the Gideons, who have a ministry providing free Bibles to travelers. So I took it. For Denise. But I didn't let Aunt Susan see. It's in the bottom of my suitcase. We just passed Mr. Zion-Crittenden Road, which reminds me of Zion City and John Alexander, First Apostle. I want to remember everything about this trip. I'm so excited. Here are a few things I noticed today:

1.   Uncle Steve does not like McDonald's. Aunt Susan made him stop there for lunch because it's the kids' favorite. It sounded like an argument. Aunt Susan told him what to order. She took the pickles off Rebecca and Nicholas's Happy Meal burgers and put them on her own Big Mac. She ordered a regular cheeseburger and fries for me without asking if that's what I wanted. The cheeseburger tasted tangy, and when I finished it, I immediately wanted another. (I didn't ask for one, though.) Uncle Steve ate a fish sandwich and an apple pie. No one else had dessert. I helped the kids put their plastic toys together: a blonde-headed man in a space suit for Nicholas and a red and black car for Rebecca. They didn't like their own toys and started to cry, so I told them to trade. There is always a peaceful solution!

2.   Uncle Steve turned on the radio to Whitney Houston ("Greatest Love of All"), followed by "Wind Beneath My Wings" (Bette Midler), plus other songs I liked but don't know. Then Nicholas asked to watch *The Fox and the Hound* (the first time) with the volume super loud. He's only five years old and already very disobedient, probably because he's so spoiled. Aunt Susan buys him something every time they go somewhere, regardless of need. While

Nicholas was picking out a pop at the gas station, Aunt Susan told me to go to the van and hide the remote control. Now he can't control the volume, which he shouldn't. Uncle Steve's thin blonde hair is longer in the back, balding in the front. He wears glasses with silver wire frames. His face turns red when he's angry; a purple vein pops on his forehead, and his face turns putty grey. I can see him in the rearview mirror. Once, our eyes accidently met.

3. Aunt Susan would rather listen to Christian tapes. We've heard Carmen, DeGarmo & Key, and Evie, all several times. When Aunt Susan doesn't like something, she presses her lips together in a thin line and smacks her lips. Mom does that same thing. Last week at Meijer, Mom bought me three polo shirts and two pairs of Bermuda-style shorts, plus a new pair of fake Keds. My favorite is the mint green shirt and matching mint-green shorts with their awesome black geometric pattern. I look good even if I have to repeat outfits. On the Friday before I left school, everyone but Angie signed my shoes. Even Jennifer Hartman wrote "Jennifer Hartman" with a heart over her "i." I made them use my new Bic four-color ballpoint and pick their color: red, blue, black, or green. Denise drew an enormous green smiley on the top of my left toe, with a tongue hanging from the mouth and red stars for eyes. Aunt Susan asked if I brought other shoes. I have light pink flats to go with my dress outfit, in case we go to church. Aunt Susan asked if my mom was upset about me ruining my shoes. I didn't know what to say, so maybe I didn't answer. I don't care what she thinks—I like my shoes.

She began thinking of adolescence as a place one inhabits. First in the body, then in books and films, in art. Adolescence as location, time plus space, as tone or atmosphere. She recovered the feeling of existing within a visibly shifting body, the feeling of lost control, of overwhelming anger, of loneliness, as if you were the only one experiencing the world and the world itself had gone mad. How the days felt longer when you were thirteen, and how, by seventeen years old, thirteen felt like ages ago. How the everyday felt more present-tense when you were younger, punctuated by moments of excitement, happiness, fear, despair. Or maybe, she thought, that's how it seems as you grow older, when there's more to remember. When the remembering is more difficult. When you grow older, it's more tempting, seemingly easier, to let the days, months, years pass by while you stay in a trance.

She began spotting hypocrisies, not in her parents (they were too close) but in her aunt and uncle, who professed to be Real Christians even as they made her feel so bad. So low. Underclass. She felt similarly with some families at school but figured that money was another lie they had bought into because they were still Catholic and thus "of this world." She had noticed Father Berne's hypocrisy, the way he smoked a cigar and said words like "dammit" at Friday-night bingo or during the annual pancake breakfast. "Oh," she said to her sister. "What a role model for children." This made her sister laugh. But she did not understand her aunt and uncle. They had all the keys to joy and ease; that's what it seemed like—they were wealthy Real Christians. They were white in a country that she knew, like everyone knew, discriminated against people who were brown or black. With her aunt and uncle, she mostly felt their striving, not their love.

She began thinking about memory, recognizing how writing often jogged something within her, how a scene, situation, or image written evoked remembrances, as well. She could feel them in her body, feel the old shame or envy, the fear of forever wrongness, the desire to be good. To be right. As she wrote, she began uncovering languages: the language of the schoolyard, of Christian radio, her mother's sighing tongue. Over time, the many written revisions became her new memories—until she could no longer remember beyond them. She had become, she realized, less certain about what had actually happened but clearer, more accepting, of what it had meant. To her. So this, she thought, is writing one's life.

TENNESSEE

U ncle Steve isn't Irish, so Nicholas has never tasted a
McDonald's shamrock shake. We saw one pictured
on a billboard yesterday, and I began telling Nicholas
stories about St. Patrick—the saint who escaped slavery
and carried a staff, like Moses, and who spread good-luck
shamrocks throughout Ireland, driving out the snakes
and saving the potato crop. I remembered his story from
our third-grade advent play based on *The Lives of the
Saints*. Parts of St. Patrick's story are obviously a myth,
but so is Santa Claus, and Aunt Susan acts as if he is real
since that's what Nicholas and Rebecca believe. When she
heard me talking about St. Patrick, however, she called
him "imaginary" and said that if I'm going to tell stories
about miraculous men, I should tell Bible stories because
they're actually true. So when Nicholas asked for another story, I told him about how Moses's brother, Aaron,
cast his staff down before the Pharaoh and it became a
snake, to which the Pharaoh's wise men responded by
turning their staffs into snakes. But Aaron's snake was
from God-Jehovah, so it was bigger and able to swallow
their smaller snakes. Nicholas asked if snakes were good
or bad, and I said both. "That's not true," said Aunt Susan.
"Snakes will hurt you, so stay away from them—do you
hear me?" When Nicholas asked for another story, I said I
was too tired and that we should watch a movie, instead.

This wouldn't have mattered, except we went to Mc-
Donald's again today and they didn't have shamrock

shakes. Uncle Steve tried to distract Nicholas by pointing out a mountain, but Nicholas didn't care. He called
me a liar and would have sucked his thumb, but Uncle
Steve swatted at his arm, so Nicholas sat on the back of
his hands instead, shaking. At first, he wouldn't eat; then
he was eating only fries. Then Aunt Susan said he better
eat his meat, and, when he said "No," she took his fries,
saying he had to eat half his burger to get them back.
Nicholas's face turned red, and he got ready to scream,
but Uncle Steve covered his mouth, yanking him from the
chair and marching him right into the bathroom. Aunt
Susan just sat there, brushing crumbs from the table, her
hand jerking back and forth. I think she agrees with Mom
about not spanking in anger. It's better for the child to really understand what they did wrong and how your mom
has to spank you because, otherwise, she would be disobeying God.

When they came back, Nicholas was whimpering, but
Uncle Steve told him to cut it out or he'd get another. Then
Uncle Steve narrowed his eyes at me. "No more about the
s-h-a-k-e-s," he said. It hurt to swallow. He told me to wrap
the food for the car, and Aunt Susan glared at me, I swear.
But it's not my fault they give Nicholas whatever he wants.
So then when he doesn't get something, he tantrums.

When I'm in charge, I lock Nicholas in his bedroom
until he accepts the rules. I usually have to pick him up
and physically put him there, and I've seriously been
covered in bruises from his punches and kicks. I never
spank in anger, but Nicholas and I usually have three or
four rounds of time-outs before he obeys. Which he never
does if Aunt Susan is there. He's not stupid. He knows
she's the boss of me.

It was tense and gross in the van, but maybe Uncle Steve felt bad because he eventually turned on the radio, and, even more surprisingly, he sang along to a song about time making us bolder and children growing older. (Note: He told me later it's called "Landslide," by Fleetwood Mac, so, see, he was being nice.) But Aunt Susan turned off the radio as soon as that song stopped, saying Nicholas and I should find a book. I've read *Oh, the Places You'll Go!* five times today, at least, and Nicholas watched *The Fox and the Hound* twice, once with headphones. When Aunt Susan asked about my book, I had to show her: *The Story of a Soul: The Autobiography of St. Thérèse of Lisieux.* "It's for Religion class," I told her, which is true. Sister Mary Francis wants me to write an extra report to make up for missing so much school. Aunt Susan fake-smiled. I know she doesn't like the saints, either. Now Mom will know and get mad.

GEORGIA

We've finally reached Atlanta, where the freeway sometimes has five lanes on each side and there are skyscrapers and endless lights. Coming into the city, we were stuck in rush-hour traffic, which upset Uncle Steve—he cussed at other cars and swore he would never live here. We went to The Old Spaghetti Factory for dinner. The inside was decorated in an old-fashioned style with at least twenty-eight hanging lamps and chandeliers (Nicholas and I counted). The walls were dark wood with a candle on every table. I ate fettuccini Alfredo (one of my favorites!), broccoli, and at least eight pieces of garlic bread. Plus unlimited refills on strawberry lemonade, which was so good. Uncle Steve thought I ate too much, even though the bread refills were also free—so why should he care? I didn't realize he was being sarcastic when he held up the empty bread basket and offered to ask the waitress for more. "Sure," I said, and he laughed in a funny way and raised his eyebrows. That's when I felt stupid. Kind of sick. After all, I didn't mean to pig out, but who knows if I'll eat at The Spaghetti Factory ever again. It's not like my family goes on vacation or eats at restaurants, which are more expensive than eating at home.

That was last night.

Today, while waiting for Aunt Susan outside the restroom, I was holding Rebecca on my hip, swaying back and forth and talking about animal sounds. A lady with purple-gray hair and hands that shook like an old woman's asked Rebecca what a cow says. "Moo," said Becca, and the lady asked me, "How old is your daughter?" The lady looked like a horse—her jaw was long, and her ears, small. She didn't look old. "Rebecca just turned three," I said, and the woman looked at me so strangely. "Is that so?"

Then Aunt Susan came out of the restroom, and Rebecca cried, "Mommy!" The lady and I just looked at each other. I never said I was Becca's mom.

We were at the Atlanta Zoo, which is larger and more crowded than the one in Grand Rapids, with many more animals. The giraffes and hippopotami are my favorites (Aunt Susan told me that both plurals—hippopotami or hippopotamuses—are correct). Nicholas and I loved the tiger cub, which is so cute, even though, as Uncle Steve noted, it could claw and bite us to death.

We went into the Cyclorama, which holds the largest painting in the world! It's a panoramic called *The Battle of Atlanta,* and it circles all the way around a gigantic room. According to a brochure on the ticket counter, a Union General commissioned eleven German artists to make the painting as a campaign advertisement. The General was running for Vice President and wanted people to know he could win. Back then, people just ran for President or Vice President, and the winner was the person with the most votes. (They changed the election rules because it was too difficult having a President from one party and a Vice President from another.) Sadly, the General got sick and died before the painting was finished, and the brochure didn't mention the election results.

Rebecca started fussing during the informative movie

they make you watch before seeing the painting, so I had to take her to the lobby, which meant missing many interesting facts. That's the worst thing about babysitting—you can't pursue your own interests because the children always come first. This is probably double or triple-true for moms who can't afford babysitters. Luckily, I took a bunch of free hard candies from The Old Spaghetti Factory last night and told Rebecca she could pick one if she quit crying. She always wants orange, the grossest color. I put a purple in my mouth, and we rushed back in time to enter the main room with everyone else. The painting was really, really big, and there were bleacher-style seats in the center of the room, longer and taller than our base-ball-diamond bleachers at Sacred Heart, and these were inside, too. Isn't that cool? The usher said the best seats are at the top. When he noticed me, he winked. I was only looking at him because he was talking. Then Uncle Steve sat in the second row, even though the best seats are at the top—the usher said so. "Oh," said Aunt Susan. "Are you sure?" Uncle Steve shrugged and said it would be easier. But the worst part was the usher, who sat in the front row, just a few feet down. He kept turning and looking at me, even though he was probably twenty or even thirty years old. I pulled Becca onto my lap to hide behind her. Because I wanted to see the painting, and it was still a good view. Even the ceiling had glowing stars, and they covered the floor with fake grass and real plants. It smelled like actual dirt. When everyone quieted down, we could hear the sound of running water. Behind that, the hiss of a cassette tape.

The show started with the sound of gunshots and a

recording of a man's voice talking about the people in the painting—some fourteen-year-old boys from Mississippi, a farmer from Wisconsin, a colonel and his foot soldiers—who fought and were brave. Meanwhile, a spotlight moved across the painting, highlighting the individually painted boys and men. It seemed as if the painting was moving, but actually it was the floor. We were on a giant, slowly-turning platform—we were the ones in motion. While the people in the painting were still—dead. That thought made me nervous, I hugged Becca closer. I put my chin on the top of her head. The usher, I noticed, was still sneaking glances, so I slouched lower. If you close your eyes, will they go away? We circled the room slowly, one full rotation as the entire painting passed in front of us. When a painting is a giant circle, you can't see the whole picture all at once, and it doesn't have a beginning or an end. But a story being told has to start and stop somewhere, and the talking man ended on two brothers from Kentucky—or maybe it was Tennessee. One brother joined the Union army; the other, the Confederacy. In Atlanta, they fought on opposites sides of the battle, and no one knows what happened. Maybe they killed each other, which would be more tragic and more meaningful than if they were strangers. The talking man never mentioned slavery, though slavery was the main reason for the war.

I'm glad I'm not a boy. If I only get married and have children, no one will think anything of it because taking care of your husband and children is always considered good enough for girls. But boys have to prove themselves. Every boy I know has been in a fistfight, and, during wars, it's the boys who go to battle. Otherwise, they're cowards.

I don't want to be a killer or a coward. I don't want....

Had to stop fast. Aunt Susan came into the room, yelling because Nicholas and Rebecca were sleeping past their nap time. That's one way to wake up your kids. She thinks they won't be tired at night if they nap longer during the day, but it's nighttime now, and they're sleeping, so Aunt Susan was wrong. Again. She accused me of letting them sleep on purpose so I could write in my "silly notebook." What if I did?

Today we went to the Atlanta History Center and Tullie Smith house—an actual plantation. It was very small, much smaller than I would have thought, with literally only four rooms on the first floor and two upstairs. The kitchen was outside in a shack. The tour lady said the kitchen had to be separate because they didn't have a stove, just a fireplace, and houses burnt down all the time. The Smiths owned eleven slaves, which the tour lady said wasn't very many in comparison with large plantations who usually had over two hundred. But that's still eleven people, which is a lot. That's how many eighth-graders attend Sacred Heart. She said that farming was an impossible amount of work: the land was wild; the weather, hot and humid; the settlers had to do their own blacksmithing. They used salt to preserve their meat because they couldn't get ice for an icebox. She made it sound like they needed slaves in order to survive. I've noticed that, when people talk about history (including in history text books), there's this hint that you're supposed to be grateful because, if people hadn't settled the land and faced such dangers (like Indians), you and I wouldn't exist. But that's not true for everyone because I realized today that, if I were black, I wouldn't want to be anywhere near the Tullie Smith house. If I were Cherokee or Creek (two Indian tribes the tour lady mentioned from the area), then strangers coming and plowing the land wouldn't make me feel safe.

In the museum, there was an actual bill of sale from a purchase of a fourteen-year-old girl named Alice. It described her as having "a sound mind and body" and called her a "slave for life." In the gift shop, Aunt Susan told me it was illegal for slaves to read or write. That's another stupid law I didn't know we had. She bought me a book called *Incidents in the Life of a Slave Girl,* by Harriet Ann Jacobs. She's glad I'm taking an interest in history—that's what she said. I don't know if I am, but I liked seeing how things were different than I imagined. Also, the beds and uniforms in the displays looked too small for regular bodies. Maybe people were shorter back then.

Aunt Susan and Uncle Steve left again this evening. Last night, they went to some famous theater to see a play, and when Uncle Steve came in this evening to kiss Rebecca and Nicholas goodbye, he was whistling "I Wish I Was in Dixieland."

Aunt Susan is right—my family could never afford a trip like this.

I can't sleep, so I'm sitting in the bathroom with the tiny night-light that Aunt Susan bought, just like the one in the kids' bathroom back home. Aunt Susan peeked in a bit ago, but, thankfully, I had just turned out the light. I had been reading *St. Thérèse of Lisieux*, or Jesus's Little Flower. She was born in 1873, which makes her thirty-three years younger than the Tullie Smith house. Previously, I thought every saint had been dead for hundreds of years, but when St. Thérèse was born in France, slavery in the US was already over. Even as a young child, Thérèse wanted to be a saint, but only God can choose you for sainthood, so she prayed to be selected. Can you ask God for that? In the convent, Thérèse began writing her life story because the mother superior told her she must. Thérèse was the youngest child—her mother died when she was four years old, and her older sister, Pauline, raised her, which is why Thérèse called Pauline her "second mother." Thérèse hated school—but only because she was obviously smarter than the other girls, who teased her and wouldn't let her play with the group. Wow. Some things never change.

Wait—okay, Nicholas was just crying in his sleep. I rubbed his back until he stopped. It's 4 a.m., and although it's dark outside, I can hear birds singing. If my mom dies, like Thérèse's did, I would probably be the daughter who takes care of Dad. Even though Michelle knows more about cooking. But she's also lazy. She hates to care for anyone but herself.

She began in a class called "Life Writing." Seven years later, she began again by enrolling in an M.F.A. program. She wanted the instruction and deadlines, the encouragement, a broader exposure. She began by starting a writing group or trading writing with a friend. She began by hosting a monthly salon where, for years, she read excerpts from the book she was trying to write. She practiced reading at local events and published several excerpts. She began attending writers' residencies—some official, some of her own making. Like a week alone in the desert. She began editing other people's writing. And reading books as if they were buildings, situations as if they were novels, people as energies, her insides as cosmic terrain. She began to understand reading as another form of writing. Reading cards, too.

She gathered resources, saved her babysitting earnings in a college account. Her aunt and uncle had gone to college; her parents had not. She could see the difference in their later lives, even as she did not want to marry a dentist or have her aunt and uncle's life. In Florida, she heard other languages. Spanish. Japanese. Italian. What would that be like, she wondered, to live in another tongue? In Florida, they visited Disney World, then Epcot, and while she tried to imagine these pretend places as real countries, she couldn't ignore the loud tourists with their strollers and fanny packs. Mostly, the showcased worlds were places for people to eat or to shop. That's what she noticed. She began to want something different, something she wanted to imagine. Beyond the fear.

FLORIDA

I've heard about Disney World my whole life, but it's nothing like the commercials, with their smiling families and magical princess transformations. Not that I want to be a princess and wear hot, ugly dresses and be nice to everyone—and everyone having to be nice to me in return. So how would I ever know who was a true friend? In real life, the Disney magical castle is a small fake building that covers six feet of sidewalk, followed by a very stupid plastic-seeming bridge. There isn't even water beneath the bridge—it's just a five-second pass-through at the park's entrance, to control the crowd. But I kept my criticisms to myself and didn't complain about pushing Becca's stroller all day or how I had to take Nicky to the bathroom every time he had to go. He has to go a lot, and there were always long bathroom lines and even longer lines for the kiddie rides, which were the main ones we had to go on: the teacups, the Pirates of the Caribbean, "It's a Small World." The line for Space Mountain was the longest, and when Aunt Susan finally gave in, she made me go alone. I thought they'd wait in line with me, at least.

Epcot was definitely better, though obviously fake. "Italy" and "Morocco" were my favorites. I wanted to buy a carpet bag but didn't have enough money because I bought a Minnie Mouse sweatshirt on Saturday. It's bright white with her giant face on the front, kind of dorky but the best thing I could find at the time. I felt like I should have something Disney, not just a pencil box or coffee mug.

I like Minnie more than Mickey. I had to pick fast because Uncle Steve was irritated about being in a gift shop. Again. Becca and Nicky didn't like Epcot and wanted to go back to Disney World, which also put Uncle Steve in a bad mood—those tickets were more expensive—so he went to "France" without us. We found him later, having a glass of wine. But the absolute worst was Busch Gardens. (Oath: I will never babysit for Aunt Susan again.) The park itself was nice. It felt like a jungle, with parrots and cockatoos, macaws, and even a toucan. There were flowers in every color—pink, yellow, red, blue, purple, and orange—plus so many plants and varieties of green. I didn't know green could do all that. But I was stuck all day with Nicholas and Rebecca, even though Nicky wanted Uncle Steve's hand, not mine, and Becca kept crying for Aunt Susan to push the stroller, not me. Which annoyed their parents, as if I was doing something wrong.

Then Uncle Steve started talking to a dad from another family, who happened to have a daughter, Jessie, my same age. She looked really cool, like a smaller, younger version of Christie Brinkley but without the big hair. She was so excited to meet me because she wanted to go on the Scorpion but didn't want to go alone. The Scorpion is the biggest roller coaster at Busch Gardens, way bigger than Space Mountain and much more thrilling. And it would be so fun to go with Jessie, who kept raising her eyebrows and saying, "Do you want to?" while I kept asking Aunt Susan if I could.

When suddenly Aunt Susan totally lost it. She flung out her arms and yelled right at me, there in front of everyone. She called me selfish and said they waited for me once already for Space Mountain, and I'm there to babysit, not play, and don't look at her like that because she's done with my spoiled-rotten teenager routine. When she quit yelling, everyone was quiet. Then Uncle Steve and Jessie's dad began talking, and Aunt Susan said, "Excuse me," and walked away. Jessie and her parents left a few minutes later. Jessie didn't look at me when she said goodbye.

Aunt Susan used to be my favorite, even though she has the most spoiled and bratty children I know. We were by a pond, so I took Becca and Nicky to look at tadpoles. I felt like pushing those kids underwater, but I didn't. It's not their fault. I didn't cry, either, though my face was stinging and Nicholas said my ears were all red. I haven't spoken to Aunt Susan since. Not that she's noticed. Seriously, she's that self-absorbed.

We're in Clearwater, staying at the conference hotel in a connected suite, with our own kitchen and living room on the kids' side and a jacuzzi in Aunt Susan and Uncle Steve's. This makes the Best Western look like a shack. There are giant chandeliers in the lobby and an enormous swimming pool shaped like a kidney bean, though the hotel is right on the beach so that you can swim in the ocean just as well. There are waiters at the pool, and all the women wear jewelry with their swimsuits, which I know is supposed to be fancy, but I think it makes them look kind of dumb. Since they're obviously not going swimming. Yesterday at noon, I counted at least five pairs of diamond earrings and three pearl necklaces. I prefer the waves at the beach, but of course Aunt Susan wants to sit by the pool and fit in with the other ladies. Today she wore a gold necklace and a small pair of emerald earrings.

Aunt Susan caught me writing, so she's giving me stupid chores. Like ironing the kids' t-shirts, which she made me do tonight after Becca and Nicky fell asleep. At least I could watch TV. On *Growing Pains*, Kirk Cameron (so cute) discovered both his parents were previously married. No kids. They had a good reason for keeping this information secret, but it still raises a question: Is not telling the same as a lie?

I had another bad dream. Mom was peeling carrots and potatoes, making stew, and she told me to find a pot in the basement. Downstairs, I saw the box where Snickers had her babies. Empty except for straw. There was a black cast-iron cauldron with three short legs. What was Mom trying to hide? The cauldron swarmed with spiders, hundreds of tiny thick bodies and short legs crawling out of the pot, onto the floor, and over the tops of my boots. They rushed up the sides of my legs, wanting and biting. I couldn't breathe so hard, I woke. My legs were tingling. I rubbed them against the sheets and felt something down there. A creature in the bed. I jumped up, tore the blanket off the bed, and shook it away from my face. I didn't see anything. Becca began to cry.

Selfish Aunt Susan and stuck-up Uncle Steve are finally off to meet their superficial friends for dinner. I thought they'd never leave. I talked to Mom today. Aunt

Susan called to tell her how I'm doing. "Such a treat to have her," Aunt Susan said. What a liar! I'm never babysitting for them again. "Your mother wants to talk to you." Aunt Susan thinks she's so great because she has money and uses words like "mother" when "mom" is perfectly good. Mom asked if I'm enjoying myself. and I had to say yes because Aunt Susan was standing right there, eavesdropping. What a snitch. I don't care if that's not the right word—she's a snitch and a liar and conceited. Mom said she had to tell me something. It's really the worst. Denise and Jennifer Hartman were caught shoplifting. Why is Denise hanging out with Jennifer Hartman? Mom said that's not the point. "Is that something you do, too?" Her voice was angry, suspicious.

"No, Mom," I said. I needed to sound calmer. "Wait," I swallowed. "How do you know this?"

Mom said she doesn't agree with gossiping, but she's glad Angie's mom called and told her the news. "So," said Mom, "you've never stolen?"

"No," I said. I was speaking too hard, and Aunt Susan was still listening. "It was probably Jenny's idea because you know what?" I paused for emphasis. "Denise just became born again."

Mom said she doesn't know. She doesn't know what Denise is like, not really. "Or you," said Mom. "Who are you when I'm not there, watching?"

"Oh, come on, Mom," I said. "Did you hear me?"

"Well anyone can say a prayer," said Mom. "It doesn't mean anything unless the words are in your heart."

She began asking of her nighttime dreams and listening to silence.

She began feeling how something taken is also something gained.

She began to know God as a shape-shifter, a trickster, with a wonderfully perverse sense of humor.

This was the hardest beginning; it meant losing her life.

FLORIDA, CONT.

We were at the pool all day and my back's so sunburnt that it hurts to lie down. It's hard to put sunscreen on yourself. I've nearly finished with St. Thérèse of Lisieux. All she wanted was to join the convent, beginning at four years old until she turned fourteen, when she couldn't take it any longer. The Carmelites' rule was you had to be twenty-one, so Thérèse asked her father if she could join early. He said no—until one day, mysteriously, he came to her crying. He gave her a special white flower still attached to its roots. He said he understood they would always be connected, and, finally, he said yes. But for some reason, Thérèse needed her uncle's permission. Can you imagine if Aunt Susan had such say in my life? Her uncle was adamantly against it. "No, no, no," he cried, and Thérèse began to weep. As she left her uncle's, the sky opened with rain that lasted all weekend. Three days, three nights, while at her father's house, Thérèse wept and prayed. On the fourth day, she woke and knew something had shifted. It was sunny as she traveled back to her uncle's, where she found a changed man. God had spoken to him, he said, early that morning: "Thérèse is a blessed little flower." Then he kissed her and gave his consent.

But Thérèse also needed permission from the church superiors, and because they were a committee, it was going to take them so long to do anything except for meet and meet. Again, she wouldn't know their decision for six to nine months, if she was lucky. To help pass the time,

Thérèse traveled to Rome along with her sister and father, where the three of them lined up to see the Pope. While they were waiting, they were told the one rule while greeting His Holiness was to *not speak to the Pope*. But Thérèse knew that God is bigger than any church leader. When it was her turn, she kneeled and kissed the Pope's hand, begging for his blessing. "Please, Holy Father, I want to enter Carmel early." They rushed her away, but the Pope heard her words.

Note: If the Pope says yes, no other Catholic can say no.

So the church superiors suddenly granted her request.

Which doesn't mean everything turned rosy. In fact, that's when Thérèse's problems really began. She had to face Mother Mary of Gonzaga, the Prioress, who didn't want Thérèse to think she was special for joining the convent early. Especially because Mother Mary saw her as a spoiled and lazy child who needed constant criticism for her own good. She refused to notice any of Thérèse's hard work. Like when Thérèse hand-washed the whole front entry, even the stairs. Lesson: Sometimes your elders don't see you clearly.

Then a convent rumor began about how Thérèse was a brat because her real sisters, Marie and Pauline, who were also nuns at Carmel (in fact, Pauline was sometimes Mother Prioress until Mary of Gonzaga would retake the title; they kept going back and forth like that), gave Thérèse whatever she wanted. So Thérèse quit asking to receive anything for herself, and anything she did receive she gave away to others. On the night before Thérèse took her full vows, she was physically confronted by the devil.

He entered her room and accused her of being a fraud. She actually saw him, as if he were flesh. You don't deserve to be here, he said. And maybe you can trick the others, but I know your weakness, how you're selfish and prideful inside. Thérèse felt such anguish and doubt that she ran from her room while the devil chased her through the convent, down one long dark hall after another, the stone bricks cold and dirty, filled with spiders and other crawling bugs. Finally, she saw a door slightly opened, and, inside a warm, well-lit room, she found the Novice Mistress and Mother Prioress sitting there together. Thérèse began to tell them what was happening, and as she spoke, the devil fled!

Because the devil can't stay when you speak Truth to the Lie.

Picture this: Thérèse was lying on her deathbed, forced there because she had tuberculosis, and Mother Mary wouldn't call the doctor—not because she believed in faith healing, like Elmer Schmelzenbach, but because Mother Mary decided Thérèse's illness was mostly in her head. Which would be so frustrating, not to be believed even though you're coughing up blood—it's right there on your hankie. Yet Thérèse didn't despair or start complaining, which she had every right to do. Instead, she turned toward death, choosing another vibration and vowing to spend her time in heaven by helping people on earth. She promised to sign her miracles with a shower of roses. Sure enough, after Thérèse's death, a Carmel nun prayed and received healing while roses fell from the sky. Because if God can turn rivers to blood, like He did in Egypt, He can make the heavens rain roses. If God used Moses to work miracles, He could have used St. Thérèse just as well.

I'm not saying that Catholicism is correct, but it seems reasonable for there to be more than one way to worship God. Because I think Thérèse truly loved Him.

I wish God would give me my own miracle—something to show me I'm not alone.

The best I can do is tell you what happened.

It was late.

I was alone.

Aunt Susan and Uncle Steve had been gone all day, coming back only once in the evening to change clothes and bring us groceries. I prefer it when they're gone. I made macaroni and cheese and fruit salad; then the kids and I watched *Fantasia* and had microwave popcorn. When it was time for bed, we couldn't find Becca's Boo-Boo bear. I looked in Aunt Steve and Uncle Susan's room—I mean Uncle Steve and Aunt Susan—but Boo-Boo wasn't anywhere, not even under the bed. I had knelt down to see beneath it, and when I stood up, that's the first time I felt it—that creepy feeling of not being alone. The sliding glass door curtains were open, and I could see the room reflected in the window. Including me, life-sized, but it wasn't me, also. I don't know how to explain it. I closed the curtains quickly. I get this feeling all the time and see things, too, from the corners of my eyes. That's what I thought was happening. I started singing a praise song. When I turned around, there was Boo-Boo, in plain sight behind the swivel chair.

OK. Everything was OK.

Nicky wanted to hear a story, but I didn't have one inside me. So I read to them, instead. One fish, two fish, red fish, blue fish. I kept my voice soft and slow, to help them fall asleep.

I made my bed on the couch—that's where I've been every night since we arrived. I wanted to finish St. Thérèse. It's the part with all the prayers and answered miracles. Lots of stories about pulmonary tuberculosis, how she gave people new lungs. People also asked for her "childlike faith"—become a little child, or you'll never enter the kingdom of God (Matthew 18:3). But what does being a child mean? I definitely had that thought. I started hearing strange sounds in the hallway, like someone was out there. More than one person but not regular people staying at the hotel. I don't know why I thought that. I picked up my song, "You alone are my heart's desire." I made myself go to the door, look through its peephole. No one was there.

"You alone are my strength and shield." I lay back down and turned off the light. It was quiet; I could hear the refrigerator or the air conditioner. Some machine—it didn't matter. "To you alone may my spirit yield." I inhaled the soothing melody. I almost fell asleep.

But then the people were there, in the hallway—this time they were running. Their footsteps didn't make any sense. They were heavy, then lighter, then heavy. They sounded loudest when they were furthest away. I heard them rush toward our room and turn at our doorway; deliberately, quietly, they were entering the walls. Not possible, I thought, although I could hear them. Scurrying, like a stealth army of mice. They circled the room, north, west, south, east, moving to surround me. I was holding my breath, I realized. I needed to pray. I pictured angels stretching their wings in a hedge of protection. Please, God, keep me safe. The scurrying was softer. I listened. Nothing. I listened. I hoped I'd made it up.

I was almost asleep when the sounds started again. A rougher, bigger scampering inside the wall, like cats or snakes directly behind me. I almost opened my eyes. But I stopped, because it's better to seem like you're sleeping. The sounds were shifting. Until. I felt something inside the room. My body frozen. Something was moving. Now it sounded like wind. Outside? Or not? The more I listened, the more I heard it inside me, just inside my ears. Yet out there, too, in the space beyond the horizon: a steady rush of air growing louder. I felt a weight hovering above me, then pressing down, imprinting my chest, harder and thicker. The wind even stronger. The rest of the room fell dead away. It was me, just me, lying in the dark, on the couch. My body so heavy, I couldn't move. I'll be torn to pieces, I thought—dust to dust, clay to clay. This had to be demons. I needed to speak, but my tongue was leaded. I saw two stones in the back of my throat, grey and smooth, pinning down my vocal chords. No breath. No words. I couldn't move my fingers. I was all cement. Only Christ could save me. I tried to say Jesus but couldn't open my mouth. Help me! I cried inside as the stones grew larger. Try again, I thought. My jaw moved; the stones shifted; the winds blew stronger; my chest ached with two tons of air trying to reclaim me. If they could push me into nothingness, they would.

Try again, I thought.

My eyes opened. I saw a fog-like shadow and sensed the pillow rising around my head. My chest hurt with weighted pressure. I could not let the fog consume me. I sucked in air and pictured the stones shattering. Like glass. I summoned everything inside.

"JESUS!" I cried. This time, I heard the words aloud.

Everything stopped.

Total quiet.

I released my breath. Only silence and the sound of whirring. The air conditioner, I knew. I looked, and the room was normal. On the bedside table, the clock glowed orange-red numbers: 11:13.

now remember this when I am there in it now
        –Akilah Oliver

How the tomb is a theater and desire is a hammer
ringing in the teeth.
        –Selah Saterstrom

She received a travel fellowship to research the life of St. Maria Maddalena de' Pazzi, though, once in Florence, she spent far more time considering the saint's death. Or, more specifically, her dead body, entombed in a glass casket in a monastery just north of Florence, about an hour's bus ride away. Everything around the saint was golden: the casket's decorative edging, the blankets covering her corpse, the jeweled crown propped upon her lifted head. The saint's body had been declared incorrupt during her canonization in 1668, and now, even her shrunken brown face had golden undertones. It cost a euro to light a candle in the sanctuary; she lit one every visit, reciting the saint's words as her prayer:

Oh, loving Word, the time of missing light will come to an end;
   it is the dark light and the clear darkness....

1990-1991, WESTERN MICHIGAN

The Best I Can Do Is Tell You What Happened

Mom was waiting for me in the living room. She was mad. She told me to sit, then pulled my Depeche Mode cassette from behind a couch cushion. "What's this?" she asked. I tried to remember hiding it there, but it didn't make sense.

"A tape," I said. I glanced at the bookshelf cupboard and saw my cassette carrying case, unzipped.

"Violator?" she asked. "Who is that referring to?"

I didn't answer.

"Personal Jesus? Policy of truth? If you think this is truth, you have another thing coming." Her voice sounded like spit.

Sometimes, if you hold real still, it passes.

But rising from the couch, she flung the tape in front of me so hard the case split in two. "Smash it," she said.

I didn't move.

The air was thick. I'm not convinced that music is my problem. I wasn't going to destroy it. Not anymore.

She stared at me, then jerked forward, stomping hard on the tape. I heard the plastic crunch beneath her heel. She grabbed the carrying case from the bookshelf and began pulling the cassettes out, one by one. She was wearing Mike's old tennis shoes—dirty white Adidas with cracks down their backs and soles the color of a smoker's teeth. She complains that people see her as some kind of country bumpkin but then walks around wearing Dad's tattered blue flannels and shoes that do, in fact, make her feet look abnormally large, a little too country. Maybe that's mean to notice, but pretending otherwise won't change the facts.

When she pulled out the mixtape Chris gave me, I couldn't stay quiet.

"Wait!" I said. She paused to look at his blocky handwriting on the back of the case. "That's a tape Chris made. Let me return it to him, at least." She was reading the song titles, pushing her eyebrows together into what Mike calls her disapproval line. Right between her eyes. Amazingly, she thrust the tape at me.

"If you know what's good for you, you'll break it off with him, as well."

I'm not going to dump my boyfriend. Or listen to only Christian music for the rest of my life. Even Amy Grant is singing crossover songs now, and, no, they're not very good. But that's not the point. Most Christian rock stays on the surface, never diving down to get lost or wet. No tension. No suspense. I'm sick of being told that I should feel only God-praise and a desire to serve Him better. I will never be like Rick Stone from church, who says "praise Jesus" to everyone he meets—it doesn't matter if he's at Sunday service or a Sunoco station. He's not paying attention—that's the issue. He doesn't notice how other people feel. It's all about his glory feeling, just like Mom is all about her need to control.

"Wait," I said to Mom. She was holding my Housemartins tape. "They're Christian," I paused. "I got that at Cornerstone."

"Well, I don't know about that," she said. She looked at the album cover and list of songs. "Happy Hour?" she sniffed. I could hear Dad come in from the garage. "I'm not so sure about Cornerstone, either."

I sighed and shook my head. I've been to Cornerstone only once, but it's basically the best thing that's ever happened to Christian music. People are happy there. They were running around, singing in the parking lot, which is also a campground. It was fun. Even though Michelle and her best friend, Laurie, ditched me every chance they could.

"Look, Mom," I sighed again. "They say, 'Don't believe it.'"

"Don't believe?" she said. "Maybe that's their problem. They need more faith."

"Mom," I said. "I'm talking about the song. They say happy hour won't make you happy. That's what they're singing about." I took the tape and pointed to the bottom of the case, where, in all capital letters, it read TAKE JE-SUS – TAKE MARX – TAKE HOPE.

Mom cleared her throat.

"So I can keep it?" I paused, waiting to feel her shift.

Dad stopped in the living room entrance, feet pointed down the hall. "What's going on?" he said.

Neither Mom nor I answered. We looked at the pile of plastic pieces and loose ribbon on the floor.

Mom coughed. "We're cleaning out her music," she said.

Dad nodded, "All right, then." I avoided his eyes. He continued down the hall.

There were eight cassettes left in the carrying case. I waited. When Mom didn't move, I let out a deep breath. I walked over and held the carrying case so she could better see it.

"What about these?" I said. When she didn't respond, I continued, "Look, most of them are Christian. Altar Boys. Undercover. Steve Taylor." I picked out the one Pixies album still left. "This isn't." I handed it to her, but she didn't look. Which was good, since the cover art had a monkey with a halo. "The rest are Christian. I swear."

"You swear?" she said.

"Not like that." I sighed. "I mean I promise."

She dropped the Pixies tape onto the pile with the others.

"I'll clean this up," she said. "You'll have enough to tackle in your room."

In My Bedroom I Find

1. A total mess. My drawers have been dumped empty, and the closet doors, pushed open. My clothes are on the floor with the spiders. She even checked beneath the mattress—I could tell. I don't remember whether I left a *Vogue* there. Gone now.

2. My black and white geometric-patterned tights—cut at the knees.

3. Two minidresses, cut in half at the waist. And the brown one looked so good on me, too.

4. She smashed my owl figurine.

5. And broke my candles. And incense.

6. Two boxes of mementos, pulled from the top shelf of the closet and emptied onto the bed. Some items from box #1: rainbow-colored Psalm prayer cards, made in Religion class; 1986-87 sticker book calendar with dates from the stupid Florida trip with Aunt Susan; outline for ninth-grade research paper on the Ouija board; birthday note from Denise, signed as a Russian spy; sixth-grade essay entitled "How I Can Change the World, One Friendship at a Time – One Day at a Time." (Main strategy: "Being a real good friend to someone." Another strategy: "I think the world could change if they knew Jesus as their personal Lord and Saviour because Jesus brings people closer together.")

7. Inside box #2: my old duck-duck-goose journal from eighth grade. I'd forgotten that I wrapped it in Grandma's green chiffon scarf, which I hid beneath my Rosebud paper dolls. The ones I never played with because I didn't

want to ruin them. God, it's embarrassing to read what I wrote.

When I told Chris about the music, he wanted to make sure the tape from him was okay. That's sweet, right? He's going to pick it up from me at work later this week. If he comes while I'm on break, we can sit in the car and be green together. I can't believe it's only been three months—I feel like I've known him forever. I didn't tell him about Mom destroying my clothes or dumping my boxes. He already calls her "Church Lady," after that character on *Saturday Night Live*, which is annoying though I know he's only joking. I should probably lighten up. Chris thinks the world we live in is the only world there is, so he doesn't understand that Mom is trying to protect me. Once you've had spiritual experiences like Mom and I have, you can't pretend God doesn't exist.

I just don't want Mom's idea of God to be the only one there is.

We knew our religious childhoods made us freaky. We didn't catch seemingly simple cultural references, like who sang which classic pop or hip-hop or rock-and-roll song. We didn't know the lyrics. We couldn't sing along. We hadn't seen the movies or watched the same television. We learned to smile and nod. Because to admit not knowing meant leaving the conversation. And we, too, wanted to belong.

In her fellowship application, she wrote about visiting the Florentine Carmel to view Saint Maria Maddalena de' Pazzi's relics and archives; her uncorrupted body; her spiritual commentaries and transcriptions of her ecstatic visions, as recorded by her sister nuns. Once in Florence, her surprise discovery was the Convent of San Marco and Fra Angelico's frescos. She had seen images in art history but hadn't expected such brightness and lightness, such contemplative weight and presence. Her deeply visceral response.

San Marco, cell seven: *Mocking of Christ,* with the Virgin and Saint Dominic. Christ sits on a platform, a blindfold masking his eyes and most of his nose, even as these features remain structurally visible beneath the fabric's thin gauze. In his right hand, he holds a branch (like a scepter); in his left, an orb (or the world). Later, she would recognize this posture and these same items in the tarot's Emperor card, major arcana IV. In Fra Angelico's painting, five disembodied hands and one bodiless head surround the Christ figure. The head is male; he's blowing air or spit at Christ while one of the hands tips the man's hat to the figure that he mocks. On Christ's left, another hand holds a stick that strikes the top of Christ's head, right above his thorny crown. Two more hands seem to be slapping the air around Him. Christ is dressed in white. Or beige. Or ivory. Or the color of Florida sand. He sits on a red box with a seagreen rectangle, the width of the platform, rising behind him. A frame or contrast. A canvas pressed against the wall. For this rectangle contrasts with the wall behind it, the ceiling molding, the vast empty space behind or above. An image of Christ as a painting (and sculpture) inside another painting of this room, where the blessed mother and St. Dominic (there in the foreground) meet to read, contemplate, and pray.

We weren't "we" anymore. Some decided that church was all bullshit while others refused to think about it: suppress, repress, move on. Some numbed themselves with alcohol or drugs, or joined LGBTQ groups or centers, or looked for a new leader, a new purpose, to rally their lives. Others declared themselves asexual or became sexually promiscuous. She had moved through most of these ways of being, for longer or shorter periods of time.

She became skeptical of "we" itself, that singular plural pronoun that often assumed the most powerful person or people's perspective to be "true" reality, while those who questioned this, asserting the alterity of their experiences, were quickly labeled as crazy, lazy, not as bright. She wanted a different way to conceive of "we" and began wondering about the younger selves inside her. Like the voice of her thirteen-year-old—who, or what, was she?

Cell thirty-nine: *Adoration of Magi and Man of Sorrows*. The infant Jesus sits on his mother's lap while the three Magi and their entourage gather before the holy family, a crowd that becomes more crowded, less monied, the further people stand from the Christ child. One Magi, with a flowing pink robe, prostrates himself before Jesus and Mary, offering a crown. The lines in his robe echo the cuts and angles of the distant mountains, which rise before a stone-gray sky. This painted scene covers the upper third of the cell's wall, touching the room's arched ceiling. In the bottom center is a niche filled with another painting, this one of the adult Christ as he emerges from a casket, wrists crossed, palms bleeding, a wound in his side. The sky is midnight blue. The composition of painting plus niche allows each moment to be held within the other: The Magi recognize the divinity of the Christ child, simultaneously present as the adult Christ to come. For the viewer, both Christ bodies have already lived, died, and risen. In this way, time past exists within these multiple presents, which script a future already now.

She came to understand this as ritual time.

Avoiding Mom

She has obviously forgotten what it's like to be in love. She hates it when Dad's in the room, pulling away if he so much as bumps her arm. Like he did tonight in the kitchen. She looked repulsed, wounded. When I'm married (if I marry), I promise to keep the intimacy alive.

Mom doesn't trust Veronica because Veronica is Goth and Mom can't look past appearances. She doesn't like Mr. Redfield because he's a Democrat, and she doesn't want me to go to a non-Christian college because she's convinced they'll pressure me to have liberal views. I don't consider myself liberal, per se, but I'm definitely not Republican. I'm trying to think for myself.

I agree that cults and the occult are bad, but I think it's fine to read your horoscope. It's like entering a raffle—that's what it feels like—as silly and random as the date you were born. Mom overheard me tell Michelle that the baby will be an Aquarius, like Mom is. I was looking at the daily horoscope in the newspaper, just for fun, though I should know better than to mention the baby to Michelle. She gets mad and defensive every time, even though everyone's relieved that she and Matt are getting married, saying it's the right thing to do. "Her sign?" said Mom. "Oh, that's a bunch of lies."

Always, always remember what it's like to be a teenager. Last week, I asked Mom about when she was seventeen, and she said nothing, that she was nothing. That she was probably not right. "Don't use me as a model," she said, her face going foggy, unfocused. What is she trying to hide?

I Join a New Club

What a strange day. I feel like I've been called from one idea into another. Which sounds crazy when I write it, but let me explain.

I wanted a Little Debbie Star Crunch for lunch, and Veronica wasn't at school, so I was standing in line alone. This is important. There were sophomore girls behind me, a group of JV swimmers who were spazzing out, laughing about something that happened during morning practice. They were loud, and I was hungry. The line was moving super slow. One of the girls accidently bumped me, and I said what-the-fuck—or something like that—and glared, I'm sure. Of course, that's when I noticed Andrea and the other Youth for Christers. They were sitting at the table right by us; Andrea probably heard the whole thing. We haven't spoken since last year, when she invited me to a meeting. "We miss you," she said, but I knew she was just being nice. She knows Veronica is my best friend, and they've been enemies since tenth-grade Speech class, when they were opposite-side team captains for a debate on euthanasia. It did not end well.

Veronica thinks Andrea is an idiot, and I don't disagree. She's overly focused on waiting for the "right one" and won't date or even kiss until marriage. What if you finally kiss and realize he's gross? Seriously, I've had that happen. Honestly, I don't feel bad anymore about quitting Youth for Christ. You don't have to be in a group in order to have a relationship with God. Plus, I couldn't sit through yet another conversation about the pros and cons of condiments—that's an actual conversation they've had several times during lunch. Andrea calls sweet people "ketchups" while "mustards" are sour, grumpy people, or "tarts." Though she has no idea that, in England, "tart" is another word for slut, which Veronica and I find hilarious. Holding up "Jesus Hearts the Plainfield Pythons" signs at football games is dorky. And kind of creepy. It doesn't show school spirit (which is seriously something I don't care about), and I highly doubt Jesus would be a high school football fan. He would rather we feed the homeless than run around a chemically treated lawn, knocking each other down. Jocks are stupid and annoying. Ray Hemingway was a jock, and he bullied me that whole first semester of ninth grade—though he was the one in remedial reading who couldn't imagine a world outside himself.

I won't go to Teen Life conferences, either. The Youth for Christers attend the annual state conference in Lansing, and this year they're raising money for the National "March for Life" in Washington, DC. I still believe abortion is a moral decision and don't know if I could have one myself, but I definitely think the government shouldn't tell people how to live their lives. I mean, isn't democracy all about letting people make their own decisions? And so many pro-life brochures and pamphlets (including mine from that "Teens for Life Teen Day" conference, which I'm still saving in memento box #1—not sure why, but it seems important) cherry-pick their details. Or outright lie. Like saying abortion is medically riskier than pregnancy. That's not true. Or using the word "life" when what they're actually talking about is the moment a soul enters a body, since the soul is the part of the human that matters, that makes us different. And we don't know if the soul arrives at conception. Probably not. To say that the moment of fertilization is the same as a baby is kind of insulting to babies. Just like when there's a fertilized egg in your carton, which you know from the red dot in the yolk—we don't call that a baby chick. It's an egg you'll probably scramble and eat for breakfast. Is this Veronica's influence on me? Probably. But I don't care. I'm sick of being told what to do just because I'm female. In the past, girls couldn't vote or take out mortgage loans without a male signature. If a girl wrote a book, no one would publish it unless she pretended to be a man. (George Eliot's real name was Mary Ann Evans, and Charlotte Brönte said she was Currer Bell.) They say legalized abortion is legalized murder, but I know girls at school who have had abortions—Shannon Kirkstra may have had two—and she's not a murderer. She doesn't make very good decisions, that's true, so maybe she's not ready to be a mom. It would be different if she was twenty-two and still living at home, like Michelle is. With a boyfriend who wants to get married. Okay, why not?

All this is to say I did not want to make eye contact with Andrea today. I turned and studied the cinder block wall, instead. It's pale blue, and I thought "bare and blue" would be a good description. The cafeteria line moved forward, and I heard someone call my name. Or thought I did—and that it was Andrea. So I ignored her. But when the voice called again, I turned my head before I meant to, and Andrea and I locked eyes. Only for a second, though, because she immediately shifted her gaze past me. What?

Is she too good for me now? Just because I used the word "fuck"? When I turned back toward the wall, I saw it: a bright orange flier announcing the school's new chapter of Amnesty International. I swear it hadn't been there a moment before. I even asked the JV swimmers, and while most of them hadn't noticed, Carley Schupel understood and began freaking out.

"What is happening?" she said.

By this point I felt a sharpness all around me. "I don't know," I said, "but look." Mr. Lee was listed at the teacher sponsor. "That's where I'm going right after lunch." Carley looked confused. "Because I have Mr. Lee for fourth period Government."

"Whoa," said Carley.

I like her. She's cool.

Isn't all of this so strange?

Our first AI meeting is tomorrow. I saw Carley after school, and she may come. She really should. It's important. Tristan Dalton is the chapter president, and she's one of the smartest girls in the senior class. I told Carley what Tristan told me: that Amnesty is an international organization to defend the weak and wrongfully convicted. Did you know there's still racial segregation in South Africa? They call it apartheid, and the South African government wrote and adopted it as their official position. I had no idea. It's all too weird to be a coincidence.

Cell one: *Noli me Tangere.* Touch me not. The title re-
fers to John 20:17, when Mary Magdalene meets the risen
Christ outside his tomb. She is the first person to see him.
Or, rather, he appears to her first. This English translation of Christ's words, "Touch me not," appears in the
King James Version of the Bible—though scholars now
agree the original Koine Greek phrase is better translated
as "cease holding on to me" or "do not hold on to me"
or "stop clinging to me." "Touch me not" is a command
given for a moment; "Cease holding on to me" is an invi-
tation to the process of letting go.

In the painting, Mary Magdalene is positioned between Christ and the tomb. She bows on one knee while
Jesus stands beside her, bare feet crossed, wounds clearly
visible. He holds a stick in his left hand and looks over
his right shoulder, eyes fixed on Mary, who returns his
gaze. Small red flowers dot the ground between them—
the same red, as Didi-Huberman has noted, of Christ's
piercings, hands and feet. The color and tone of Christ's
garment matches that of the tomb, and the rock's concave
lines echo the swoop and hang of Christ's garment. In this
way, the separation between one form and another—flowers and blood, stone and fabric—is called into question.
She looks again and sees how Christ's body, the stick over
his shoulder, the way he seems to float, is reminiscent of
the Fool card in her tarot pack. Major Arcana 0: Begin
again, let go, move into the unknown.

She met a young man who had grown up as a Branch Davidian in Waco, Texas. He was eleven years old during the Waco siege, living in the compound with his mother, who was still, from what she understood, a believer. The young man hated to talk about Waco or for people to know this biographical detail. She felt his embarrassment (or was it shame? what's the difference?), even as she was fascinated—she wasn't sure why. Similarly, she was intrigued by a coworker's story about growing up in a cult in Colorado. The group was led by her coworker's father, described as a preacher, very charismatic, with a message more loving than the church's, so the family didn't mind. Her coworker laughed about her dad—he was a very bad cult leader, repeatedly changing the group's name and never really attracting followers, apart from his wife and seven children. "And what do you believe now?" she asked her coworker, who shrugged and said, "It's complicated. You know what I mean." She did. For years she had been trying to write a book about the difference between faith and dogma, or spirituality and religion. It wasn't as easy as embracing Enlightenment ideas of science and reason—two ways of knowing that had, it was clear, ushered in worlds of possibility, of good. But she also intuited something lost, an unexplained interconnectedness between one form and another. Flowers and blood, stone and fabric. A leap into the void of not knowing, a journey that she, like each of us, must undertake alone.

If It's Love, It's Worthy

What does love feel like? Does it make you try things that you wouldn't have tried before? Chris is so cute and short—it's hard to believe I first saw him as a turtle-face. I'm glad I know there's more to a person than physical looks. Because his personality has definitely won me over. Now I honestly see him as exciting. We're basically the same height, a perfect fit when we're standing, hugging, and rubbing—it feels so good. We've both wanted this for so long. His school offers real sex education (not like the video I saw at Sacred Heart), so he knows about anatomy, though, until me, he hasn't been able to test that knowledge. Like how certain parts are more sensitive than others. More nerve endings equals more responsiveness to stimulation. I love how he's so curious. I've never been able to talk like this with anyone, to touch while talking, to figure things out. He didn't touch me tonight (I'm raggin'), but I went down on him, his whole thing in my mouth. He wants me to try again, next time slower. He wants to eat me out, too, he says, but made me promise to bathe first. Which made me feel a little weird, actually, like I'm dirty or smelly, but that's probably not what he means. He knows I'm saving sex for marriage. That's another thing I love about Chris—he's willing to meet me halfway.

There's so much more, but I don't want to write it. I don't know—I think I'm really falling in love.

So Sick of Dad

I don't care if Dad thinks he makes the best burgers. I'm not going to eat one. I'm not going to eat meat. I didn't quit for health reasons, either, so I wish Mom would quit saying that. Not mine, anyway. But for the health of the whole planet. Because factory farming and deforestation, and using land to raise cows instead of corn—these are #1 causes for global warming, and if we don't do something about it, we are all going to die.

Dad thinks it's un-American not to eat meat.

He wouldn't drop it.

I made a lettuce, cheese, and tomato sandwich. With pickles.

He said if I really want to clean up my diet, I should quit eating candy bars and snack cakes. He said rats fall into those vats of chocolate, and they're not going to stop the whole factory production line just to pull out one fat rat. "Yum," he said, "rat-flavored chocolate bars and kisses."

So, yeah, I got mad and left the table. I don't care if I'm too sensitive. I'm tired of not being taken seriously. And Dad just wants to freak me out.

Whoever said we date versions of our parents is stupid. Chris is nothing like my dad.

I Watch My Sister Marry

When Michelle entered the chapel on Dad's arm, I began to cry. I couldn't help it. I'm glad she's gone, but it finally hit me: We'll never be sisters like we were. That part of our life is over.

Mom was already weeping, but Dad was proud, his face beaming as he walked Michelle down the aisle. "One down, one to go." That's what he said while we were standing in the greeting line. I don't want a wedding like Michelle's—and not because of the horrible peach-colored dresses or the excruciating fakeness of the women at the hair salon. I think Michelle is happy, but it's weird to call her by a different name. Does she feel changed? If I get married, I want something more elegant than the American Legion banquet room, with folding tables draped in peach and white linens and bland centerpieces made from carnations and baby's breath. Those are the cheapest flowers, and nothing felt personal to Matt and Michelle. That's what I noticed. It was as if they were playing roles instead of being themselves. Even Pastor Marks used the ceremony to preach about the sanctity of Christian marriage and God's supposed command (because it was Paul, not Christ, who said this) that husbands should love their wives and wives should serve their husbands. But you can't command love, and, as any restaurant worker can tell you, service often breeds contempt.

Michelle and Matt have been meeting with Pastor Marks for premarital counseling. Does he even see the fear in Michelle's eyes? It's older than Matt and the baby;

it's been there as long as I can remember. Telling her to serve her husband will probably make the fear worse.

I know I'm being very negative. Chris says I need to work on that.

Here's a positive I noticed: Michelle was beautiful. She wore her hair in a low bun, and her dress was amazing—nothing I would choose, but the V-cut neckline and empire waist were perfect for hiding the baby (does Grandma C even know?). Before the ceremony, we crowded into a Sunday school room to finish prepping, and Laurie, who brought a full-length mirror, fussed around and arranged Michelle's veil. Mom was there, too. I wanted to catch Michelle's eye to see what she might be thinking—not that she would ever want me to know. I watched her taking in her reflection with a look of near acceptance, her face soft and relaxed. Our gaze met in the mirror, and her eyes snapped back. The problem, I realized, was that I had noticed, if only for a moment. Does being truly seen hurt?

At the reception, Mom was laughing and drinking champagne, which I didn't know she liked. Matt's brother, Ron, kept clinking his glass with his knife so the couple would have to kiss, and when Michelle started looking visibly annoyed, he did it even more. Until Mike started grabbing Ron's arm to make him stop, and they almost got into a fight—but didn't, thank God. It was time to dance to oldies-but-goodies. Aunt Susan was there with her new husband, Steve, a short, frumpy man quite the opposite of the old Uncle Steve. Grandma C declared the wedding cake delicious and asked if I would book the American

Legion Hall for my wedding in a few years. I couldn't help laughing. I told her I'll probably never marry. She thought that was funny.

"Oh dear," she said, lightly tapping my arm.

A few nights before she left for Florence, she had sex with her friend Tonya. They'd met months earlier in a summer language class and had immediately begun flirting. She recognizes this now, though at the time she couldn't see it—how she wanted only to be with Tonya, who was so funny and charming, only a few years older yet seeming so much wiser, who had been out as a lesbian since freshman year of college. Her parents wished she were straight, Tonya explained, but there's a certain acceptance of eccentricity in the South. Tonya was white, from North Carolina. She had a flare for storytelling and turning the ordinary into something worth talking about. Several times over the days before her departure, the air between them became thick with tension. She kept touching Tonya's shoulder or arm, half hoping (though not realizing even this) that Tonya would cross that other boundary, would lean in, would kiss her. When she finally did, they were both a little drunk. The next morning, Tonya apologized. Which confused her. "You don't have to apologize," she said. But nothing more. For she understood Tonya's apology as her escape, as if the sex had been Tonya's seduction instead of something they did together. On the flight to Florence, she kept replaying everything. Tonya was the second woman she'd slept with, which meant she could no longer dismiss the first woman as an accident. She felt knotted and anxious. Like the world was falling apart. She decided that, while being gay was okay for others (she didn't think Tonya or her other friends were evil or going to hell—she really didn't), she needed to choose heterosexuality for herself. Because she didn't know if she could do it. If she could be with a woman and still feel spiritually safe.

She was beginning to understand the power of interpretation, how perspective creates the social imaginary, makes the frame, determines the picture. To view the Bible as a history, for example, turns the stories literal, which lessens, in some ways, their metaphorical weight. Alternatively, to view the Bible as a hybrid of poetry, literature, chronicles, and epistles, collectively written and collaboratively assembled, is to see the Bible as a stranger, perhaps more dangerous, book—alive and mutable, crossing and de-creating categories. That's how she felt, too. She was trying to write a life story that didn't move from one clear frame into another.

San Marco, cell three: The room itself is a round arch filled with other arches. The painting is another *Annunciation*. Gabriel's wings remain rainbowed, and Mary kneels and looks down, holding an open book in the crook of her left arm. Behind the angel, St. Peter of Verona stands, palms pressed together in the same prayer gesture she was required to hold under the nuns' watchful gaze during weekday Mass at Sacred Heart. In the painting, St. Peter of Verona fixes his eyes on Mary as blood drips from a wound on his head, the same spot where, in other depictions of the saint, a Cather's sword is left lodged in his skull. But this painting shows a moment of grace, the witnessing of divine articulation. There is light emanating softly from the angel, while a door is visible behind Mary, whose shadow marks the wall. Gabriel's shadow is fainter, barely there, while St. Peter of Verona is shadowless, his body crossed instead by the obscure tips of Gabriel's wings. The three figures stand in a room ceilinged with arched lines, which correspond to the arch of picture's painted frame, which is, itself, rendered to mirror the architecture of the cell. To the painting's right is a prayer nook, a segmental arch with a window inside. The window's shutter, another kind of arch, opens so that, when sunlight shines through, another temporary arch is made on the cell's mahogany floor. Frame inside frame inside another way of seeing: plaster, paint, wood, sound, and light.

In Florence, she stood before Savonarola's cell staring at the ecstatic saint painted in a circle above its entrance. This must be Maria Maddalena de' Pazzi, she thought, though it could be St. Teresa, St. Cecelia, St. Catherine— this woman who levitates, back arched, arms opened, gazing into the unseen-by-the-viewer beyond. She's surrounded by cherubs, and there's a male figure, too, who tries but does not touch her, who looks away as if he cannot bear her sight. For her experience is as sensorial as it is metaphysical, a serious act of liberation manifest in multiple realms. Her body: a hinge, a spine. A book, opened to divine inscription, to being re-known, re-read, re-connected. To being re-cognized as light and love, the source from which she comes and comes and—yes, yes, yes, there, my love; that's right.

She tried to be straight. But couldn't. Because she wasn't. To be otherwise would be to choose the lessening light.

IN THE MIDDLE OF THE NIGHT

When I fell asleep, the candle was burning. A white taper. I bought it at Meijer and didn't know the holder I found in the mudroom was plastic, not glass. Well, it wasn't even a holder but a flower vase I decided to repurpose. I thought I was being clever. Skillful. I love Berlioz's *Symphony Fantastique*. To really hear the music, the melody's haunting recurrence, it's best to turn off the lights.

I learned that in Music Appreciation class.

I didn't know the holder would melt.

When I woke, my whole bedside table was burning. The flames reached the ceiling, as big as a bonfire, but I didn't comprehend what was happening. Instead, I looked and saw a pitcher of water on my dresser. Seemed normal in that moment, though I didn't recognize the vessel. Or remember filling it. I poured the liquid over the flame.

And the fire went out. Just like that.

Which is when I realized that my electric clock, still plugged in, had been burning.

I pulled the plug from the wall, and nothing happened.

Everything was okay.

I didn't want to wake Mom or Dad. I sat on the edge of bed and looked at the smoldering table. The whole top was burnt black; the inside of the clock, literally melted. My head had been right there, that close to the fire's flying sparks. The wall was spotted with soot, the shadowed shape of a figure. I touched my head and felt my long, unsinged hair.

Grandma C used to talk about guardian angels, how everyone has an angel protector who is just always there. Because someone—or something—helped me tonight.

Just this evening, before listening to the music, I moved my duck-duck-goose journal from that same bedside table to one of the dresser drawers.

WHAT'S THE TEST?

I hate physics, and Miss Hohum Adams is the worst. She can't teach! It's her second year at Plainfield, but it's my senior transcript, and I have to get into a good college, with scholarships, or I won't be able to go. Because Pastor Marks is right: The spirit of debt wants to bury you alive.

I got a C+ on HoHum Adam's exam. I don't get C+'s. I don't even get Bs. I stayed after class to ask about extra credit. She was wearing tan slacks and a pale button-down blouse. Her hair is stuck in the '70s. Feathered in front, long in back. She may even crimp it. She seemed surprised to see me. She said, "If you fully understand the material we've been discussing, those questions should have been easy."

I hate her whiny, nasally voice.

"But we haven't had discussions," I said, and she looked at me blankly.

"Marie," she said. "What are you thinking about during class?"

I don't know. I'm trying to pay attention. Or sometimes writing a letter to Chris. Because I love him. And we call her Hohum because she reads the textbook in a monotone and draws stupid examples that make no sense.

"Maybe," she said, "you're not cut out for science."

She was holding an eraser. I looked at her stupid short unpainted nails. No wedding ring, no wonder. She turned to write something on the whiteboard. The third period class was already almost there.

"Can I have a pass?" I said. I was going to be late to English.

She took one from her drawer, signed it, and pushed it toward me. She avoided my eyes.

"Thanks," I said, as sarcastically as I dared.

"See you tomorrow," she said, still not looking up.

God, she's pathetic.

I should have requested Mr. Brighton when I had the chance. Sure, he's a pervert, but he knows his stuff, and, if you don't wear a skirt, you're not an issue. Which is admittedly annoying after a while. That's why I requested Miss Hohum in the first place—I didn't want another year of Brighton's Bulging Eyes. Because everyone knows what The Bulge is doing when he walks around the room, talking about the importance of multiple perspectives. He's looking for the best place to get the best look before he drops his sad, droopy eyes and squints at that day's preferred target. He holds that position while speaking several long sentences that invariably end in a question, at which point he refocuses on our faces as if we've just arrived. The boys say the girls have it easier because we can "hike up" our grades, if you know what I mean. But none of the girls do that, even the cheerleaders, who are required to wear their "cheerful" outfits to school every day there's a home game, football or basketball. All the girls keep their legs crossed, and the cheerleaders wear jeans beneath their skirts—but just for The Bulge's class. Michelle used to complain about him to Mom, but, to be honest, I didn't believe Michelle until last year, when I had The Bulge myself.

I Try to Break Up, But...

Chris is right: I don't want to break up with him. Yet part of me still feels like I should. It sounded crazy when I tried to explain it—there's certain stuff I just know. Like how Chris won't be my forever boyfriend, and something inside me is saying get out. Go.

"Like God?" he said.

I shook my head. I don't think so.

"Wait a minute," he said. "Is God telling you to break up with me?"

We were on the phone. I was in the mudroom, twisting the pea-green phone cord around my index finger, then my thumb. It was already late, and that's the question—how do you know what you're supposed to do? I don't think God would necessarily approve of our relationship. That's what I told him. Chris laughed.

"Marie," he said. "You know that's crazy, right?" He paused; I waited. "You can't break up with me because God told you to. That's not even a reason I tell my friends."

It did sound silly when he said it, but....

"You're not listening," I said. And who cares about his stupid friends?

If I knew for sure, it would be different. I was sitting on the floor, legs stretched, no shoes. I shifted into a cross-legged position. I could feel the cold air beneath the door. I like Chris—I really do. He's the only person I talk to every day. If we broke up, would anyone notice that I exist?

"Look," said Chris, "do you like being with me?"

Of course I do.

"And if God even cares about things like boyfriends and dating...."

"And bugs," I added. "God cares about bugs and swallows, and the very hairs of your head are numbered—Matthew 10, verse 30." I was only partially joking.

Chris laughed again, this time lighter. "Yes," he said. "God cares so much that He actually wants you to be with someone you like." He paused. His voice went softer. "Someone who really, really likes you."

Him saying that made my chest hurt.

I smiled. I don't want to break up with Chris. Plus, he may come to youth group with me, maybe even this Sunday. He would need a ride, and, if I pick him up, we could leave early and have a little time in the car. Mom has been bugging me about skipping meetings, so this might actually work out. There's also a youth group retreat in January. I wasn't planning on going, but if Chris agrees, I could change my mind.

Convent of San Marco, Corridor, *St. Dominic Adoring the Crucifixion*: The saint clings to the cross as blood flows from holes in Christ's feet, which are crossed themselves, one over the other, so delicately, almost sensually, as if Christ is using the bottom of one foot to feel the texture and curve of the other. There are lines everywhere: in the wood grain and in the skeleton of Christ's body, his rib cage visible beneath the skin that wraps his frame, like the loincloth that covers his genitals. Lines in the fabric crease, fold. Blood lines stream away from his body to the foot of the cross, where St. Dominic kneels, gazes with— worry? grief? regret? The saint wears a cloak of night-sky blue.

Does spiritual safety *heart-clenched stop stop this fear of annihilation*

St. Dominic. They say he received the Rosary as a gift from the blessed mother. Pope Innocent III had charged him with converting the Cathers in what is now known as southern France, but it seems the Cathers did not want to convert. They were a dualistic Christian sect, meaning they believed in both a lesser, evil god who ruled the material earth realm and a greater, more powerful god who embodied goodness, light, and love. To the Cathers, humans were immortal souls held within material mortal bodies. The soul wasn't gendered or classed, which meant women or working people could be priests and spiritual leaders. Each lifetime was one round in the soul's greater spiritual journey, for each soul was moving toward perfect knowledge, or enlightenment, and would reincarnate until it finally reunited with perfect love, the source of its existence. To this end, Cathers disavowed material pleasures and were critical of the Catholic church, its hierarchal and increasingly corrupt leadership; the priests, bishops, and cardinals pursing power and wealth above all else.

She first learned about the Cathers while in Florence, wondering about the saint who appears in so many paintings with a sword lodged in his head. St. Peter of Verona, or St. Peter the Martyr, was born into a Cather family, though his parents sent him to Catholic school, where he converted, unlike them. He was evidently quite the preacher and was thus appointed as inquisitor of northern Italy, a term which famously ended with his assassination by a Catherist. St. Peter the Martyr was quickly canonized the following year. The information about the Cathers is less documented, more partial, given the mass killings and how history is written by the victors. Thus, to speculate about a world-not-this-one, she weaves threads from various sources, creating a picture that's somewhat Buddhist, somewhat New Age Pagan, somewhat Manichean. She weaves with words, for language can do this: create a picture, cast an interpretative spell.

The Cathers rejected Catholic sacraments such as baptism and marriage. They rejected the very act of reproduction (flesh should be renounced, not multiplied). They rejected the divinity of Jesus Christ (flesh is evil, so why in heaven's name would the good god take the form of a human body?). In 1176, the Roman Catholic Church declared the Cathers heretics, and in the early part of the thirteenth century, St. Dominic sought their conversion by engaging Cathers in debates. After all, they were reasonable, cultured, scholarly; Cathers and Catholics lived alongside each other in peace.

But Pope Innocent III was growing impatient. He had already replaced many of the bishops in the region with more severe, dogmatic clergy. In January 1208, when a papal legate was murdered the day after a meeting with Count Raymond IV of Toulouse, the Pope ordered what is now called the Albigensian Crusade. Conquered land was offered as payment, along with "indulgences," or punishment reductions for one's sins. The Crusaders were charged with fighting the heretics, and when someone (who?) asked an abbot (so the story goes) about sorting the faithful Catholics from the heathen Cathers, the abbot replied, "Kill them all for the Lord knoweth them that are His" (2 Timothy 2:19).

In their first attack, the Crusaders killed everyone living in Béziers, an estimated 20,000 people. Just the beginning of this new holy war.

For years, she thought the phrase "without a shadow of doubt" was in the Bible. *Without a shadow of doubt:* isn't that how she was supposed to be? Especially about God and His supposed teachings. A felt conviction turning her and other followers into messengers of a truth declared *the only way*, a truth that (there is safety in numbers) should be her truth, too. They promised the gift of certainty, which was, she later realized, what authoritarian energies do. She'd met these energies at church, yes, but also on US American radio, behind the preachers and blustering talk-show hosts who told their listeners to just say "ditto," if the listener agreed and loved the show. She felt a similar self-righteousness in some political activists and in certain academics or artists who insisted on one form, one lineage, one genre as the great-and-only-way-to-be. She felt this energy within herself, when she strove to give an agreed-upon-correct-and-thus-absolutely-right answer. Or during those times when she performed an idea of someone else rather than connecting with her inside knowing, which was often more difficult to reach.

They say St. Dominic wandered into the forest, where, for three days and three nights, he prayed fervently, flagellating himself into a coma. Thus suspended, the blessed mother appeared with a vision of the Rosary: a prayer, a circular strand of beads. Fifty roses strung together, punctuated by Our Fathers. When you pray the Rosary, you repeat a Hail Mary for each small bead, moving around the circle three times: once for the Joyful Mysteries, again for the Sorrowful Mysteries, a third for the Glorious Mysteries. There is no glory without sorrow, and we know sorrow because we were made with perfect joy. Thus, a complete Rosary is one hundred and fifty Hail Marys, which is why the Rosary is also called Mary's Psalter, for there are one hundred and fifty Psalms of David. They say St. Dominic began preaching about the Rosary, and the Catholics won against the Albigensians (the Cathers) with the help of Our Lady of the Rosary—victories "so famous," writes St Louis de Montfort, "that the world has never seen anything to match them."

Was St. Dominic there as thousands of children, women, and men were slaughtered? Did he watch as Catholic Crusaders marched the Cathers, naked, into the street?

Paul Tillich writes that to call one's own truth the ultimate truth is a form of demonic bondage. The force behind the authoritarian energy—is this what Jung calls "the shadow"? The part of yourself that part of yourself wants to destroy. (The part of the social body that part of the social body wants to destroy.) She submerged this part deep within, alongside her inner knowing. Shielded with defensiveness, righteousness, bravado. She tried to ignore ancestral patterns of spiritual indecision and confusion, fear of lunacy, shame. She blamed herself but didn't know how to change it: a fog so heavy, cloudy within her head.

Does spiritual freedom *inhale and deeply center imagine release the heart a rose unfolding notice a thousand possible movements into other sight*

She sits now. It is raining.
So still, she hears the water move.

I Learn from Unlikely Sources

Mom married Dad because she thought she should, which doesn't mean his mom approved the marriage—Grandma C taught me that. Grandma also taught me about violets and that it's okay to call on St. Christopher when the person driving is likely drunk. Dad told me to be careful because alcoholism runs in our family, and Uncle D showed me the body of a heavy drinker: I can hear his wheezing breath before he enters the room, his nose practically falling off his face. Denise helped me learn that sometimes money isn't worth it. She quit babysitting for the Schmidt family even though they paid almost double. Later, when I took that same job, she warned me about getting into the car with Mr. Schmidt when it was time to go home. Pastor Marks teaches that alcoholism is an evil spirit who wants to control you while real freedom means turning your life over to God. I feel near-dead when he says that, like I'm being buried alive in should-do's and never-enoughs.

Chris doesn't drink because he thinks alcohol makes you stupid, but Veronica says Chris needs to lighten up. Because it's sometimes fun to go to parties, that's what she says, and will I please be the designated driver for her and James this Friday after work? James is gay and goes to Northridge; he came out last year at school but not to his mom, not yet. He says he can feel it when people look at him and see only "gay." I used to do that, but now he's more "James" than anything else. Every day on the way to school, I pass the tree that killed Kelly, Brad, and Natasha.

Well, the tree didn't kill them. The alcohol did. Because sometimes drunk bodies don't make it through a crash, even though, at work, Derek Spelman is always talking about how people get hurt in car accidents because their bodies tense and resist the impact, and everyone is more relaxed when they're drunk. Derek is a dishwasher. And a good example of someone who talks so much that no one listens. I never want to be like that.

In the Early Dawn

I was walking through the woods, so beautiful and relaxing. There were yellow butterflies fluttering above the path, and the sun sparkled sound in the trees' green leaves. As I walked, the trees began changing, from oaks to pines to cedars. The ground covered in needles. I saw a cone hidden and knew it was for me. In my palm, it felt warm. My spine began stretching, growing, rooting into the deep, dark earth. I felt happy for a moment. The sun shifted. I wanted to go home.

But couldn't move.

Roots extended from the base of my spine, and a trunk grew from the back of my neck, branching into a triangle-tipped top of a tree. I should be scared (I thought this), but, instead, I was curious. The butterflies returned with a brown horse, who nuzzled my face with her nose. I wanted to pet her, but I couldn't. I wanted. She licked my cheek. My tree-spine wiggled, tried to move.

Wake up, I thought.

I breathed easy for a minute.

Until the strange sound in the closet. Not a rustling or rearrangement but a whirring, a flapping, like flying creatures caught inside. I did not want to open the doors, my beating heart now frozen. Cover my head. Sing a psalm.

DENISE AND I CHANGE COLORS

I saw Denise today while leaving school. She was smoking a cigarette near the bowling alley, and, when she returned my wave, I went over to say hello. We ended up walking to the 7-11, where she bought a blue raspberry Slurpee and I got lime. She told me about breaking up with Jessie for the one-thousandth time, then showed me how she turned his name into "Justice." I tried to eraser burn myself once but stopped before I broke actual skin. "Now I can wear short sleeves," she laughed. The word is big and red on the inside of her left forearm.

"Hey, Denise," I said. "I see blue in the shape of a mouth."

She looked at her tongue in the reflection of the store window. "So perfectly monstrous," she said, in the best-fake-dorkiest British accent.

"Let me see," I said, trying to mimic her voice. I found my compact mirror and checked my mouth. The lime Slurpee had turned my lips only slightly green.

"Marie," said Denise, in her regular voice. "Do you like the tarot?"

No. My skin prickled. Why do you ask?

"That's why I chose 'Justice,'" she said.

I felt a familiar panic. Why does Denise always do stuff that scares me? It was the same thing when we got to high school and she immediately began hanging out with the burnouts. Michelle said Denise was being stupid, that everyone was going to judge her as a druggie and a loser, which they did. I didn't want to be labeled a burn-out. Denise's new friends didn't like me, either—especially Sherry. She called me Little-Miss-Do-Good, not as a compliment, and said I was a nerd-snob for using words like "equivalent," which isn't even that big of a word. The smaller "equal" is literally inside it.

"I think you might like them, the cards," Denise said. We were back by the bowling alley, and Denise wanted one more cigarette before going back into work. I held her Slurpee while she found her lighter. "Anyway," she continued, "justice is about so much more than laws, you know? A law might be unjust. Or mis-justice."

"Just-free," I countered, which made her laugh.

"But cereal," she smiled, like we used to say for "serious." "Justice is about more than cause and effect. It's also how the present moment makes the future. Because what will be is already inside us. Not fated but here, in this now."

I nodded even though I didn't, and still don't, understand. Seeing through a glass, dimly, and Denise hardly ever makes sense. She may still be friends with Jennifer Hartman and Angie—I didn't ask her. "Are you high?" I joked.

She laughed again. "I wish... but not with these new meds."

Denise and I Did Not Talk About

Denis's old "friend" from the across the lake, Mr. Henry. He died last year (heart attack), and Michelle heard they (who?) found some stuff in his house. Photos and videocassettes—not of Denise, I don't think, but the whole thing creeps me out. Denise has never mentioned him, not his death, not nothing. I don't want to bring it up.

Our other friends. Not Jennifer Hartman or Angie or anyone from Sacred Heart. Not Veronica or Sherry or anyone else. I've quit mentioning Denise to Veronica, too, because Veronica always shakes her head. "I can't believe the two of you were friends," she says.

Denise's meds. She been on them since ninth grade. "Chemical imbalance in my brain," she joked, and I laughed. I didn't know what else to say.

A plan to see each other again.

A Bad Night Out

It was one disaster after another.

We were late to pick up Chris because James wasn't ready. Chris was grumpy because he hadn't eaten dinner and didn't know we never order full meals at Cha Cha's, since they give free unlimited chips and salsa. So I told him I would treat, even though I really don't have the money. He ordered steak fajitas—the most expensive thing on the menu—which means he's obviously not vegetarian anymore.

He hadn't bothered to tell me.

Veronica kept calling his food dead cow flesh. I must have given her a look because she said I shouldn't be annoyed with the truth. "Can you handle what's real," added James. "That's the question."

Meanwhile, Chris wanted to tell us about his daily energy levels with and without meat, but James and Veronica seriously did not care. And Chris couldn't see it.

James started asking Chris a series of questions, like what music he likes and how long he's been skateboarding. I don't think James was being insincere, but Chris started to get weird, and when James went to the bathroom, Chris asked Veronica if James was hitting on him.

Veronica laughed and called Chris homophobic, which Chris thinks is a stupid word.

"Are you talking about Marie?" said James, who was back before we noticed. "Oh wait," he said, "it's only lesbians who scare you—I wonder why."

James was referring to the one lesbian we saw last

month at Denny's. Evidently I was staring at her—I liked her blue hair, that's all. But James has decided it was more than that, especially when I wouldn't say hi.

Why would I introduce myself to a random stranger just because she's gay?

Chris asked James if he wants everyone to be gay.

"Everyone but you," said James. He was obviously joking.

But Chris took the bait and started in on his whole thing about how "homophobia" is a stupid word because not agreeing with a lifestyle doesn't mean you're afraid of the people who make that choice.

"Do you really think it's a choice?" said James.

"To act on the feeling, yes," laughed Chris. "We all do that. It's just that gays, no offense, like to flaunt it. Like they're special. Or more important than they are."

James laughed. "You really think that?" he said.

"But Chris," I said, "you were 'afraid' that James was hitting on you."

"What the fuck, Marie," said Chris. "You can't even back me up?"

"Look," said Veronica. "Male jocks and beauty queens flaunt their sexuality all the time."

Chris turned toward her and quit scowling. "They have big egos, too," he laughed.

Chris felt nervous and ganged up on. That's why he was being a jerk.

We should have gone right home after Cha Cha's, but James and Veronica wanted to stop at Meijer, where they completely ignored Chris, who kept falling behind us, sulking. I stopped to wait for him a couple times, but he would punish me with silence. For a minute, I thought we might break up after all. But, driving in the car, I squeezed his leg, then moved my hand up. We were in the back seat, so Veronica and James couldn't see. Chris got hard. I stroked it.

"What a mopey bastard," said James as we pulled away from Chris's house.

"Good luck with that one," he said after a long silence. Veronica just laughed.

Neither James nor Veronica have had a serious boyfriend, so what do they know about relationships? Chris isn't perfect, but certain patterns aren't so easy to change.

Cell thirty-one, *Christ in Limbo*: He fills the doorway, leaning slightly forward, right hand clasped within both hands of a penitent, the first in a group of haloed men, their nimbi creating a sea of light, rounded waves in a larger movement toward this one who has come to redeem them. To release them. From this place between here and there. A place of torment but not surrender. A place created, she heard, by the Catholics. Show me Limbo in the Bible, Pastor Marks used to say. Or was that her mother? Or her own mixed soundtrack, some version of some preacher, of someone on the radio? In the painting, Christ is surrounded by a larger glowing light, lines extending from his body, which is clearly protected from the devils and demons who rule this place on the edge of hell. See them on the left side of the painting, their human-shaped bodies covered in reptilian-like skin—twisted grimaces, eyes as empty sockets, faces rendered to emphasize the anger or stupidity or fear that rules their being. Which is how we, too, become demonic, our reptilian brains activated for survival: flight, fight, freeze. Necessary, to keep on living. A feeling experience that overwhelms the body, which might break apart, ignite in flames, spin out of orbit. What holds us in place?

She returned from Florence and stayed with her parents, got back together with an old boyfriend. She could say it was love or fear or because what follows sex is marriage. It was all true, but, when he proposed, she left him, instead, finally coming out to herself and then to her mother. Who said she was in the clutches of Satan and loving it. *Dear mother, please don't misrecognize my love.* In the painting, Limbo's entry is a hinged entry that Christ has pushed open as if it were a trap door, its thick stone-gray metal falling flat to the ground, over a same-gray armored body. Or was that armor etched into the door? Fra Angelico has painted black arrows above this collapsed and windowless barrier: a diagonal arrow pointing to Christ; another arrow pointing down, tipping right. This way out.

Things I Haven't Told Chris
and Probably Won't Ever

1. What a dork I was in eighth grade. I won't let him see pictures. He doesn't know about Jennifer Hartman and Angie, how they turned on me after I led them to Christ. He already calls me a "zealot." The first time he said that, I was mostly surprised he actually knew that word.

2. How much Veronica and James don't like him. They say he's an insecure baby for making others (me) responsible for his low self-esteem.

3. That I regret letting him copy my English essay on global warming. Of course he got an A; I wrote the paper. He seems to forget that when he tells me how great he did.

4. Anything more about the kitten I found, Iris, or her miraculous healing. When I told him that Mike accidently ran over her in the driveway, he laughed and asked if Mike had been drinking. Chris doesn't like cats (he's allergic), so maybe he can't understand why it's sad to lose your cat.

5. That two guys have gone down on me already. Chris assumed his first time was mine also. The other two didn't ask me to wash first.

6. That I still get freaked out in the dark and sing praise songs to clear the demons. My favorite is from Psalm 42.

7. Any of my dreams.

8. That when I reread this list, I wonder if we should even be together. Then I remember how much I like him. He's so funny and cute. Everybody is insecure—I don't want to judge him for that.

Another Energy Blows into the Room

Chris was at Denny's last night, and there were some people from my school there, including Tricia Cormack. She's a junior, and while I've never spoken to her personally, she has a reputation for giving it away. They say she's had three abortions, at least. Chris says I'm being judgmental and I shouldn't complain about double standards if I'm willing to use one myself. Point taken, though I wouldn't recommend dating a player, either. (As Veronica notes, we call her a slut and him a player, which means he wins and she gives it away. Question: What's the prize?) Chris said Tricia was friendly, that's all. They started talking on his way back from the bathroom, and then he and Jason moved and joined Tricia and her friends. He said Jason thinks she's pretty, and, to be fair, she is. She has full lips and dark wavy hair; her eyes are bright sparkle-brown, and her nose is thin and angular. She's skinnier than I am but slightly pigeon-toed—that's her main flaw—which is especially evident when she walks. It makes her seem unsteady. I've heard so many bad jokes about her, like how she's easily toppled, smells of day-old tuna, and is as creamy as spoiled tartar. I will be so embarrassed if Chris develops a crush on her. I am not that low.

Chris laughed and told me not to worry. They only talked, and she had been drinking, which Chris hates.

I have to remember that reputations aren't necessarily true. One of Pastor Mark's favorite television preachers, for example, was recently caught having sex with prostitutes, even though Pastor Marks always calls him a godly man. And there was a "family values" politician who just made news because he likes to cruise men's bathrooms. Pastor Marks says the media likes to exploit these stories as an argument against Christ, but when we had to write a news article for English class, Mr. Redfield said our stories should be about uncovering truths to help citizens make better decisions, since we live in a democracy with a government created by and for us, the people. I don't think it's bad to write a story about a dishonest preacher. Most people don't like to be lied to. They also love to discover that their suspicions were right all along and that those in high positions aren't genuinely better than them. Some people would rather have no reputation (be and do nothing) than risk a bad one. I figured that out freshman year, since no one at Plainfield, including the teachers, remembered Michelle, even though she had just graduated the year before. But that's Michelle's strategy: stay under the radar and hope you don't die.

I WONDER AT LANGUAGE AND BODIES

Michelle and Matt were over for hamburgers. No, Dad, I'm still not eating meat. Michelle and Mom were talking about some birth thing in Mom's room—maybe Lamaze, but I'm not sure because Michelle snapped when I tried to listen. I wanted to hear how she's doing. It's stupid, but I kind of miss her. Mom said, "Don't you have homework to do?"

Michelle is replicating Mom's life—even worse. Because at least Mom can say "bra" and "tampon," while Michelle says "slingshot" and "equipment." She won't change her clothes in front of anyone (Mom can, just not undergarments), and when Michelle and Laurie were younger, I bet they never dared each other to run around the outside of the house naked, like Denise and I used to do. How is she going to stand giving birth with multiple people staring at her vagina? Mom can't say "vagina," either, which makes me want to write it all over this page:

Vagina, vagina, vagina.

P-ssy, vagjayjay, kitty, c-nt.

(Whoa! I just wrote that…. Kinda fun….)

One time I asked Mom about my birth, and she went hazy. "I don't know," she said. "It's all a blur." She went to bed early that night. Migraine.

Veronica calls hers my-vagine, and says she doesn't have body hangups since her mom was a public health nurse. "She would have liked you," Veronica says. Her mom died the summer before we met. Cancer. She still has her mom's anatomy books, which is how I know about the clitoris (oh! so that's what I've been touching all these years). Veronica takes bubble baths in front of me and leaves the bathroom door open since she's an only child. The baths are one of our things. She likes it when I sit and watch her or look at *Vogue* or read Emily Dickenson poems aloud, which we analyze while she makes bubble mountains or slowly shaves her legs. Emily is one of our favorites. Has been since we met in ninth grade honors English. Because how can you resist

My Cocoon tightens – Colors teaze –
I'm feeling for the Air –
A dim capacity for Wings
Demeans the Dress I wear –

A cocoon: what the caterpillar wraps herself in before transformation. A cocoon is pressure, being squeezed into a space too small for one's potential, though that same space is what allows the caterpillar to grow wings. Maybe the speaker feels confined because she's female and stuck at home when she wants something more expansive, a "feeling for the Air." Cocoons are made of silk, and that's what makes fancy dresses. So herein lies the paradox— one of my favorite words—because without the pressure of the too-tight cocoon, she might not realize her desires and abilities or become the person she was always meant to be. The cramped space creates awareness, which makes the small space of the home even more unbearable. Especially when you're legally allowed to wear only dresses in public, no pants.

I get it, Emily. I really do.

A Woman Shows Me Another Woman Shows Me

I went to the school library today to research our historical person essay, due in two weeks. Mr. Redfield advised us to take the assignment seriously, especially in light of any upcoming college essays or interviews. He said they like to ask about "someone of historical importance who has influenced you."

I can't think of anyone, besides Jesus and Emily Dickinson.

I don't think I should write about Jesus, and Veronica has already picked Emily for herself.

Ms. Kempe, the librarian, pointed me to a row near the back of the room. The library shelves are double-stacked, meaning you can slide the top shelf over to reveal a second layer of books. It makes browsing slow, but the glide has a nice slippery quality. In any case, I had just slid a top row over when a book from the back literally popped out and fell to the floor. It's called *Maria Maddalena De'Pazzi: Selected Revelations*.

"Love love, oh God, you love the creature with a pure love, oh God of love, oh God of love."

That's the sentence I opened to, and it reminded me that Mary Magdalene is the patron saint of repentant women—something I realized I knew right then.

Holding the book, I felt a chill surround me. Not a creepy one but a thrill, moving like a wave from my forehead to the back of my thighs. The room became very still. I could feel myself focus. A sensation tickled the back of my neck. Very clearly, I could see the edges of shelved books, and between the silence, I heard the sound of buzzing fluorescents and the click, click, ticking of the clock. Almost three.

Maria Maddalena de' Pazzi lived in sixteenth-century Florence, Italy, where she was a nun and mystic who had extended ecstatic visions about the love of Christ. She was often in a trance for days at a time, speaking to or as the "Word," or "Love." The mother superior instructed the other nuns to record Maria Maddalena's words and visions, which seemed to occur without warning, as if the curtain between the physical and spiritual realms was suddenly torn or lifted. One time, during a ceremony for a novice receiving the veil, Maria Maddalena saw a cherub recording the girl's sung words. Later, alone in the novices' dormitory, Maria Maddalena (who they call "our blessed soul") entered into a rapt state, crying out in pain as she witnessed how sins, including cuss words, wound the Lord.

Yet, mostly, Maria Maddalena de' Pazzi spoke of love ♥

Next to the gap left on the shelf by *Maria Maddalena de' Pazzi*, I saw her biography, compiled in 1852 and later translated by a priest in Philadelphia. It's called *The Life and Works of St. Mary Magdalen De-Pazzi*. The names are spelled differently—spelling used to be irregular—but it's the same Carmelite nun. Ms. Kempe smiled when I handed her the books.

"Fear not the language of this world," she said. Or that's what I heard, which felt strange.

"Beg your pardon," I said. Which also surprised me. I never talk like that.

Ms. Kempe smiled again. She's the only teacher at our school who calls herself "Ms." Mom says that's for women who think they don't need husbands. (But Mom, maybe some women don't!)

Evidently, the book with Maddalena's writing came in just the day before. "It is," said Ms. Kempe, "a pre-order." She whispered, as if telling a secret. I nodded. Ms. Kempe pushed the books across the counter, leaning close and saying, "Remember: The Holy Ghost asks for us with mournings and weepings *unspeakable*."

Or that's what I thought she said. Because, as the library door closed behind me, I wasn't sure Ms. Kempe had said anything at all. But my uncertainty wasn't frightening. I felt like the answer must be in these books. Or in Maria Maddalena's name, because when I saw Veronica a few minutes later, she glanced at the titles and told me, in one long breath, that Mary Magdalene is the patron saint of prostitutes, hairdressers, apothecaries, perfumers, and women ridiculed for their piety. It was strange that Veronica—a self-declared atheist—would know anything about a saint, especially more than me, though she explained it's a virgin-whore thing, which interests her. Historically, men have portrayed women as one or the other, but Mary Magdalene is both at the same time. A contradiction.

"Like you," she laughed, and I must have scowled because she flicked me and said, "Just kidding."

A Webbed Text I'm Happy to Be In

I got caught up in reading Maria Maddalena and forgot to call Chris. He didn't call, either, but it's probably okay. I'd rather think about Maria Maddalena's two kinds of vision.

1.   Information about others, seen on the insides of her eyes, including which priests were being unfaithful and which nuns were breaking their vows.

2.   With her "corporeal" eyes, she saw spiritual entities who were actually in the room: devils and angels, Christ and the blessed mother. (Remember Ma Mbele, who saw her husband's actions while he was away? Or Johanna Nxumalo, who could smell evil?)

The first time Maria Maddalena was attacked by demons, she heard horrible screams and howls as fleshy devils pushed her down a flight of stairs, wrapping themselves around her body and biting her arms and neck. None of the other nuns could see the devils, but, afterward, her body was covered with wounds. Usually, though, the devil attacked her thoughts, filling her with doubts and fears about her choice to live a holy and austere life. At first the other nuns were uncertain about the righteousness of Maria Maddalena's visions; they said she looked "crazy," almost possessed, especially during the night when she jumped out of bed, grabbed a small crucifix, and began running around the room screaming "Love, love, love!" while smiling in "a sweet and cheerful manner." But the church authorities ruled her visions to be good and thus from God, and the mother superior commanded the other nuns to write down Maria Maddalena's words as she spoke them. One time, Maria Maddalena found these pages and quietly gathered them, her dark hair hidden beneath her veil as she burned them in a fire. Or maybe she snatched them in a fury and threw them into the flames before anyone could stop her. Either way, the mother superior ordered her to never do that again, as her visions were gifts from God; it was selfish not to share them.

Who did Maria Maddalena see when she said love? "Oh, love, make every creature love you, love."

"You are infinite and eternal, immutable, incomprehensible; love, you are inscrutable. What does *inscrutable* mean? Who knows, who knows, who knows? Please, who knows it, please tell me—because I know nothing about it."

Reading Maria Maddalena reminds me of that night in Florida, and the demonic attack. When I got home and told Mom what happened, she pressed her lips into a thin tight line. We were in her bedroom. She was sitting on the bed, rifling through her button tin with one of Dad's flannel shirts on her lap. She sighed and patted the space next to her, and we sat in silence for fifteen or twenty seconds—though it felt longer.

"What were you doing that night?" she finally asked. Her voice sounded like when I was four years old and she'd caught me with my hand in my underwear, trying to fall asleep. After that, she wouldn't turn the bedroom lights off until my arms were outside the covers, hands clasped for prayer. She sighed again and asked if I had anything with me that night, an object that might invite spirits into the room. I began shaking my head even as I remembered St. Thérèse of Lisieux—that I had been reading her book.

But that's not what Mom meant.

"I know about your diary," she said, and my mind emptied. "Does your writing glorify God?"

If Writing Opens Spiritual Realms, Maybe I Can Write

Maria Maddalena's mother didn't want her to leave, either. She refused to allow Catherine (Maria M's baptismal name) to enter the convent, crying for her to please marry and have children, that it was pure selfishness to do anything else. Catherine-Maria had plenty of rich suitors; if she married, she could go with her mother to the theater, and, afterwards, they could talk while enjoying deliciously beautiful food. Her mother didn't want to lose her daughter. Because when you take religious vows, you release your identity, like a snake shedding her skin, and become someone new. But Maria Maddalena was destined for God, so she began praying, saying, "Please, God, may my mother love me less. Please, help her cease holding me."

Maria Maddalena did not want to break her mother's heart.

But if she had stayed Catherine, she may have lost her soul, her very essence. She may have become bitter, resentful, angry—that's what happens when you're being dishonest with yourself. She would have continued to change, since change is inevitable and constant, like the dark and light of the earth's daily rotation.

Who would she have changed into?

Does God also change?

San Marco, cell eight, *Resurrection of Christ and Women at the Tomb*. They can't see him, though he stands, floats, behind them, body glowing within an aureole, feet obscured by clouds. Beneath him, Mary Magdalene (yes, that must be her, dressed in red) leans on the sarcophagus, right hand pressed to her forehead, as if she may faint. From exhaustion. From grief, loss. From the thing she feared, resisted, happening here in this now,

becoming her mother, her mother's mother, her own mother, mother-who-has-lost-control, mad-mother, mother-to-blame, mother-always-right, always-wrong, mother-needs-to-know because epigenetically-imprinted-mother with PTSD, murdering-mother, mother-illegible, wise-mother, marian-mother, mother-witch, mother-everywhere, mother-in-the-cards and of-the-sea, blessed-mother-made-manifest, mother-me-enough-with-a

vision. Of acceptance. The tomb as void.

I Read the Signs Around Me

Tricia Cormack came into the shop and bought a small vanilla soft-serve. When I handed her the cone, she asked, "How's Chris?"

I haven't spoken to him today.

She smiled, "Say 'hi' when you do."

I watched her grab napkins from the dispenser on the counter. She has feathery fingers, and her nails are small and pointed, painted glittery navy blue. Booby stick: that's what she looks like. She's probably a C cup even though her arms and legs are too thin and she was wearing black tights with cutoff jean shorts and black fake-leather boots. She kept adjusting her thin purse strap on her shoulder— ugly, something from Meijer. She was obviously trying to be cool. Yet nothing can disguise her pigeon-toes; when she walks, her butt sticks up and out like a bird's.

<u>Penny</u>: Immediately after Tricia Cormack left, I grabbed the broom and swept from behind the counter toward the front of the shop, out the door. I saw Tricia in a dirty white Pontiac Sunbird with a big scrape down the rear quarter panel. She was waiting to turn left though her blinker wasn't on. I looked down, saw a penny, heads side up. So someone's looking out for me. I put the coin in my pocket. As I walked inside, my coworker, Cyndi, handed me some leftover strawberry shake. "For sweetening," she said.

<u>Straw wrapper</u>: I tied my empty straw wrapper into a knot and pulled while thinking Chris's name. The knot stuck, so I did another. That one stuck, too. Not thinking about me doesn't mean he's thinking about her. Remember: logic. Cyndi came in from a smoke break. Her boyfriend, Tim, didn't stop by tonight. She figures he was at the bar, instead. "Take my advice," she said. "Don't give Chris the message." I must have looked confused. "It's not lying, honey," she said, with a small smile. "Don't help that bitch get inside his head."

<u>Flavors</u>: The two most popular flavors at the shop are mint chip and chocolate. I flipped my penny to see who got mint chip: it came out tails for her, leaving chocolate for me. By the end of the night, there were seven chocolates and only five mint chips, so, by the count, I won. Yet right before we closed, Mr. Brighton came in for a double waffle and ordered chocolate on bottom, mint chip on top. When he left, Cyndi said she remembered him from when she was at Plainfield. "I always thought he was cute," she said, "in a pathetic sort of way."

<u>Clocks</u>: When I got into the car to drive home, the clock said 10:10, and a double number is always good luck. Yet, walking through the kitchen, the microwave clock said 11:13, and it's worse to barely miss than to be completely off. Mike was home, and we sat in the mudroom, talking about Michelle and other stuff, like how Dad wants Mike to take a bigger role in the business but Mike doesn't want to be a builder his whole life. Mike asked if I'm still dating "that scrawny punk"—the way he said it made me laugh.

His eyes were red, and he was relaxed, friendly. Probably stoned. He was sitting on the bench while I was on the floor, leaning against one wall with my feet on the other—the same spot I used to sit in when Chris and I would talk every night on the phone. "Listen," said Mike. "You're going to college, right?" I shrugged and said hopefully. But Mike says I have to go, or it would be a waste. He made me pinky swear, then said he will personally cut off each and every one of my fingers and toes if I break my promise. "Michelle can stay here and be married," he said. "But that's no fate for you."

How to Make Sense Of

Let me write this as clearly as possible. I climbed a strangely familiar staircase while remembering another (the same?) staircase leading down. At the top, a door opened onto a grassy meadow, and, as I passed through the portal, a sharp pain pierced my heart. I began to weep. No—sob. Sudden convulsions, such aching. Until I saw, in the distance, a group of figures sitting in a circle. A woman stood and walked toward me. She wore a veil and radiated light. I knew, then, that I wasn't there to reflect on my own pain but on the pain of others. I bowed my head as she extended her left hand and gestured toward me. A light moved from my heart down. "There are many ways not to be seen," she said. "They called me a prostitute because they feared my intelligence; when they call you false names, speak back in truth." A single eye appeared on my stomach, just beneath my navel. "A guide," she said. She took my hand and led me to a picture. A woman sat in a boat with a small child while a ferry man pushed them along. Their heads were covered; they moved toward night waters. "In silence," she said, "they emerge."

"Show me," I said. I saw a page turning. Saul becoming Paul as he fell from his horse in a moment of blinding light. A sword, with a scroll for a hilt. Who holds the message wields the blade. That's what I woke to.

Except I Don't Remember Anything for the Next Three Months

I wanted tonight to be special. I wore a new brown mini-dress (to replace the one Mom cut). Chris and I went to the Olive Garden. I didn't mention Tricia Cormack, not once, because the more I thought about Cyndi's advice, the better it seemed. Chris and I ate way too much garlic bread, and he was in a great mood—he's probably going to get hired at Wind, Waves and Wheels, which is a big deal. Only the best skaters work there, and, if the manager doesn't respect you on both boards, he won't even accept your application. I drove the station wagon and brought a sleeping bag so we could put the back seat down and have plenty of space. We chewed Extra peppermint on our way to the cemetery near his house—no one's ever there, and they don't lock the gate at night.

He wanted to touch me, but just with his tip, to see what it felt like. We had our clothes on, my dress pushed up. I was wearing thigh-highs. He knows there's a line. I've said no so many times. It was cold outside but warm in the car, and the windows were fogged. Our breath felt like curtains. Plus, the way he talked—he murmured, "I'm so warm and wet,"—and he loves me, he loves feeling me, he's so much more sensitive down there. It must be amazing, with all those nerves running to and through it. He wanted to feel it, just once. He wasn't complaining, only curious. I know it's not right, but the way he talked made me want to make him happy. I'm the only one who can do that for him. He said, "You're my first serious girl-friend." He sounded like a little boy asking for candy.

So in a moment of silence, I said okay. But just the tip and on the outside only. His giddiness filled the car. He asked if I was sure, and his excitement made me smile. I moved my hips as he easily pulled off my underwear, and, for a moment, he held me, stroking me and kissing me deeply on the mouth. Then I was on my back and he was pushing down his pants, which were already unzipped. I said ok but only on the outside. Only the tip. That's where he was. He said it's amazing. The way he said it sounded funny, like he was somewhere else, not in the car. It was and was not happening. He was touching me, but I could have been any girl. He was rubbing it across my length, warmer than his fingers. Flesh to flesh. I was on my back, and he was kneeling, touching only on the outside, like we said. But then he went in. I mean, I thought he did, not super far, but I felt him. I jerked up and away. What are you doing, I said.

That's when we saw it. The car behind us. It was driving slowly toward us, its bright lights making shadows outside and in. I scrambled into the driver's seat and turned the key in the ignition. The doors were already locked. Plain black sedan with tinted windows. It followed us to the edge of the cemetery, but when we turned onto the street, the car stopped, stayed on the graveyard side of the gate.

We've never seen a car there before.

We didn't talk on the way to his house. It's not a long drive. Chris was humming—I don't know which song. When we arrived, I pulled to the curb. I needed to know what happened. That's what I said. I asked, "What happened?"

He was confused—"What happened what?" He thought I was talking about the sedan and laughed.

"Did we just have sex? Because it kind of felt like you went in."

He said he did, kind of, but not really. He said that was definitely not sex. He laughed. But I don't understand because, if he went in, which he did, then it was. There was a pressure in my head, and I couldn't cry. It was dark. He couldn't see me. He said that wasn't sex—we didn't have sex—but I don't understand. If he went in, which he did, then it was.

"I told you not to," I said.

"No," he said, "that was nothing,"

It was late. He had to leave, or I wouldn't make it home on time. When he said goodbye, I didn't answer. He gave me a quick kiss and said he'd call tomorrow. That's what he always says. He went in—I know it. When he got out of the car, it was dark,. I didn't watch him. He tapped the car window, waved goodbye.

I still don't know what happened.

But if he went in, then it was.

⁙

⁙   ⁙

⁙

Bimbo Dressing

Mr. Redfield asked to see me after class. I missed another due date, but only by a day, so my grade will drop only one letter and just on this essay, nothing else.

"I'm concerned," he said, "about your priorities." He was leaning back in his desk chair, working a blue powerball ring with his left hand. He says that it helps with muscle cramps and any serious writer should have one. I apologized, said it won't happen again.

But Mr. Redfield wanted a better explanation. "You seem distracted lately," he said. He leaned forward and raised his eyebrows. "Is something going on?"

I couldn't tell him the truth: That on the day before the due date, I met Chris after work and we messed around in the car. I had my opening paragraph and figured the rest would come easy, but then I accidently fell asleep before midnight, forgetting to set the alarm. I realized that's what happened last time, too.

When I didn't respond, Mr. Redfield audibly sighed. "Look," he said, "dressing provocatively will just make people think you're a bimbo, and if you miss due dates, their suspicions will only be confirmed."

Everything was wrong with his words. And despite my total embarrassment, including the flush I felt across my face, I heard myself saying that I have had just a lot of stuff happening. My voice didn't falter. I forced myself to smile. I said, "Don't worry. I won't be late again."

He leaned back, and I could see him appraising the situation, slowly squeezing and releasing the powerball ring. "OK," he said, with a slight nod. "But if it happens again, it will impact your total grade for the class. Understand?"

My top lip began twitching.

He handed me the ring. "Here," he said. "You'll need this."

I Feel Spotty, Barely Present

I wrote Chris a long love letter, and he gave me a heart-shaped box of milk chocolates. We used a condom for the first time. He wanted to know what it felt like to finish while still inside. Might as well—doesn't matter, since it's already happened. Back home, I burned jasmine incense until Mom knocked on my door and told me put it out.

At midnight we agreed to kiss and drop it. He left a few minutes later, and I stayed the night at Veronica's.

Michelle had a girl. Ariel Carter. Seven pounds, eight ounces. Not a terrible name. I didn't go to the hospital. I'll meet her tomorrow. Wow, I'm an aunt.

Dad keeps trying to get me to listen to Rush Limbaugh. "For the real news," he said. But Dad has no idea what's really going on.

Ate a giant bowl of popcorn and read *Things Fall Apart,* by Chinua Achebe, because Tristan Dalton insisted. So good—so many feelings about it. I don't like what they did to twins or how men could have multiple wives (so Old Testament). Keep thinking about this sentence: "The church had come and led many people astray." Is facing change different from facing your fear? It seems like Okonkwo was so afraid of cowardice that he became a coward. Or was he brave yet profane?

Late.

Sometimes the only thing worse than waiting is a yes.

Blue +. Really tired and have to pee between every class.

Turned my paper in on time, regardless. An interview with Ms. Kempe. She studied library science at UCLA, where she held a manuscript draft of Virginia Woolf's *Mrs. Dalloway*, written in purple pen. I checked out *To the Lighthouse,* as well.

Chris wants me to confirm at the doctor's. Made an appointment at pp for Thursday. Before work.

Confirmed.

Right and/or wrong, I thought I was better than this. That I would get out.

IN THE MIDDLE OF THE

I saw a large brick house with smoke or clouds or fog coming from its windows. Making the shape of a horse or an angel. I looked down. My cousin, Becca, was tugging at my sleeve. Paint me in, she said. I didn't understand, though we had to walk toward the house—I knew that. It took so long to reach it, and, when we did, it was only ashes, though Mom and Michelle were there, whispering about the girls' locker room. Becca tugged my sleeve again. "Why won't they answer?"

"I don't know," I said. I was angry. I thought I heard Chris, but when I turned, I saw three veiled women instead.

"Darling," they said, "turn over this stone." I did and saw another time and place, parallel, simultaneously present. Behind the woman: another brick wall. The neutral one handed me a dagger. That's how I learned about stepping through canvas. On the other side, Dad smiled despite himself.

I peeked back to say, "Goodbye, Becca." But she was gone.

Question: If you leave your painting, are you still you?

Haven't gone to school for two days. Mom thinks I have the flu.

Such an idiot. So stupid.

GRACE FILLS EMPTY PLACES

I didn't want to go home after work, so I drove downtown. Passed the skating rink and the turn off to Grandma C's house. Wasn't sure where I was going, but then I was at the cathedral and there were people milling around. I pulled into the parking lot. It was drizzling. I looked at my outfit—jeans and an orange turtleneck sweater. OK, enough. I put on lipstick and powdered my nose. The bells were ringing as I hurried for the door. People dress more casually for Saturday evening Mass. That's still true.

I'm not Catholic and never will be. Yet dipping my finger into the holy water and crossing myself—in the name of the Father, the Son, the Holy Ghost—I felt calm. I know how to do this, follow this script. I flashed on attending Mass for our eighth grade graduation ceremony. Sister Mary Francis let me sing "Friends" as part of the program, which I now understand to be ironic, though I hadn't yet learned that word. At the cathedral, I genuflected and entered a pew, not in the very back, but not in the front, either. I put down the kneeler and knelt, palms pressed together. It was quiet. I could hear the bells' lingering peals.

I sat back and traced the arched pattern in the ceiling above the altar. Such geometry and so many shades of seagreen and Mary's blue. To the right of the sanctuary stood a statue of a woman dressed like a nun with a bloody mark on her forehead. Later, I read her as St. Rita, Saint of the Impossible. How to explain the way my eye felt pulled, repeatedly, to her wound?

Everyone shuffled and stood, and the organist began to play as we sang "Be Not Afraid." I remembered that hymn from Sacred Heart—*I go before you always*. The priest had a Goddish beard, and the primary altar server was a grown man with beady eyes and thinning straw-colored hair. I didn't like him, though the priest seemed kind. I don't know why. His voice rose and fell as he led us in an opening confession—*through my fault, through my fault, through my most grievous fault*. Why is the pattern Lord, then Christ, then Lord have mercy?

We sat. My body relaxed into the rhythm and my mouth opened with the others to say, "Thanks be to God." Two older women sat in the pew before me. Short hair, pressed slacks. One of them held a tissue in her left hand. A few pews up and to the right was a middle-aged lady and a young woman who looked like her. Mother and daughter, I supposed. We began singing Psalm 91, "Be With Me, Lord, When I Am in Trouble." I didn't even pretend to sing.

The priest read from the Gospel of Luke—the parable of the Pharisee and the tax collector, and how a prayer made in judgement is not a prayer at all. Three nuns sat in the chamber to the left side of the alter. Their habits were blue and white, their heads bowed. On the wall behind them hung a painting of Mary as our Lady of Guadalupe. The priest was talking about how public religiosity is different than holiness. I half listened. Do people not know this? Who did Mary appear to, and was she surrounded by such glowing, radiant light?

I haven't told Veronica because I know what her advice will be. That's what Chris wants, and to choose otherwise will be to go it alone. But that's not the reason I don't want this—these cells growing inside me. It's not time. I felt a burning in my heart. The priest was still talking, something about inner thoughts and outward behavior. "Help us," he said, "to embrace your merciful love."

Then he began the prayers and petitions: for the Pope, for peace, for persecuted Christians. He paused after each one as we said, "Lord, hear our prayer." He ended with the elderly and the unborn, his voice still rising and falling in that sing-song rhythm. He called them "our most vulnerable populations." Lord...I didn't finish the response. Because how can he can equate a full life lived to a life that never was? I closed my eyes and felt a surging, almost dizzy. We were sitting, again. Dear God, do you hear me? No movement, nothing. Until I finally felt my dread.

Dear God. I whispered, "Show me."

I looked to my right and saw two twelve- or thirteen-year-old girls beneath a clear glass window, its pane crisscrossed with strips of lead to create a diamond pattern. Or when I tilted my head, they became squares in diagonally-moving lines. Through the glass, I could see vines growing on the outside wall of the cathedral, which seemed strange. I wasn't sure why. Their heart-shaped leaves framed the window with a green that seemed to pop out at me, as if they wanted my attention. I began to feel a thrumming—between my eyes, first, then moving down into my throat, my heart. My stomach. An aliveness. Between my legs. I heard a voice, then, so clear inside me. "Cease holding; let go."

Warmth and solidity moved through me, straightening my spine. *Inscrutable*: the word given to Maria Maddalena. She would not approve. Am I certain? *Who knows, who knows, who knows.* Who knows that which cannot be read or comprehended? Who knows the intimacy of transubstantiation? If bread can become the body of Christ, can my body become the bread of my life?

I hadn't planned on going up for communion. I had, in fact, assumed I wouldn't, as receiving communion without first going to confession is a mortal sin. Father Byrne, and all the priests, say so. *Through my fault, through my fault, through my most grievous fault.* The priest was moving through the Eucharist, washing his hands, praying over the host, lifting the chalice toward us, then to the right, to the left.

We began singing "Here I Am Lord," and when the time came, I stood with the others. I moved into the center aisle. My heart began beating so nervous. What if the priest somehow knew? What if refused me, called me a sinner and withheld the host? Should I lift my hands or let him place it on my tongue? I took a deep breath. Oh, holy darkness. *Oh, God, you love the creature with a pure love.*

"The body of Christ," said the priest.

"Amen," I said.

I looked into purple-grey eyes.

Leaving the building, I felt light and free and clean. Possible.

Used the phone at Veronica's house to call and make the appointment. Veronica says she'll come with me; Chris promised to help pay.

Over the river and through the woods

They always made it sound like the people here are absolutely evil, and, to be honest, the woman sitting behind the counter does look a little wrong. She has thin ash-blonde hair (dyed) and is weathered and skinny. She's chewing gum and is at least forty or forty-five years old. She wasn't rude, though, as much as distracted. They were out of medical history forms, so she had to make more copies in the back. "If the buzzer sounds," she said, "don't answer. I'll only be a moment." They keep the door locked for security. I waited, staring at the stuffed plush bear sitting by her phone. It's off-white with a heart-shaped nose and a neck ribbon covered with green and rose-colored hearts. I could hear the mechanical whir of the copy machine. "The paper's always warm when it comes out," she said, back at the front desk and snapping several sheets onto a clipboard. "New client form, medical history, consent and release, follow-up questionnaire. We want to know if and how to contact you in a way that's safe and confidential." They didn't leave enough space for actual writing, so my name and address looked gross. On the medical history, I marked nearly four pages of "no's" and checked "do not contact" on the questionnaire. When I handed her my completed forms, she asked how I wanted to pay. Duh—$250 in cash. This obviously didn't surprise her.

I came early because I knew the roads might be icy (weird, late spring storm), and now I have nearly an hour to kill (bad joke). Veronica called this morning to say she wasn't feeling well. When I pressed her to come anyway, she refused. "Don't take this wrong," she said, "but it's too much for me today." I was staring at the bulletin board by the kitchen phone. Mom had copied Grandma's chocolate Wacky Cake recipe onto a blank three by five note card. It's the vinegar and three holes that make it wacky, plus the way you mix it directly in the cake pan, so no dirtying an extra bowl—which is actually sensible, if you think about it. Beneath the recipe card, I saw a phone list I'd tacked up years ago: the number for every girl in my eighth-grade class. My handwriting was so big and loopy, especially compared to Mom's. Or to mine now.

"OK," I said.

"It just doesn't feel right to me."

"OK," I said. What else could I say? She was quiet, like waiting, so I said thanks for calling. (I didn't mean it, I wasn't grateful.) I said I had to go.

"Wait," she said. "You're still going?"

Out of everyone to get weird about this, who thought it would be Veronica?

"Don't worry about it," I said.

"It's just I thought…." She didn't finish. Finally, she told me to call her later.

I said I would.

But I won't.

The only other person here is an older woman, probably in her early thirties, kind of fat. She's sitting by the water cooler and keeps refilling her to-go cup from home. Earlier, she left to have a cigarette—you have to go out back where no one can see you. She was buzzed back in but not out, which means the door is locked on the outside only. I could leave without asking. It stopped snow-ing early this morning. Soon, even the side roads will be plowed.

Mom was in the shower before I left, so I threw up in the mudroom bathroom. Denise and I used to make up stories there, using the wallpaper as our guide. It's a newspaper print—advertisements, mostly—from the late 1800s. In one of them, a woman wears a hat with a feath-er while leaning on a sign: "Beauty Outlooking toward Hope's Land of Promise." Nearly every line is a differ-ent-sized type. She was our favorite, with her strangely lettered sign and swept-up hairstyle—no matter what di-rection the story took, we always had to have her in the final scene. That was the rule.

Worst-first, best-last. That's how Michelle ate her din-ner.

Rules are rules.

Any minute now,

she will

call my name.

Holy Mary, mother of god,
Love the little ones inside you
Forever
Held within your heart....

March 1981, Western Michigan

Dear Diary,
Do you like that name?
Love,
Marie

Dear Diary,

Do you want to know a secret? If you listen, trees will tell you.

See you later,

Marie

Dear Diary,

Do you have a favorite color? Mine is red today, but tomorrow may be different.

I like to wear some colors and eat others.

Your friend,

Marie

Dear Diary,

Does your mom make dessert? My mom made apple crisp tonight.

I like pie more than cake, especially berry.

Your friend forever,

Marie

Dear Diary,

I told my sister I want to be the fat lady in the circus. She laughed because fat is ugly.

I didn't know.

Your friend,

Marie

Dear Diary,

Are you going to heaven? Here is a prayer to help you.

Dear Jesus. I admit I'm a sinner.

I believe you died on the cross for my sins.

I accept you into my heart as my lord and savior.

Thank you for saving me.

Your child,

Marie

Dear Diary,
Acorns are baby trees waiting to crack open.
Later alligator,
Marie

Dear Diary,
Thank you for burying my rosary in the garden.
Does your mom get headaches? Mine does.
Your friend,
Marie

Dear Diary,

Mom says I have to be the apple among the oranges.

Do you know that feeling when mad people are in the room?

Miss you,

Marie

Dear Diary,

Polish sausage gives me a headache. Dad likes Mikey because he's a boy.

I can't have a cat because Michelle already has one.

Best friends forever,

Marie

Dear Diary,

I met a new girl, I still love you.

Guess what? Colors change shapes. Maybe people can, too.

Love always,

Marie

ACKNOWLEDGEMENTS

Excerpts from earlier versions of *The Reconception of Marie* have been published in *Edna, Eleven Eleven, Bombay Gin, Fold Appropriate Text, NAP 2.9, Drunken Boat*, and as a Woodland Editions chapbook entitled *My Spiritual Suit of Armor by Katherine Anne*. Thank you to the Millay Colony for supporting this project through an artist's residency. This book emerged over a span of more than twenty years, in and alongside workshops at The Evergreen State College, Antioch University, and University of Denver—thank you.

I am grateful to the following friends, family members, colleagues, and teachers:

Adam Rovner, Aditi Machado, Alexandra Forman, Alyssa Brillinger, Amanda Annis, Amanda Montei, Andrea Rexilius, Amy Hood, Anna Moschovakis, Andrew Wessels, Angela Buck, Anna Joy Springer, Barb and Ray LaForge, Bin Ramke, Brandi Homan, Brian Evenson, Brian Kiteley, Brian Teare, Cameron Venuti, Christopher Rosales, Clark Davis, Coco Owen, Connie Samaras, Dodie Bellamy, Dana Green, Danielle Pafunda, David Arata, Diana Khoi Nguyen, Divya Victor, Dorna Khazeni, Douglas Kearney, Elisabeth Sheffield, Eloise Klein Healy, Emily Culliton, Jamie Robles, Janet Sarbanes, Janice Lee, Janis Butler Holm, Jeffrey Pethybridge, Jennifer Calkins, Jenn Seif, Jessica Mintz, Jo Ann Beard, Johanna Blakley, Jon Rutzmoser, Joseph Mosconi, Juan Carlos Reyes, Judith Freeman, Julian Smith-Newman, Kanika Agarwal, Karla Kelsey, Karen Carmody, Ken White, Kimberli Meyer, Kristen Nelson, Laird Hunt, Larkin Higgins, Lidia Yuknavitch, Lindsey Drager, Lucy Corin, Mairead Case, Marie Celeste, Matias Viegener, Matthew

Timmons, Melissa Buzzeo, Michael du Plessis, Mildred Barya, Militza Jean-Felix, Molly Corey, Mona Awad, Pam Ore, Patrick Greaney, Paul Lisicky, Patty Yumi Cottrell, Poupeh Missaghi, Prageeta Sharma, Rebecca Goolsby, Roxanne J. Kymaani, Ruth Forman, Ryan Rivas, Sabrina Dalla Valle, Sawako Nakayasu, Sarah de Heras, Sarah Gerard, Sarah Shun-lien Bynum, Scott Howard, Sean Pessin, Selah Saterstrom, Serena Chopra, Sissy Boyd, Stephanie Garzanti, Susan McCabe, Susannah Dyckman, Sylke Rene Meyer, TaraShea Nesbit, Tayana Hardin, Thirri Mya Kyaw Myint, Tracy Bachman, Vidhu Aggarwal, Yolanda Pourciau, and Zach Forrester.

Thank you to Aurelia, Tod, and everyone at Spuyten Duyvil. I'm incredibly grateful for your support and enthusiasm, and for your visionary publishing.

Thank you to Stetson University, especially the English Department, the M.F.A. students and faculty, Jacklyn Gion, Maribel Velazquez, Paula Hogenmiller and Terri Witek—thank you.

Thank you to my mom, Janice Carmody. And to my siblings: Ann, Maureen, Dan, Karen, and Casey. I love you, all.

My love and gratitude for Maude, Fergus, and Vanessa Place. Always.

TERESA CARMODY's writing includes fiction, creative nonfiction, inter-arts collaborations, and hybrid forms. She is the author of three books and four chapbooks, including *Maison Femme: a fiction* (2015) and *The Reconception of Marie* (2020). Her work has appeared in *The Collagist*, *LitHub*, *WHR*, *Two Serious Ladies*, *Diagram*, *St. Petersburg Review*, *Faultline*, and was selected for the *&NOW Awards: The Best Innovative Writing* and by *Entropy* for its Best Online Articles and Essays list of 2019. Carmody is co-founding editor of Les Figues Press, an imprint of LARB Books in Los Angeles, and director of Stetson University's MFA of the Americas.

https://www.teresacarmody.com/

Made in the USA
Las Vegas, NV
23 March 2021

20028770R00184